THE PROBLEM AT TWO TITHES

An Angela Marchmont Mystery Book 7

CLARA BENSON

MOUNT STREET PRESS

clarabenson.com

The Problem at Two Tithes

On a reluctant visit to her painfully respectable brother and his wife, Angela Marchmont finds herself once again caught up in murder when a local farmer is shot dead, apparently at the hands of his sworn enemy. But the case is not as simple as it seems, for other motives and suspects soon come to light. With reporters hot on the scent and her friend Inspector Jameson battling a conflict of interest, Angela must use all her ingenuity to unravel the case and bring the murderer to justice—or more than one person will suffer the consequences.

Chapter One

SIR HUMPHREY CARDEW was a man for whom the word complacency might have been invented. As a young boy his natural intelligence, obedient disposition, and preference for quiet games and cleanliness had prompted many a visitor to exclaim that he was a darling of a child—a delight, in fact—and to observe to his parents that they must be tremendously proud of him. Faced with such adulation, the precocious Humphrey had quickly learned that to stand in the drawing-room, his hair combed and his hands folded smartly behind his back, and recite, with the merest hint of a lisp, *Come Down, O Maid* or *Now Sleeps the Crimson Petal*, before an audience of relatives and family acquaintances, was the quickest and surest way of earning a handful of sixpences and shillings (and even the odd half-crown on festive occasions, after the sherry had been passed round). So successful was he in his efforts to please that he saw no reason to change his approach as he grew older, and by the age of forty he had, through the continuing application of the arts he had learned as a boy, combined with diligence and hard work, attained one of the most senior positions in the Department of Labour and earned himself a knighthood to boot. Now, at forty-eight, he could justifiably look about him—at his fair and frosty wife, his quiet and dutiful sons, his large, comfortable house in Surrey with its nine acres of land, and his position as squire of the nearby village—and feel that he had earned all this; it was his, and he fully deserved it. Even if there *were* one or two dissenting voices (for even the best of men will have their naysayers) who decried him as the worst kind of pompous ass and wished him, if not precisely at the devil, then at least at a place in which his self-satisfaction might be duly punctured, they were in the minority and could be safely disregarded.

Aside from the occasional annoyance, then, there was little to blemish this otherwise idyllic state of affairs, and for the most part Humphrey's life proceeded in harmony and serenity. There *was* one particular irritation, however, which, while it could for the most part be forgotten, occasionally required his attention. When Humphrey was ten years old, his parents had, most inconsiderately, presented him with a sister. Humphrey was not the sort of boy who needed playmates—and indeed, what was he supposed to do with a child ten years younger than himself, other than regard her with faint puzzlement and then return to his carefully-catalogued butterfly collection?—and so he naturally passed much of his time in pretending the new arrival did not exist. Unfortunately, this interloper could not long be superciliously ignored, for as soon as she learned to walk she began to demonstrate a regrettable tendency to get up to mischief, break his toys, and trample the cabbages in the kitchen garden. Such destruction of neatness and order disturbed Humphrey greatly—especially since Miss Angela immediately and mystifyingly became a great favourite of the servants, who fed her sweetmeats and taught her to whistle. Nobody had ever taught Humphrey to whistle, but he consoled himself by rattling the coins in his pocket and reflecting that, while artlessness and good humour might have their attractions, they did not pay.

As the two of them grew older, however, Humphrey found it more and more difficult to comfort himself thus, for his sister, far from losing that early spiritedness and determination to do things her own way, grew even more independent-minded and inclined to draw attention to herself. By rights, as soon as she grew up she ought to have married a suitable young man, produced some children and dedicated herself to quiet country pursuits; instead, as soon as she was of age she announced her intention to earn her own money, and when objections were raised, declined to argue the point and merely ran away to London and did it anyway. Being a conformist by nature, Humphrey could not understand why on earth anyone should want to defy the wishes of their family, when it was so much easier to do what was expected of one, and he was even more astounded at the idea of a woman's supporting herself, so in his confusion he found the safest course was to pretend it had never happened. This approach stood him in good stead over the years, as his sister first disappeared to the United States to work as secretary to an important financier, then married some dreadful American, and at last—and worst of all—returned several years later (having apparently discarded the American), took up detective-work and began to get her name in the newspapers. There was no falling-out—nothing so extreme as that—but over time Humphrey and Angela found that the best way to get along was to meet as infrequently as possible, since when they did meet their incompatible personalities tended to lead to some little friction. Inflexible and rigid as he was, Humphrey never realized that it was invariably his headstrong sister rather than himself who made the allowances while they were in company together, and was secretly convinced that she set out to vex him deliberately, although he would have deemed it beneath him to voice the suspicion out loud.

Now she was coming to visit—at his own invitation, for he was not one to shirk his duty and it had been many years since she had visited Two Tithes, the house in which she had grown up and which he had in due course inherited. Whenever they had met since her return from America it had been on neutral ground, but the longer this went on the more uncomfortable Humphrey became. He was a fair-minded man, and moreover did not wish to be thought unfeeling. It would be right and proper for his sister to be welcomed back to her childhood home. Despite her odd proclivities and her many years' residency among the Americans (whom Humphrey considered to be little more than barbarians), she appeared to know how to conduct herself in company, and could presumably be trusted not to do anything to embarrass or inconvenience him—or so he had thought until a week ago, when he had received a telegram from her out of the blue to say she was stuck in Italy and could she please come next week instead? That confirmed him in his suspicion that she had not changed a bit, and while he naturally replied in the affirmative, his heart sank at the disorder she was likely to bring with her. Still, he comforted himself with the thought that at least she would not get herself mixed up in any murders or other similar unpleasantnesses during her visit, since nothing of that sort ever happened here, deep in the Surrey countryside.

On the morning of the expected late arrival Humphrey and his wife Elisabeth sat, as they always did, in the breakfast-parlour at Two Tithes, which overlooked the croquet lawn and the rose garden, and drank their tea from china cups that were never permitted to be chipped, while Humphrey read *The Times* and Elisabeth her post.

'Mother says she will arrive at four,' said Elisabeth. 'What time is Angela coming?'

'She said three o'clock,' replied Humphrey, 'although I shouldn't rely on it. She may well arrive later than that.'

'Well, I suppose her turning up at all will be something,' said Elisabeth. 'She's already a week late. An hour or two more won't make much difference, will it?'

Humphrey nodded in heavy agreement.

'It's tremendously inconsiderate,' said Elisabeth for perhaps the fifth time. 'What made her think we could accommodate her this week? Why, for all she knew we might have had a houseful of guests coming.'

'Perhaps that is what she was hoping,' said Humphrey. 'As a matter of fact, I was rather surprised that she accepted the invitation at all.'

'Well, if she does turn up she can certainly help with the fête. We shall need all the assistance we can get. Do you suppose she can bake? I am starting to feel quite over-whelmed by the cake stall. I know Margaret Tipping promised to help but after last year I don't quite trust her to do a good job. Another competent pair of hands would be such a relief—although of course Angela lives in a flat, doesn't she? One of those modern buildings. Hardly conducive to baking. She probably has her food sent up. Perhaps I won't ask her, then. I should hate to have to put her right as I did Mrs. Tipping. It does rather create bad feeling.'

'I'm sure you'll do a fine job by yourself, my dear,' said Humphrey. 'I know Mrs. Hunter is especially grateful to you.'

'I should think so, too,' said Elisabeth. 'I happen to know she doesn't get that sort of help from anyone else.'

'Well, after this perhaps they will stop asking us for money for a while. The church roof can't possibly have developed another hole already.'

'Oh, no,' said Elisabeth. 'There's always something. I fancy it will be the organ next. I happened to mention the other day that it was starting to squeak on the higher notes, which of course was a mistake on my part as Mr. Hunter's eyes gleamed immediately, and so I had to make my escape before he could broach the subject.'

Before she could expand further on this topic, she was interrupted by the entrance of a visitor who bore a certain resemblance to herself, being slim with the same fair hair and blue eyes. Where Elisabeth's habitual expression was a mixture of haughtiness and impatience, however, the newcomer looked much more cheerful. This was Kathleen Montgomery, Elisabeth's younger sister, a widow who lived with her young son in the nearby village of Banford Green. She was invited to sit down and did so.

'And how is Peter this morning?' said Elisabeth. 'Have the spots quite cleared up? Do you suppose he is well enough to go back to school yet?'

'He's much better today, but he's still looking very pale and thin,' said Kathie. 'I think I shall keep him at home for another week or so, just to be on the safe side.'

'You oughtn't to spoil him,' said Humphrey. 'A little hardship will be good for the boy. He is becoming soft.'

'Oh, but he had it so badly,' said Kathie. 'I was quite worried about him last week. Measles can be such a dreadful illness. A few more days won't do him any harm.'

'Perhaps,' said Humphrey, 'but that's a few more days' school fees wasted. Of course I am happy to pay them, but I should hate to think I was throwing money away.'

'You know how grateful I am for the help,' said Kathie, 'and I promise I'll send him back as soon as I can—but you wouldn't want him to get sick again and miss even more school, now, would you?'

'No, I suppose you are right,' said Humphrey. 'That reminds me—I saw Norman Tipping yesterday, and he said that he was going to send a man along to mend your fence in the next few days.'

This may have seemed rather an abrupt change of subject, but in fact it was not, for Humphrey—if not Kathie—had expectations of Norman Tipping, and hoped very much that before long he would be relieved of all responsibility for young Peter Montgomery's schooling, being very fond as a rule of keeping his money to himself.

'Oh, yes,' said Kathie. 'He did say something of the sort, although he didn't say when. I must say it's very kind of him.'

'I only wish he would get to the point at last,' said the forthright Elisabeth.

Kathie did not reply to this, but instead said:

'And so Angela is coming today. I shall be very glad to see her again. I thought she was rather good fun when we met her in London.'

'I do hope she's going to behave herself, at any rate,' said Elisabeth, who had only a passing acquaintance with the notion of fun. 'Mother is coming and I don't want her upset. You know how easily shocked old people are. Perhaps I had better have a quiet word with Angela to let her know what sort of thing will be acceptable in conversation. We don't want her mentioning that husband of hers —wherever he may be—or all that horrid business with dead bodies.'

'I have already written to her with full instructions,' said Humphrey, 'although I'm not sure whether the letter will have reached her in Italy, especially since she seems to have moved about rather a lot. I wrote to her in Florence but her telegram came from Venice.'

'I shall speak to her anyway, to remind her,' said Elisabeth.

'That is probably best, my dear,' said Humphrey. 'Then we shall have nothing to worry about. It will just be a pleasant family party, with no unwelcome surprises.'

'Unwelcome surprises?' said Kathie. 'Why, what do you mean?'

'Nothing in particular,' replied Humphrey. 'It's just that my sister is rather modern in her ideas.'

'Positively *outré*, in fact,' said Elisabeth. 'She's not quite the thing at all, and if you'll take my advice, Kathie, you won't let her influence you.'

'Influence me?' said Kathie with a laugh. 'Why should she try to influence me? Don't be silly, Elisabeth. She's jolly nice, and I'm quite sure she'll behave perfectly well.'

She then went out and left the Cardews to finish their breakfast.

Chapter Two

MRS. ANGELA MARCHMONT rested her chin in her hand and gazed out of the window of the Bentley as it ate up the miles along the Surrey road. Her maid, Marthe, was sitting in the front with her driver, William, and all three of them were uncharacteristically silent. At last, William cleared his throat and said:

'I guess it must feel a little funny to come back home after all these years, ma'am. Do you suppose much will have changed?'

Angela made no reply but continued to gaze out of the window. William and Marthe exchanged glances. After a minute or so, Marthe took out a pocket-mirror and held it up. She appeared to be examining her own rather pretty face, but in reality she was observing her mistress in the back seat. She was most disconcerted. Angela had returned from Italy on Tuesday evening, almost a week late, with only a terse telegram regarding the collection of her luggage to explain herself beforehand. When she finally did arrive, she said very little but wore an abstracted, almost dazed air, stared into space, and was inclined to put butter in her tea and sugar on her toast if not duly fore-stalled. On polite questioning she claimed to have been ill, but that was clearly nonsense, since she was bright-eyed and rosy-cheeked and had in fact never looked better. Marthe was offended. Something had happened and she had been left out of it. She wanted to know what it was, although she already had the strongest suspicion, since in her view only one thing could explain her mistress's general demeanour. She replaced the little glass in her pocket and narrowed her eyes. She was determined to get the secret out of Angela by hook or by crook, and she began idly pondering the best approach.

They passed the sign for Godalming and William said:

'Not far now, I think, ma'am.'

At his words Angela turned her head, then visibly pulled herself together.

'Yes, we're nearly there,' she said. 'Keep a careful lookout for the turning as it's rather difficult to see. There, that's it.'

William successfully navigated the sharp bend. The new road headed downhill into a valley, and from the top commanded splendid views. Below them was a pleasant landscape of rolling fields and hedgerows, and ahead they could see that the road led directly to an agglomeration of white, red and brown houses, from the centre of which a church spire stood out proudly. The sky had been overcast all day so far, but now the clouds parted and the sun cast a ray or two onto the village, showing it to its best advantage.

'It is very pretty,' said Marthe. 'Then this is where you grew up, *madame*.'

'Yes,' said Angela. 'If you look slightly to the left you can just see Two Tithes. It's that house standing a little apart from the rest. I wonder if any of the old servants are still there. If they are, no doubt they will tell you all kinds of hair-raising tales about the things I got up to as a girl. I should advise you not to believe any of them. Or not more than half, at any rate,' she added fairly.

Very soon they drew up before the great house and Angela alighted. In some obscure way she felt that this visit to her brother constituted a sort of penance for her sins, and so she marshalled her forces and determined that *this* week at least nobody should be able to say she had not behaved impeccably.

Humphrey and Elisabeth came out to greet her, stiff and formal.

'Hallo, Angela,' said Humphrey and shook hands with her, since the idea of kissing her would never have occurred to him. This had always irritated Angela, but she smiled and instead kissed Elisabeth before that lady could step back.

'How lovely to see you both,' said Angela. 'I do hope you'll pardon my dreadful unpunctuality, but I'm afraid it simply couldn't be helped. I was laid up all last week, you see, and couldn't make it back in time.'

'How unfortunate,' said Elisabeth politely, noting Angela's sun-tan and general air of well-being. 'You seem much better now, though.'

'Yes, I am, thank you,' said Angela. 'You look very well yourself, Elisabeth. Goodness,' she went on, as they stepped through the door and into the hall, 'It must be more than fifteen years since I was here, and it still looks exactly the same. I always loved this rose pattern on the wallpaper, and you've kept it just as it was when I left. How delightful.'

'Oh, that. Yes, I've always hated it,' said Elisabeth, 'but we have somehow never found the time to change it. Perhaps we'll do it next year.'

'Oh,' said Angela, momentarily disconcerted. 'Well,

I'm sure that whenever you do change it, it will be quite splendid. You have such good taste, Elisabeth.'

Here she stopped for she felt she was beginning to gush.

There was an awkward pause, then Humphrey said:

'Shall we go in to tea?'

They all seized upon this thankfully and went into the drawing-room. This had evidently been redone since Angela left, for she barely recognized it. She looked about her and was mildly interested to note that she felt no sadness or feelings of nostalgia, but merely a polite interest in what had been done to the room. She stepped over to the window and saw that the garden looked much the same as ever, which pleased her, for she had been fond of running around outside as a girl. A man she did not recognize was trundling a wheelbarrow along the path, and she wondered again how many of the old servants remained. Many of them had undoubtedly gone to war and most likely some of them had not returned, while it was not unreasonable to assume that others had merely found work that paid better and left.

Tea, of course, was very stiff and proper. Angela sat, straight-backed, on the edge of her seat, and nodded politely while Humphrey recounted some interminable story about the sale of half an acre of land to a neighbouring farmer. She was just about to ask a pertinent question to show that she had been listening when her attention was caught by the butler, who happened to be passing.

'Why, it's Joseph, isn't it?' she said without thinking. 'How nice to see you again.'

'It's Doggett now, if you please, madam,' he said, with an embarrassed glance at Humphrey.

'Oh, of course,' said Angela. 'I can see you're terribly important now. Well, I must say you hardly look a day older than you did the last time I saw you. Is the swing you put up for me still there? I must look for it tomorrow.'

'Doggett, do stop bothering Mrs. Marchmont and go and see to the silver,' said Elisabeth coldly.

'I beg your pardon, your ladyship,' said Doggett, and went out. Angela smiled apologetically at him as he passed, and reminded herself that chatting with the servants was not considered the done thing now that she was a grown woman. It was rather a pity, she thought. Joseph Doggett had been one of her friends in the old days, when he was a young under-footman, and she determined to speak to him later, when Humphrey and Elisabeth were not about.

'You won't mind visiting Mrs. Hunter, of course,' said Humphrey then. 'She knows you are coming and is very keen to find out what you have been doing for the past few years. I have told her you will visit tomorrow.'

Angela's heart sank, for she remembered the vicar's wife of old. Mrs. Hunter was a big-boned woman with a booming voice, who had the tendency to bombard one with impertinent questions and then pass on the answers— real or imagined—to the entire neighbourhood. She would much rather not have visited, but saw that she had been presented with a *fait accompli* and could not get out of it.

'By the way, I've given you your old room,' said Elisabeth. 'I thought you'd like it. Peter sleeps there sometimes, but otherwise it's quite unoccupied. The weather is pleasant enough at the moment so it oughtn't to be too cold.'

'Oh, no, I'm sure it will be quite warm,' agreed Angela, who was starting to feel that her penance was a little more than she deserved. Her old room was at the side of the house, overlooking the kitchen-yard, and had little to recommend it, being dark, damp and poky. Angela was quite certain that it would never have been given to any other guest, and could only assume that Elisabeth had chosen it out of some misplaced desire to make her visitor feel at home, since it was not to be supposed that any deliberate humiliation had been intended.

The conversation was beginning to flag when Humphrey suddenly remembered that Angela had been travelling in Italy, and began to question her closely about what she had done there. Since Angela had spent much of her holiday investigating a murder and consorting on the friendliest terms with a known criminal—neither of which pursuit was likely to impress her brother with the idea of her respectability—she was forced to tread very carefully when replying so as not to give herself away. Fortunately she was rescued by the arrival of Kathie Montgomery and her son Peter, and shortly afterwards, of Mrs. Randall, the mother of Kathie and Elisabeth. Kathie greeted her cheerfully, and for the first time in the past hour Angela felt as though *someone* at least was genuinely pleased to see her.

The teapot was replenished and the newcomers all sat down, and Angela was happy to be spared the necessity of talking for a while, since the others all appeared to have plenty to say to one another. She sat, lost in her own thoughts, until she suddenly became aware that young Peter was staring at her fixedly. He blushed and looked at the floor when he saw that she had spotted him, and Angela took the opportunity to rub hurriedly at her face, just in case he had seen a smudge of something there. After a moment he raised his eyes cautiously to her again, and she pulled a face at him. He looked away and seemed to be trying not to laugh. After that, tea became much more fun as the two of them engaged in a game to see which of them could make the other giggle first. Angela thought she was winning until Peter pulled a face of such startling and appalling monstrosity that she let out a laugh before she could stop herself. She covered it immediately with a cough, and said:

'I forgot to ask about the boys, Elisabeth. How are they getting on at school?'

As she spoke, she saw Peter wrinkle his nose in disgust, and guessed rightly that he did not think much of Horace and Clarence, the Cardews' sons, who must be about sixteen and fourteen now, if she remembered correctly. She had thought them rather beastly herself when she had met them, although Humphrey and Elisabeth evidently believed them to be the finest boys who had ever lived. Angela listened as Elisabeth enumerated all the certificates and prizes her sons had won that term alone, and offered her congratulations. Her entrance into the conversation had evidently brought her to the attention of Mrs. Randall, for the latter now observed her closely through a lorgnette, and then entirely without preamble or tact said:

'And where is Mr. Marchmont?'

Angela opened her mouth to reply, then looked at Elisabeth and closed it again.

'In America at present,' she said at last. It seemed the safest answer.

'Of course, you lived in America for many years, didn't you, Angela?' said Elisabeth in an attempt to divert the subject away from personal matters. 'And how did you like New York?'

But Mrs. Randall, undaunted, was still eyeing Angela through the lorgnette. Suddenly her brow cleared.

'Ah, of course,' she said in triumph. 'I remember your name now. You were mentioned in the newspapers in connection with that dreadful murder down on the Romney Marsh. You were the one to find the body, I believe.'

'Er—' said Angela, glancing once again at Elisabeth, who had pursed her lips.

'And they *said* you solved the murder, too,' continued Mrs. Randall. 'Of course, one can never believe a word one reads in the newspapers, but there must be something about you if it's true. One doesn't see many women detectives. It must be tremendously exciting.'

There was no sense in denying it at this point, so Angela said:

'To be perfectly honest, it's been mostly accidental up to now, but I confess it has been very interesting.'

'I don't quite think—' began Elisabeth.

'I dare say you have lots of friends in the police and in the—what do they call it?—ah, yes, the *criminal underworld*,' went on Mrs. Randall happily.

'Let me show you your room, Angela,' said Elisabeth, who felt the need to act.

'Oh, yes,' said Angela and jumped up immediately, although she knew perfectly well where her room was. The two ladies left the drawing-room, of one accord for once, and Angela allowed herself to be escorted up to the small box-room in which she had slept as a child. There she found that Marthe had already unpacked her luggage and pointedly lit a fire to take off the chill, even though it was early June.

'You'll find everything quite comfortable,' said Elisabeth, 'but do ring if there is anything you require.'

She then left hurriedly, leaving Angela to gaze about her and try to summon up some feelings of warmth and regret for her old home. Pleasantly situated and comfortable as it was, she was disturbed to find that she felt nothing. She wandered over to the window and looked out into the kitchen-yard. William was down there, smoking and flirting with one of the maids, and she smiled and turned away. An old, white-painted cupboard stood in the corner of the room and she pulled open the door and looked inside. One or two items of clothing hung there, but nothing that had ever been hers. None of her old toys were here either; in fact, the house seemed to retain no impression of her at all. She had never been precisely unhappy at Two Tithes, but somehow she had never felt as though she belonged here, and odd though it sounded, she wondered whether perhaps the house felt the same. She laughed at her fancy and closed the cupboard door.

'You're going soft in the head, Angela,' she said to herself, and went out.

Chapter Three

THE NEXT DAY BROUGHT WARM, hazy sunshine, and after breakfast Angela excused herself and said she was going to take a solitary walk around the grounds and reacquaint herself with the place.

'You won't stay out too long, will you?' said Elisabeth. 'I shall need your help with the rosettes and the bunting for the fête.'

'And don't forget you are to visit Mrs. Hunter this afternoon,' added Humphrey.

Angela promised to return in good time, and set off before one or both of them could suggest walking with her. She crossed the garden briskly and passed through the field beyond, then began to climb up the hill that lay behind the house. From the other side of this hill it was possible to see as far as London on a clear day, although there was too much haze today, so she stopped a little way up and turned to look back at the house. Two Tithes was a typical, rambling old country place which had been owned by the Cardews since the previous century. It was certainly attractive enough, set as it was among flower gardens and smooth lawns, with fields and woods beyond it and a little stream running along the edge of the grounds, and yet still Angela was unable to call it home. She supposed she had never been the type to indulge in nostalgia and could not regret having left, for she knew that had she stayed she should have felt like a captive. No: Humphrey had the house and was welcome to it. She was quite content to consider herself merely a visitor.

She came back down the hill and passed through the fields and beyond the boundaries of Two Tithes, then drifted along a lonely path through a tunnel of trees, hat in hand, with only the pleasantest of thoughts in her head and a smile on her face of which she was completely unaware. She was proceeding along the path, not paying a great deal of attention to her surroundings, when she suddenly became aware of a low growling, and she raised her head to see an irritable-looking bull terrier standing on the path before her. There was no mistaking the menace in its demeanour.

'Oh!' said Angela, and stopped. The dog began to approach her, still growling, and she backed away, eyeing it nervously. 'Good boy,' she ventured. The dog gave a scornful sneeze at such patently insincere praise, and kept on advancing until it had her pinned against a tree. Then it let out a loud bark and she squeaked in surprise.

'Dear me,' she said. Glancing about for the dog's owner, she turned her head and found herself staring into the barrel of a shotgun. She gave another squeak.

'I beg your pardon,' said the newcomer, lowering his gun. 'Down, Skipper! Here, boy!'

The dog gave one last disgusted growl and padded over to its owner, who turned out to be a tall, hearty man of sixty or more with unkempt hair sticking out from under a deer-stalker hat.

'I hope we didn't frighten you too much,' said the man. 'I thought you were someone else, and one can't be too careful. I'm not fond of trespassers, you see.'

Angela stepped away from the tree, keeping a wary eye on the dog, and replaced her hat as she composed herself. She bit back the words that had initially come into her head, and said:

'It's Mr. Norris, isn't it? I remember you. I'm Angela, from Two Tithes. Humphrey's sister.'

The man squinted at her, then straightened up. His expression cleared and immediately became more friendly.

'Ha! So it's you, is it?' he said. 'Back again. How long has it been? Ten years?'

'Nearer twenty, I think,' said Angela.

'So long?' he said. He appeared to have found his manners now, and was looking at her appreciatively. 'Well, you're quite the elegant lady now, aren't you? I remember when you were barely this high, all curly hair and mischief, and would as rather be covered in mud as not. The curls are still there, I see, but I must say I hardly recognize the rest. What's your name now? I don't suppose you're still a Cardew. And where have you been hiding for all these years?'

'My name is Marchmont now,' said Angela, 'and I've been living in America and London.'

'America, eh?' said Mr. Norris. 'A man of mine was there for a while. Ben Shaw. Do you know him?'

Angela forbore to point out that the United States was not a village bowls club but a large nation with many millions of inhabitants, and merely said politely:

'I'm afraid I don't recall the name.'

'And now you're back. Visiting family, I expect. The Sir and Lady. Not as la-di-da as *her*, though, I'll bet.'

Angela affected not to know what he was talking about, and said:

'Is this your land, then? I'm awfully sorry if I was trespassing. I didn't mean to.'

He drew himself up.

'It most certainly is my land,' he said. 'I've been to law to prove that Dead Man's Path is mine, and prove it I shall one of these days. I'm not an unreasonable man: I know this is the quickest way through to Banford and I won't stop anyone from using the path who doesn't cause me any harm, but I *will* defend it if I have to. I won't let what's mine be taken from me.'

'Who is trying to take it from you?' said Angela.

Mr Norris's face darkened.

'There are some who would have it that the path is common land,' he said. 'But it's most certainly mine, and if that's the way they want to play the game then I'll show them what's right and what's wrong. There's no call to stand up against me and try to deny me my rights.'

'I see,' said Angela, and then, since he seemed to want her to ask, went on, 'Who has tried to deny you your rights?'

But he did not reply, and indeed was no longer looking at her but at something over her shoulder. Angela turned and saw that someone else was approaching. As he came closer she could see that he was a man of similar age to Mr. Norris. He was dressed in aged tweeds, and he, too, had a shotgun and a dog. The two men scowled at one another and the dogs began to growl, but then the second man spotted Angela. He nodded to her politely, then passed on without a word. Mr. Norris, fingering his shotgun, watched him until he was out of sight. It seemed to Angela that her question had been answered, and she said curiously:

CLARA BENSON

'Who was that? I don't believe I recognize him.'

'*That* is Tom Tipping,' said Mr. Norris in a tone of deep disgust, 'and if you'll take my advice you'll have nothing to do with him, for he's the worst sort of neighbour and he'll have the shirt off your back before you know it. He's cheated me out of my rights once before, but I won't let him do it again.'

'Is he the one who says that this is common land?'

'That's him, all right,' said Norris, 'and it's lucky for him you were here, or I'd have seen him off. I won't let him pass, you see. Not until he admits the truth of the matter.'

'Just to avoid confusion, then,' said Angela, 'am I to understand that you allow all those who agree that this is your land to use it, while those who don't agree are warned off?'

'That's about it,' he said, nodding. 'Most people are sensible enough about it, but there's no making Tom Tipping see sense. And he *will* walk along the path just to provoke me. I've told him I won't be held responsible for what I do if he keeps at it, but he doesn't listen. Mark my words, though, one day he'll regret it. If he thinks I won't use my shotgun against him he's wrong.'

'Oh, I do hope it won't come to that,' said Angela. She was keen to get away from Mr. Norris before he forced her to swear an oath of allegiance in exchange for permission to use the path, and so she glanced at her watch and exclaimed, 'Dear me! I had no idea it was so late. Humphrey and Elisabeth will be wondering where I have got to. It has been very nice to see you again, Mr. Norris. Goodbye.'

He returned her salute and she hurried off. As she left the path she glanced back to see him still standing there, his shotgun in his hand and his dog by his side, watching her.

Chapter Four

As IT HAPPENED, Angela *had* been walking for longer than she intended, and by the time she returned to Two Tithes it was almost lunch-time. She was rather cross with herself, for she had wanted to seek out Doggett the butler and have a comfortable chat with him about the old days, away from all disapproving stares, but now there was no time. She arrived to find Elisabeth packing armfuls of ribbon into a box with a martyred air, and remembered that she had promised to help with the bunting and the rosettes. It was hardly the best way to make a good impression and she chided herself for having spent the morning wandering about in a day-dream when she was supposed to be forgetting all that and concentrating on her familial duties.

'I'm awfully sorry I was so long, Elisabeth,' she said. 'I'm afraid I ended up walking a little farther than I meant to and didn't notice the time. Have you finished the bunting? I can do some more after lunch, if you like.'

'No, it's quite all right,' said Elisabeth with a sniff. 'I've finished it all myself. It didn't take as long as I expected, and I'm sure Mrs. Tipping has managed the cakes admirably on her own this morning. She won't mind that I couldn't come and help.'

Angela abased herself suitably, although Elisabeth had said nothing about agreeing to help Mrs. Tipping today and Angela could not help suspecting that there had been no such arrangement. Still, hers not to question: she had come to Two Tithes to cast down her eyes and act like a dutiful sister, and this she would do to the best of her ability. This morning she had made a bad start, but from now on she was determined to do better. The bell rang for lunch and she followed Elisabeth into the dining-room, where Mrs. Randall was already seated. The old lady immediately raised her lorgnette to her eyes and stared hard at Angela as she entered, then made a little noise that sounded like 'Hmp!' which may have denoted approval or disgust; it was impossible to say. Angela was starting to feel quite uncomfortable under her dispassionate gaze, but there was nothing to be done, so she merely smiled at Mrs. Randall and took her seat meekly. Humphrey just then arrived, followed by Kathie and Peter, and all talk was of the fête, which was due to take place the next day.

'Did you happen to speak to Margaret Tipping this morning?' asked Elisabeth of her sister. 'I am wondering about the cakes.'

'No, but I saw Norman earlier. He was in a hurry so didn't stop, but he did say in passing that she was just finishing the icing on the last ones,' replied Kathie.

'Norman Tipping is Mrs. Tipping's son. He is a particular friend of Kathie's,' Humphrey explained to Angela in the manner of a bewhiskered head of the family of some fifty years earlier.

'Oh?' said Angela. 'Do they happen to be related to someone called Tom Tipping? I believe I met him this morning on Dead Man's Path.'

'Yes, Tom is married to Margaret,' said Kathie. 'He is Norman's father.'

'I see,' said Angela. 'I was talking to old Mr. Norris of Low Meadow Farm when he turned up. There appeared to be some sort of dispute between them.'

Elisabeth sniffed disdainfully.

'Yes,' she said. 'It's most tiresome of them, and quite embarrassing. Of course, it's Mrs. Tipping I feel most sorry for, since she has to put up with it.'

'What exactly are they feuding about?' said Angela. 'There seemed to be a disagreement over who owns Dead Man's Path.'

'Yes,' said Kathie. 'Mr. Norris has spent the last I don't know how many years trying to prove that it legally belongs to him. He hasn't succeeded yet, but he is determined to win his cause one day.'

'Of course it doesn't belong to him,' said Elisabeth. 'It's common land, and has been for centuries, but most people have the good sense to nod and smile and agree when he starts on the subject, since it's quite impossible to convince him that he's wrong. It's only Tom Tipping who insists on contradicting him and writing to the newspapers about it whenever the case comes up. Naturally, that only serves to infuriate old Norris further.'

Kathie gave a sigh.

'Yes, I'm afraid that's true,' she said. 'Poor Margaret! And each of them is as stubborn as the other. I believe Tom has taken to walking along Dead Man's Path several times a day, and I can only imagine it's because he wants to provoke Mr. Norris, since there's no real reason for him to do it quite as often as he does.'

'I should have thought he would rather want to avoid the place,' said Angela. 'Mr. Norris was brandishing a shotgun and he hinted very strongly that he was minded to use it.'

'Oh, Andrew Norris and his shotgun,' said Humphrey. 'I have had words with him on numerous occasions about it. He is far too fond of pointing it at people. One day it will go off accidentally and then we shall have all manner of trouble. Now, Angela,' he went on, dismissing the subject of errant landowners, 'don't forget that Mrs. Hunter is expecting you this afternoon. She remembers you very well and is looking forward to hearing all about what you have been doing over the past few years. I'm sure I don't need to remind you that she is an old lady and that certain subjects are not suitable for her ears.'

Angela resisted the temptation to say, 'Yes, sir,' but merely nodded.

'I'll come with you if you like,' said Kathie. 'I promised Mrs. Hunter I'd visit her this week. I meant to go yesterday but I forgot.'

Angela accepted gratefully, for she foresaw an uncomfortable hour or two ahead of her and she hoped that Kathie's presence might ease the awkwardness. Accordingly, after lunch the two of them set out in the direction of the vicarage, accompanied by Peter. They had not gone far when they saw a man coming towards them.

'It's Norman,' said Kathie, and then as he came up to them, said, 'Hallo, Norman, this is Angela. I don't believe you've met before.'

The two of them acknowledged the introduction politely and Angela now had the opportunity to examine the man who seemed by all accounts to have been marked out for Kathie. He was solidly built and of middle height, with thinning hair. He was neither particularly handsome nor particularly plain, but his face wore a habitually serious expression which made it less attractive to look at than it might have been had he smiled more. At any rate, he looked the very essence of country respectability and as far as Angela could tell, Kathie liked him well enough.

'Hallo, Peter,' said Norman heartily as he caught sight of the boy, who was standing to polite attention. 'You're looking rather better today. You'll be back at school before you know it. Here, take this,' he said. He fumbled in his pocket and brought out sixpence, which he gave to Peter. 'I know what you boys are like—always wanting money to buy tuck. I remember it very well myself.'

'Thank you very much, sir,' said Peter.

Norman Tipping nodded and passed on, and the ladies continued on their way. Angela glanced at Peter and felt rather sorry for him. If that was the sort of largesse that his future father dispensed in general, then he was unlikely to get much in the way of extra food at school. She made up her mind to give the boy half a crown later when no-one was looking.

'So that is your intended, I take it,' she said to Kathie. Kathie blushed and glanced at Peter, who was walking ahead out of earshot.

'Not exactly, no,' she replied, 'although he is very kind.'

'I beg your pardon,' said Angela. 'I was under the impression that it was pretty much all arranged. I must have misunderstood. I do apologize.'

Kathie laughed.

'Oh, no need for that,' she said. 'I know everyone in the village talks about it as though we were on the point of putting up the banns, but they're far ahead of us, I'm afraid.'

'Has he asked you?'

'Not in so many words,' said Kathie cautiously. She lowered her voice. 'To be perfectly honest,' she went on, 'I wonder sometimes whether he doesn't consider my acceptance to be an established fact.'

'Then you think he has no intention of getting to the point?'

'He seems in no hurry, certainly,' replied Kathie.

'And is it?' said Angela. 'An established fact, I mean.'

Kathie hesitated.

'It would be a very suitable match, of course. I know that,' she said at last.

'You don't seem very sure,' said Angela with a smile.

'Oh, I don't know,' said Kathie suddenly. 'Perhaps I have been on my own for too long. For years it's just been Peter and I and we've mostly been very happy. But Peter's father didn't leave us much money, you see. Humphrey has been very kind and helped out, but he worries about school fees, what with having two boys of his own, and I know he and Elisabeth are keen for the thing to go ahead.'

'I see,' said Angela. That sounded like Humphrey, all right: he had always been very jealous of his money as a child, and she could easily see that the responsibility of having to pay for his nephew's schooling would not sit well with him. It seemed a little unfeeling of him to push his sister-in-law into marriage merely to relieve himself of the burden, however—for it was clear to Angela that Kathie was not in love with Norman Tipping in the least, and indeed, any woman who could refer to her future marriage as 'the thing' could not possibly be *wholly* enthusiastic about it. It was none of her business, however, and so she let the subject drop and the talk moved onto other topics.

Chapter Five

PETER HAD BEEN GIVEN special dispensation not to partake of the visit to Mrs. Hunter, and so when they reached the gate of the vicarage he ran off with a whoop on business of his own, leaving Angela and Kathie to knock at the door and be admitted by an aged parlourmaid.

'Is that you?' boomed a voice from a room somewhere off to their right. It was shortly followed by Mrs. Hunter herself. The vicar's wife was a woman of large and hearty bearing and a manner to match. As far as Angela could remember she must be in her late seventies now, but she seemed to have lost none of her ebullience over the years, and indeed, still insisted on riding her bicycle around the village, to the great danger of the rest of its inhabitants. She greeted her visitors loudly, and then looked Angela up and down with bare-faced curiosity.

'And so this is what time has done to you,' she said. 'You're wearing reasonably well, I suppose. I shouldn't take you for a day older than thirty-five. Not a scrap on you, I see. That's a mistake. It's all very well when you're young, but it doesn't become an older woman. You can just about carry it off now, but if you're not careful your face will collapse and you'll start looking positively desiccated in about ten years. Like one of those Egyptian mummies, you know. Still, it's nice to see you both. Come in, come in!'

Not entirely sure which was worse—being compared to a three thousand-year-old cadaver or being told she looked as much as thirty-five—Angela threw a glance at Kathie, who appeared to be trying not to laugh, and followed their hostess into the parlour.

'Stephen is not at home,' said Mrs. Hunter, 'so we can have a nice, friendly chat without having to talk about the church roof for once. Tea, Esther,' she said to the parlour-maid, who looked to be about twenty years older than Mrs. Hunter herself, and who tottered off obediently. 'Shall you be giving us a hand at the fête tomorrow, Mrs. Marchmont?'

'I believe so,' said Angela. 'I think Elisabeth has plans for me. She mentioned something about putting me on the bric-à-brac stall.'

'I see,' said the vicar's wife. 'You'll have to have your wits about you, then, or you'll be fleeced. Watch out for Mrs. Goddard in particular: she'll beat you down until you end up paying *her* two shillings to take the stuff off your hands. And she's not above helping herself to things when one's not looking. I only say what's true, my dear,' she said to Kathie, who had seemed about to protest. 'I hope you know how to stand firm,' she went on, regarding Angela narrowly, 'or you'll be flayed alive.'

Having established to her satisfaction that they were not to attend a church fête but rather a bear-baiting, she paused to pour the tea, and then returned to the attack.

'And was your brother pleased to see you again?' she said. 'I understand you hadn't seen each other for many years.'

'That's not quite true,' said Angela. 'I have seen him since I returned from America, but this is the first time I've returned to Two Tithes since I left.'

'Of course, now I remember,' said Mrs. Hunter. 'You ran off to mess about with a typewriter in London, didn't you? Broke your parents' hearts, of course. Still, as I told them at the time, it's best to let girls get these things out of their system. She'll get over it, mark my words, I said. Once she's tried to live on twenty-five shillings a week and had her fill of eating stale rolls for breakfast and sharing a bathroom with ten other girls, she'll be back and begging to be forgiven. I was wrong, though, wasn't I? You never did come back. I suppose I ought to have seen it, really. You always had that fire in you—that independent spirit. Ungovernable, they used to call you at home. Always up to something. Not like your brother, of course. He was the well-behaved one. Not that I particularly admire a boy who is never naughty. There is something about it that doesn't appeal—something a little unnatural, don't you think?'

Here she paused to take a breath and a sip of tea, while Angela tried and failed to think of a suitable reply to all this. Mrs. Hunter's memories of that period were evidently very different from hers. When she had left Two Tithes her mother was already dead, and her father had been more annoyed than broken-hearted at her insistence on earning her own living. She was about to change the subject and make some remark about how the village had altered since she had last seen it, when Mrs. Hunter found her second wind and began again with breezy unconcern for the niceties of social intercourse.

'I understand you are separated from your husband,' she said, then, as Angela was struggling for an answer, went on, 'Tell me, did he have other women? They so often do, you know, but that's no reason to separate. The marriage vows seem to be taken less and less seriously these days, I find, and just because a man can't manage to be faithful that's no reason to throw him out. We women are put on this earth to suffer, you know. You must look the other way and make home all the more enticing, to make him come back to you. How is your cooking? Perhaps it wasn't good enough for him. A man likes to be well fed at home, and he's much less likely to stray if he feels he is being well looked after. I have a recipe for a rather marvellous chicken pie which has never failed me yet. I must look it out for you.'

Kathie, in sympathy to Angela, was about to interject with a change of subject, but she had no time, for Mrs. Hunter went on:

'Or was it another man? I do hope you're not that type. Now, that kind of thing really does make me cross. One reads about all kinds of scandalous conduct coming out in the divorce courts these days, which simply wouldn't have been allowed fifty or even twenty years ago. Women like that would have been ostracized, and rightly so, in my opinion. That sort of behaviour is simply disgraceful. But you wouldn't do anything like that, would you? Of course not—why, it's quite unthinkable. What was it, then? Was it to do with money? I understand you worked when you were in America. I shouldn't be surprised if that's why he left you. Men don't like their wives to work, you see. It hurts their pride and makes them feel unimportant. A man needs to feel as though he is king in his own home.'

Angela by now was nodding politely at everything and counting the flowers on the wallpaper above her hostess's head. At last Mrs. Hunter seemed to decide that she had dispensed enough words of wisdom to resolve Angela's marital difficulties, and turned her attention to Kathie.

'And so Norman Tipping still hasn't asked you to

marry him, I hear,' she said. 'Send him to me, and I'll have a word with him. He oughtn't to keep you hanging on like that. It's not fair on a woman. You're not getting any younger and you don't want to leave it too late to have more children.'

Kathie was used to Mrs. Hunter's ways and so she merely smiled and said:

'It's very kind of you, but there's no need to worry about me. Peter and I are quite happy as we are at present. There's no hurry at all.'

'Well, just you make sure he doesn't think he can get out of it,' said Mrs. Hunter. This was a conversation they had had many times, however, and she soon ran out of things to say on the subject, so Kathie was spared any further impertinent observations, and the visit soon came to an end, after a mercifully brief diatribe from Mrs. Hunter about a spate of bicycle thefts in the village, which she suspected to be the work of some gipsies who had recently been seen in the area.

'Whew!' said Angela as they walked away from the vicarage. 'I feel rather as though I'd spent the last hour being hit repeatedly over the head with a sandbag or something of the sort. I'd forgotten about Mrs. Hunter and her —er—idiosyncrasies.'

Kathie laughed.

'Yes, she is rather forthright, isn't she? She means well, but I find it's best not to take what she says too much to heart.'

Angela agreed, although naturally it was easier said than done. The ladies parted, and Angela made her way back to Two Tithes via a path that led through the grounds and to the side of the house. As she passed the open door to the kitchen-yard she glanced through it and spied William leaning in his usual spot against the wall, smoking, and went to speak to him. He straightened up when he saw her approaching, but she motioned to him not to bother putting out his cigarette and instead said:

'Have you got any more of those? I've just had a rather bruising encounter with the vicar's wife and I'm dying for a cigarette, but mine are in the house and I don't think I can bear to go back in just yet.'

He obliged immediately and lit it for her, and they stood in companionable silence for a few minutes, although Angela could not help casting the occasional nervous glance about her in case Elisabeth or Humphrey should come upon them and tell her off for hob-nobbing with the lower orders.

'I hope you're quite comfortable here,' she said at last. 'Have the servants made you welcome? I don't know much about this lot. Most of the ones I knew seem to have left long ago.'

'Yes, quite comfortable, ma'am,' he said. 'And the servants are friendly enough.' He glanced at her sideways. 'They all seem a little frightened of her ladyship, though.'

'I'm not surprised,' said Angela. 'I'm rather frightened of her myself. But don't you dare tell anyone that.'

'I shouldn't dream of it,' he said in some amusement. He paused for a second, then said hesitantly, 'I guess she's scared of you too.'

'Scared of *me*?' said Angela in astonishment. 'Whatever for?'

'Why, because she doesn't know how to take you. She's lived all her life in the same place with the same people, but you—you've been places, and you've seen and done things that she'll never see or do. Maybe she finds that a little intimidating.'

Angela paused to absorb what William had said. She had never considered things from this angle, and had always supposed that Elisabeth's air of barely-concealed impatience when in her presence was due purely to disapproval.

'I'd never thought of it like that,' she said. 'I wonder whether you mightn't be right. Banford is a small place and most of the families here have lived in the area for centuries without feeling the need to go anywhere. I suppose they might be wary of someone who has lived abroad and developed foreign habits. Odd, though, isn't it, to think that I might be the only person from here ever to have travelled.'

'Oh, but you're not,' said William. 'There's an old fellow here who's been in the States. I met him yesterday. When he found out I was American he insisted on telling me all about his time in Chicago.'

'Ben Shaw,' said Angela, remembering her strange conversation with Mr. Norris.

'That's right,' said William in surprise. 'Do you know him?'

'No, but I've heard of him,' said Angela. 'He works at Low Meadow Farm, I believe.'

'Well, we're the best of pals now,' said William. 'At least, I think so.'

Angela laughed. Just then two kitchen-maids came out, carrying a large tub of apples between them.

'Those must be for the fête tomorrow,' said Angela. 'I'm supposed to be helping. As a matter of fact, I shouldn't be a bit surprised if Elisabeth were to give me some job or other as soon as I get in.'

'Aren't you baking?' said William wickedly, and she turned to see a mischievous look on his face. 'I was talking to Mr. Doggett this morning, and he told me all about your particular expertise in the kitchen.'

'Don't tell me he told you about the exploding blackberry pie,' said Angela. 'He was under strict instructions never to mention that again. The gunpowder was an experiment, but the cook gave notice and I don't believe they ever got the stains off the ceiling.'

William seemed to be looking at her in a new light.

'I always assumed you were a well-behaved little girl, ma'am,' he said.

'Goodness, no,' said Angela. 'I was tremendously naughty. Humphrey was the good one. My mother was the only person who could manage me. When she died I rather lost any reason to stay here.'

She looked a little sad for a moment, then seemed to realize that perhaps she had said too much. She smiled awkwardly and went away, leaving William to watch her go with raised eyebrows and some sympathy.

36

Chapter Six

THE DAY of the fête dawned and everybody looked anxiously out of their windows to see what the weather was going to be like. There was some sun, but it was more often than not hidden by heavy clouds which threatened rain at some point. The Two Tithes family were all up early, and after a hasty breakfast Elisabeth and Angela headed down to the lower field, which the Cardews had kindly given up for the day, and set to work. Angela wanted to be helpful, but rather feared she was getting in the way, since every time she finished one job she had to go and ask Elisabeth to give her another and, furthermore, to explain how to do it. In the end Kathie took pity on her and they spent a merry half an hour stringing up bunting across the stalls. Elisabeth, meanwhile, was setting up the cake stall with great efficiency, assisted by a woman of sixty or so whom Angela guessed to be Margaret Tipping. She glanced about and saw Tom Tipping setting out seats for the brass band concert which was to be held later in the afternoon.

By half past ten everything was ready, and Angela now

took the opportunity to have a look around. She was to be on the bric-à-brac stall, but there was also a jam and preserves stall, a cheese stall, a tea tent, several handicraft stalls, a hoop-la and a coconut shy. At the very end of the line was a stall that appeared to consist of nothing but a plain wooden table with a glass jar on it. By the table a man sat in a chair, his arms folded and his feet planted firmly apart. His very air said, 'I'm here and I'm not moving.' As Angela came closer she saw that just beyond the table was a makeshift wooden pen containing what appeared to be a small pig. The animal snuffled about and snorted happily, and the man in the seat said:

'Guess the weight of the pig. Sixpence a go.'

'Oh!' said Angela, looking at the glass jar, which was empty. 'Very well, then.' She put sixpence into the jar, and said, 'Now what do I have to do?'

'Guess the weight of the pig,' said the man, as one speaking to a person of limited intelligence.

'Oh, yes,' said Angela. She regarded the animal, which obligingly presented its rear end to her. 'Twenty-four pounds and two ounces,' she said at last.

The man removed a pencil from behind his ear, then brought out a dog-eared notebook, licked his finger and opened it.

'Name?' he said.

Angela gave her name and he wrote it and her guess down laboriously, then sat back and without another word began to watch the pig. Angela waited for a second, then retreated uncertainly.

'That's Mr. Toft of Lees Farm,' said Kathie, who had been watching. 'He insisted on having the pig stall because he'd heard of them doing it in some other village. It's hardly practical, of course—after all, this isn't exactly an agricultural show—but Mr. Hunter didn't want to offend him as he's the best bass voice in the church choir.'

'I think he might do better if he were a little friendlier,' said Angela.

At twenty to eleven there was much consternation when it suddenly began to rain and they all had to run for shelter. For ten minutes they watched as it threatened to become a downpour, but then, as soon as it had begun, the rain stopped, the clouds cleared away and the sun began to blaze down. Soon the ground was steaming and it looked as though the fête would take place under sunny skies.

At eleven o'clock Lady Cardew, in all her glory as the wife of the squire, triumphantly declared the fête open, and the fun began. The event had drawn quite a crowd, and Angela found herself kept busy with the bric-à-brac stall, which for some reason was attracting a great deal of attention. It was not until she had been there for over an hour that it occurred to her that many of the visitors to the stall had probably come to see *her*, and the idea quite startled her. It made sense, though—everyone must surely know that Sir Humphrey Cardew's sister, the famous Mrs. Marchmont from the newspapers, had come to visit, and there was bound to be some curiosity. And in fact that proved to be the case, for rather than selling things, Angela found herself answering questions and trying to place half-remembered faces, and altogether getting very little done. At last she decided that if everybody was going to come and gawp, then they should jolly well buy something while they were there, and so she set herself to exerting all the charm she could muster. Before long the sixpences and shillings were rolling in and she began to do rather well, much to her relief, for she had been afraid that her stall would meet with similar success to that of Mr. Toft, which was doing little business, as far as she could see from where she stood.

At lunch-time Kathie came to relieve her and Angela went off to find something to eat. Presiding over the tea tent was Elisabeth's mother, Mrs. Randall, who appeared to have left her lorgnette at home and spoke to Angela as though she had never seen her before. As Angela stood, balancing a saucer in one hand and a plate in the other, she saw Humphrey, who had been striding about all morning with an air of great superiority.

'And how are you getting along?' he said to her. 'I hope it is not too dull for you. I know you are used to more excitement than we can generally offer in a little country village such as this one.'

He might have been talking to a visiting dignitary's wife rather than his own sister, but Angela smiled and said she was enjoying herself very much.

'At half past three we will have a brass band,' went on Humphrey. 'It will be rather a forlorn affair, I fear, since there was a dispute last week between the two trumpet players which ended in one of them—the best one, unfortunately—resigning. The vicar has promised to replace him, but his playing is somewhat rusty and the quality cannot be guaranteed, I am afraid. Still, we must all clap loudly and encourage them as much as possible.'

Angela promised to do her best, and shortly afterwards returned to duty. Her efforts had been so successful that by half past three her stall was looking very bare. The brass band was due to start playing at any moment, and she thought she might take a few minutes off to go and watch it, since she judged there was unlikely to be any urgent and last-minute demand for the cracked china shepherdess or the dented pewter tankard which were all that remained to be sold. She saw Humphrey and Elisabeth sitting in the front row of seats and went to join them. Elisabeth was looking crosser than usual.

'Well, at least *you're* still here, Angela,' she said. 'Margaret Tipping has disappeared so I've had to leave the cake stall unattended. I don't suppose you've seen her, have you?'

'Not lately,' said Angela. 'Can't Kathie help?'

'I can't find her either,' said Elisabeth. 'But we'll be finishing soon and I do hope they aren't trying to get out of the clearing-up. There's such a lot to do.'

The band struck up then and they had to stop talking and pay attention. Angela did her best to enjoy it, but it was evident that the musicians had not rehearsed enough, for they made more than one false start—and indeed, at one point the vicar, a stringy little man who was the physical opposite to his wife, seemed to be playing an entirely different tune from the rest of them. As Humphrey had said, Mr. Hunter was rather rusty, and his face grew purple with the effort of getting a note out of his trumpet. Mrs. Hunter, who was sitting on Angela's other side, was quite obviously tone deaf and was enjoying it immensely, for she applauded loudly after every number.

'Bravo! Bravo!' she called. 'Stephen's musical ability was one of the things I loved about him as a young man,' she confided to Angela. 'It's very gratifying to see that he has lost none of it.'

At last the band ran out of puff and the audience began to disperse. It would soon be time for everyone to go home, but first there were raffles to draw and prizes to award, with Sir Humphrey and Lady Cardew doing the honours. Angela clapped politely when called upon to do so, but then was button-holed by Mrs. Hunter, and was standing to one side in conversation with her when she heard her name announced. She turned to find Mr. Toft standing before her, clasping something in his arms that squealed and wriggled.

'Eighteen pounds, four and a half ounces,' he said.

'What?' said Angela.

'Eighteen pounds, four and a half ounces,' he said again.

'You've won the guess the weight of the pig competition,' said Mrs. Hunter with a malicious smile.

'Really?' said Angela. 'But my guess was nowhere near that.'

'Fourteen entries altogether. Yours was the nearest,' said Mr. Toft. 'Here.' He took a step towards her and made as if to hand her the struggling animal. Angela stepped back in a panic.

'Do you mean I win the *pig*?' she exclaimed in horror. 'I thought the prize would be a jar of jam or something.'

'No,' said Mr. Toft, with a withering look. 'Guess the weight of the pig. You win the pig.'

Then without further ado he pushed the piglet into her arms and walked off.

'But what shall I *do* with it?' cried Angela at his retreating back. The pig had its own ideas on that subject. No sooner had it been handed to its new owner than it began to scrabble wildly at her frock with its muddy feet. It then stuck its bristly snout into her face, gave a tremendous squeal and with one giant leap was out of her arms and heading straight for the tea tent.

'Quick, catch it!' cried Elisabeth. There followed several minutes of confusion as people variously leapt out of the pig's way or tried to stop it as it passed. But the animal had quite a turn of speed, and easily dodged all the hands that reached out to grasp it. The children all thought this was great fun and soon a group of five or six boys and girls, with Peter Montgomery at their head, were shouting with laughter as they tried to catch the escaped pig. It reached the tea tent but swerved off to the left as someone emerged. For a second it seemed to hesitate, then it made a bee-line for the cake stall, and Elisabeth gasped in horror as it shot under the table, dragging a line of bunting with it. Unfortunately, the bunting was attached to the tablecloth that covered the stall, and there was an ear-splitting crash as platefuls of bath buns, Bakewell tarts, rock cakes, walnut cakes, sponge cakes and a very fine fruit cake were all dragged to the ground. Angela winced.

'You'll get the blame for that,' said a voice by her ear. It was Mrs. Hunter, who wore an expression of great satisfaction.

Angela glanced at Elisabeth and very nearly laughed at the look on her sister-in-law's face. Perhaps it had been worth it for that alone. The pig was now rooting happily among the ruined cakes, while a small crowd of people watched it with great amusement. This had been a fine end to the day, and as it gradually became evident that nothing more exciting was likely to happen, the visitors now began to drift off and go home.

Elisabeth had pulled herself together and was bidding a gracious goodbye to everyone as they left, while the stall-holders began to pack things away and clear up. The pig was still helping itself busily to cake, and Angela regarded it from a safe distance.

'Who will rid me of this turbulent pig?' she said to herself in consternation. 'I can't just leave it here.'

In the end she was rescued by William, who had been watching the fun with great enjoyment. He caught the animal in his coat and deposited it neatly back in its pen before it could escape again.

'But what am I meant to do with it?' said Angela after

she had duly thanked him. 'We haven't room for it at the flat.'

'Don't worry about that,' he said. 'I've had a word with old Ben Shaw and he says they'll gladly take it at Low Meadow farm. He doesn't think much of Mr. Toft but he won't say no to one of his pigs, he said.'

'Thank goodness for that,' said Angela. She looked down at her dress and sighed. If she went to get changed Elisabeth would think that she, too, was trying to avoid clearing up. She brushed at the mud with her handkerchief but to little effect. She would have to see what Marthe could do with it later.

'Come and help me take the bric-à-brac stall down,' she said to William, and they set to work with the few helpers who remained. They had almost finished when Angela noticed that Elisabeth, instead of helping to clear up, was standing by the gate to the field with Kathie, who was talking animatedly and pointing in the direction of the village. Angela packed away the last few things and then went across to join them.

'Is anything the matter?' she said.

Kathie turned to her. She looked very serious.

'I'm afraid there is,' she said. 'Someone has shot Mr. Tipping.'

Chapter Seven

IT WAS NOT long before the essential facts of the matter were established. Shortly after lunch-time, Kathie had run home for a spare tablecloth, as there had been a spill in the tea tent and the only one they had was soaked. On the way back she happened to meet Norman Tipping, who was on his way to the fête too. They walked together along Dead Man's Path and met Norman's father going in the other direction. Tom said he would see them later and they went on their way. A minute or two later they heard the sound of a shotgun going off, which puzzled them a little but not unduly. Shortly after that, they passed Daniel Tyler from Burdett's farm, who was heading in the same direction as Tom Tipping. They had almost reached the fête when Tyler came haring after them in a great state, and said they had better come quickly as Mr. Tipping had been shot. Naturally, they had rushed back with him and found Tom Tipping lying dead, shot in the head, with his dog next to him, pawing at him and whining pitifully. Kathie ran to fetch a doctor but there was nothing to be done. The doctor insisted on calling the police, and Norman came to fetch his mother and break the news, and the Tippings and Kathie had spent the rest of the afternoon at the Tippings' farmhouse talking to the police, until Kathie was given permission to go and tell everybody what had happened.

Further details were soon known. By Sunday lunchtime the word was all around the village that Tom Tipping and Andrew Norris had been seen together on Dead Man's Path earlier on Saturday, engaged in an altercation in which Norris loudly threatened to shoot Tipping if he found him trespassing again. The feud between the two men was well known, of course, and everybody nodded sagely and said that it had only been a matter of time before Norris had gone off his head and carried out his threat. On this particular occasion the rumours were slower than the local police, for by Saturday evening Andrew Norris had already been arrested on suspicion of murder and his house was being searched.

By Sunday evening, however, everything had changed, for to everyone's surprise Mr. Norris turned out to have an alibi. At the time of the murder—which, given the presence of three witnesses during the fatal period, could be narrowed down to an interval of approximately five minutes—he had been eating his lunch in the Red Lion Inn in Banford Green, in company with his man Ben Shaw. As it was the day of the fête, the inn had not been very busy, but the landlord and one or two other customers, as well as Ben Shaw himself, were willing to swear to Andrew Norris's presence there at the crucial time. This settled the matter and the police were forced to release Norris forthwith, much to their annoyance (for they had been congratulating themselves on an easy case), leaving the small matter of who had killed Thomas Tipping at present unsolved. An inquest was to be held on

Tuesday morning, but it was expected to be adjourned while the police investigated further.

On Monday morning Angela came down to breakfast a little late to find Humphrey and Elisabeth already in the breakfast-parlour. Mrs. Randall was there too, and the lorgnette immediately sprang to attention as Angela entered. Elisabeth was buttering a slice of toast and holding forth about the momentous events of the past two days.

'Mrs. Hunter says that old Norris didn't help himself at all when they arrested him,' she was saying. 'Apparently, he denied doing it, but said that whoever *did* do it had done him a favour and that he'd like to shake him by the hand.'

'Good gracious!' said Mrs. Randall, looking suitably shocked.

'I'd like to know who told her that, though,' went on Elisabeth. 'She was laid up all yesterday so it must have been a visitor. Or perhaps she heard it from Mr. Hunter. He might have heard it from someone at church. Yes—that must be it: he probably got it from Mrs. Primm. She'd know from her husband, of course, since he was the one who arrested Andrew Norris.'

It was too early in the morning for Angela to follow all this, and so she grasped at the one piece of information she *had* managed to understand.

'Is Mrs. Hunter ill?' she said.

'Not exactly,' said Elisabeth. 'She sprained her wrist and grazed her knees rather badly falling off her bicycle on the way home from the fête. Of course, she's far too old for that sort of nonsense these days, but she *will* insist on doing it. Luckily Alice Hopwell saw her and helped her home, but they had to leave the bicycle and Mrs. Hunter was terribly worried about it—the silly woman is convinced the gipsies are out to steal every bicycle in the area—but then

47

Alice said she'd chain it up until Mrs. Hunter's wrist was better.'

'I see,' said Angela. She helped herself to some toast and gazed out of the window. Sunday had been almost unbearably tedious—she had lost count of the number of times she had apologized for the pig incident, although of course it had not been her fault—and she was longing to escape and get some fresh air away from Two Tithes. She wondered wistfully whether the police were swarming around Dead Man's Path today, hunting for clues. It would be rather fun to help, she thought—although of course she had no right to do so, and indeed would probably be considered a dreadful nuisance if she *did* turn up. Still, she would certainly escape and go for a walk if she could.

She was about to take a sip of her tea when her attention was caught by the sight of a tall, gangling young man, sparse of chin and splendid of tooth, who was just then sauntering nonchalantly past the window in a regrettable yellow checked jacket. He skirted a rose-bush and began to walk along the path to the left-hand side of a large pergola.

'Who is that?' she said. The others looked up.

'I have no idea,' said Humphrey.

'He's not from around here, at any rate,' said Elisabeth. 'You don't suppose he's one of these gawpers, do you? These people who turn up and stare ghoulishly whenever there's a murder. I've heard of them before.'

'He has no business on our grounds,' said Humphrey, 'and I shall certainly warn him off.'

He stood up and was about to leave the room when a second young man sauntered past in the opposite direction, a notebook in his hand and an unlit cigarette protruding from the corner of his mouth. His hat was stuck on his head at a rakish angle and he looked most disreputable. Angela opened her mouth to say something, then closed it again. They all watched as the second man skirted the rose-bush and walked along the path to the right-hand side of the pergola, and Angela stifled a laugh at the enormous start he gave when he reached the end and caught sight of the first man. The two intruders glared at one another suspiciously for a full minute, then appeared to enter into cautious conversation. The first man said something with a smirk, and the second grimaced and seemed inclined to continue on his way alone, but the first man set off to catch him up and the two of them walked off together in what looked like a state of uneasy truce.

'Well!' said Elisabeth, once they were out of sight. 'Of all the impudence. One would think they owned the place. If you see them again, Humphrey, you must warn them off. We can't have tourists tramping across the grounds whenever they like just because someone has been killed.'

'They're not tourists,' said Angela. 'I'm rather afraid it's the press. They must have got wind of the story.'

'The press?' said Humphrey in dismay. 'How did they find out about it?' An awful suspicion began to dawn on him and he drew himself up and regarded his sister sternly. 'Now, Angela, tell the truth: did you call them?'

'Of course not,' said Angela in surprise.

'I know you are fond of appearing in the newspapers —' went on Humphrey.

'No I'm not,' interjected Angela hurriedly.

'—but I should have thought that a quiet visit to your family was hardly a suitable occasion on which to invite the press to intrude.'

'But I didn't,' said Angela. 'I promise you, I didn't.'

'Well, then,' said Humphrey. 'If you say so, then I suppose I shall have to believe you. But how did they know to come here?'

'They have all kinds of ways of finding things out,' said

Angela. 'They certainly wouldn't need me to tell them that someone had been murdered.'

'Then must we really put up with reporters crawling all over the place from now on?' said Elisabeth.

'I'm afraid we must,' said Angela. She looked out of the window again, wanting to go out and join in the fun, even though she knew nobody would approve. Her supposition was confirmed a minute later, when Humphrey cleared his throat and said:

'I do hope, Angela, that you will have the sense not to try and interfere with the police as they carry out their investigation. I am aware that you have gained something of a reputation for *detective-work,*' (this last phrase was uttered down his nose) 'but I am quite certain they have no need of your help in this instance—and, indeed, they may consider it rude of you to offer, since it might be interpreted as a suggestion that they are not capable of doing their job.'

'I'm sure they're perfectly capable of doing their job,' said Angela. 'And I never—' she stopped. She had been about to say, 'interfere,' but she realized that was not exactly true. She went on, 'Of course, it's nothing to do with me, and I have no intention of doing any investigating.'

'I am glad to hear it,' said Humphrey, with an approving nod. 'Let's leave that sort of thing to the people who know what they are doing. There is nothing worse than an incompetent amateur.'

Angela stirred her tea vigorously here, but said nothing.

They finished breakfast and Humphrey went outside to find the intruders and give them a dressing-down, while Elisabeth walked out without a word to talk to the servants. Mrs. Randall put down her cup and rose.

'You did look funny with the pig,' she remarked, and went out.

Angela waited five minutes then, as nobody seemed inclined to come back, got up and ran to fetch her hat, and was shortly walking briskly away from the house and towards Dead Man's Path. It might be ghoulish of her, but she could not help her curiosity, and if she was spotted she could always say she was going to visit Kathie. Of course, she had no intention at all of doing any investigating, but there was no reason why she should not take a little stroll into the village.

She took a different route from the one she had taken on her previous walk, and entered Dead Man's Path from the field in which the fête had been held. The sky was overcast and there was a chill in the air, and the entrance to the path where the trees met overhead had a more forbidding aspect to it than it had the other day in the sunshine. As she entered the path she was struck by the gloom and the silence, and she half-considered turning back. She pressed on, however, and followed the windings of the path until she was almost at the spot where Mr. Norris had pointed his shotgun at her on Friday. As she approached, she heard voices and slowed cautiously. Soon the owners of the voices came into view. Two men were standing in conversation. One of them was gesturing here and there as he explained something to the other, who listened carefully. Angela recognized the second man immediately, and as she approached he looked up and his eyes widened in surprise.

'Hallo, inspector,' she said cheerfully.

'Why, Mrs. Marchmont,' said Inspector Jameson. 'Whatever are you doing here?'

'Being dreadfully curious, I'm afraid,' she admitted. 'I can't seem to shake it off. But I was about to ask the same question of you. Have they called in Scotland Yard already?'

'Not exactly,' said Jameson. 'The local inspector picked this week to go on holiday, and I happened to be in the area to discuss another case with the Chief Constable when I heard about this one, so someone suggested I take a look. This is Sergeant Primm, who is really in charge of the matter. But don't tell me you're mixed up in all this?'

'No, not at all,' said Angela. 'It's nothing to do with me this time, I'm pleased to say. I didn't know the dead man—at least, not to speak to—and I didn't find his body either. I'm quite a bystander on this occasion. I was helping at the church fête when it all happened.'

Sergeant Primm shook his head in disgust.

'It's a pity it had to happen just then,' he said. 'The whole village was wandering about that day. We're going to have a terrible job establishing alibis.'

'It sounds like it,' said Angela. 'I don't envy you the task. But everybody is talking about it, so perhaps witnesses will come forward of their own accord. And presumably whoever killed Mr. Tipping must have had a motive, so it's not as though the whole of Banford is under suspicion, is it?'

'No,' said the sergeant politely, but did not go on. Angela guessed he had his own ideas as to who might have done it but did not wish to speak of them in her presence.

'If you were helping at the church fête then I suppose you must be staying here,' said Jameson.

'Yes,' said Angela. 'I'm at Two Tithes, the big house just outside the village.'

'Isn't that Sir Humphrey Cardew's place?' said Jameson. 'Are the Cardews friends of yours?'

'They're family, as a matter of fact,' said Angela. 'I am—or was—a Cardew myself. Humphrey is my brother.'

'Is he really?' said Jameson, staring.

'Does that surprise you?' said Angela.

'It does, rather,' he said. 'Somehow I can't quite picture it.'

'No, Humphrey is far more "county" than I am,' said Angela with a smile. 'I rather left all that sort of thing behind me years ago. As a matter of fact, the last time I was here was before the war. It's just the most tremendous coincidence that when I finally come back here a murder happens—at least, I assume it was murder. Am I allowed to ask you about it, or must you be terribly discreet?' Asking questions was not the same as investigating, she told herself.

'That is entirely the decision of Sergeant Primm, since he is in charge and I am merely an observer for the purposes of this investigation,' said Inspector Jameson politely.

'Not at all, sir,' said the sergeant, acknowledging the gesture. 'We're only too glad to accept whatever assistance you can give us here.'

'Well, then, I suppose you know that Mrs. Marchmont has been very helpful to the police during several recent murder investigations,' said Inspector Jameson, 'and has gained rather a reputation for her detective-work. Still,' he went on, addressing Angela, 'there's not much to tell you at the moment. I suppose you—and the entire village—know as much as I do. Thomas Tipping was killed by a shotgun blast to the head while walking along here with his dog shortly after lunch-time on Saturday, while most people were at the church fête. A man known to have a grudge against Mr. Tipping was arrested, then released shortly afterwards when he was discovered to have an alibi. I haven't seen any of the witnesses yet, but I understand the sergeant has spoken to them.'

'Was Mr. Tipping carrying a shotgun himself?' said Angela.

'Why, yes, he was,' replied the inspector. 'It was found next to his body.'

'Presumably he had no chance to use it to defend himself, then,' said Angela.

'Not much. He was shot in the back of the head,' said the sergeant. 'He won't have known a thing.'

'Then I suppose that's another point in favour of Andrew Norris,' said Angela, thinking. 'Not that he needs one, of course, if he has an alibi—but if Norris did it, then surely he wouldn't have sneaked up behind Mr. Tipping to shoot him, since he regularly threatened him with it quite openly.'

'Oh, you know that, do you?' said Inspector Jameson.

'Yes,' said Angela. 'I happened to—er—encounter Mr. Norris and his shotgun myself the other day, and he made no bones about it.'

'That's Norris, right enough,' agreed the sergeant. 'Everyone knew about it.'

'Was Mr. Tipping's shotgun still loaded?' asked Angela hesitantly. 'I mean, I don't suppose he was shot with his own gun?'

Primm shook his head.

'No, of course not,' said Angela, 'or there would have been a struggle for the gun, wouldn't there? But you say there wasn't.'

'We will need to find out if anyone was seen running around the place with a shotgun shortly after Saturday lunch-time,' said Jameson.

'Hmph,' said Sergeant Primm. 'Hardly the time of year for it. I know Tom Tipping carried his for protection against old Norris, who always carries his about with him, but even Norris didn't have his on Saturday—leastways, not according to the landlord of the Red Lion.'

'So, then, all you need is to find a witness who saw a man with a gun,' said Angela, 'and then presumably you'll have your murderer.'

'Let's hope such a witness exists, then,' said Inspector Jameson.

Chapter Eight

JUST THEN THEY WERE JOINED, rather to Angela's surprise, by Norman Tipping and his mother, who had been walking along Dead Man's Path together. It was the first time Angela had met Margaret Tipping properly, although she had seen her at the fête, and she looked at the older woman curiously. Mrs. Tipping must have been handsome once: her bones were good and her features regular, but now, in her sixties, she looked worn down and tired—although, of course, the fact that her husband had just died in violent and mysterious circumstances might have had something to do with that. If Mrs. Tipping was particularly upset by his death, however, she gave no sign of it, for her expression was closed and revealed nothing of her thoughts. As she and her son joined the others at the spot where Tom Tipping had died she glanced about her dispassionately, but said not a word. Sergeant Primm introduced the newcomers to Inspector Jameson. Norman Tipping said what was proper, and then went on:

'I'm afraid Mother insisted on coming here this morning. I tried to dissuade her from it but there was no putting her off. She would come.'

Mrs. Tipping appeared not to be listening. She was still looking around expressionlessly.

'I always knew something dreadful would happen here,' she said at last in a flat voice. 'And now it has. The place is haunted, don't you think? Dead Man's Path, they call it. Well, whoever named it was right enough.'

The day was dull, and thin fingers of grey light penetrated weakly through the branches of the trees overhead and onto the path. Angela glanced about her involuntarily and for a moment could not help but agree with Margaret Tipping's description. It was quite different from how it had looked the other day, when the sunshine had dappled the place with cheerful patches of yellow and green.

Inspector Jameson glanced at Sergeant Primm and said:

'I'm very sorry about your husband, Mrs. Tipping, and I'd like to find out what happened to him. Should you mind if I asked you one or two questions? We can do it at your house if you would prefer not to stay here.'

'Oh, it's all the same to me. We can do it here if you like,' said Mrs. Tipping, still with that expressionless tone.

'Thank you,' said Jameson. 'Very well, I understand from Sergeant Primm that your husband went out at the same time every day.'

'Yes,' said Mrs. Tipping. 'He always goes for a walk after lunch—used to go, I should say.'

'Did he always come the same way?'

'Yes,' said Mrs. Tipping. 'He always came along here. Always along Dead Man's Path. I told him not to do it—not to provoke Andrew—but he would never listen.'

'Do you mean Mr. Norris?' said Jameson, glancing at Sergeant Primm, who nodded. 'I gather there was a dispute between your husband and Mr. Norris over this path. What was it about, exactly?'

'Andrew has a bee in his bonnet about it,' said Mrs. Tipping. 'Everyone uses it, but there's some doubt as to whether it's common land or whether it belongs to Andrew. Andrew insists it's his, of course. He says that anyone can use it who likes—but only because he says so. When he and Tom fell out, he withdrew his permission and forbade Tom from using the path. I know he's a stubborn old thing but it was partly Tom's fault, as he *would* deliberately provoke Andrew about the path and taunt him about its being common land, when he ought to have kept quiet. But Andrew always had a vengeful temper on him, and that's why Tom never went out without his shotgun, because he never knew when Andrew would turn up and threaten him.'

'It was quite ridiculous,' said Norman Tipping. 'Two grown men behaving in that way. They were forever glaring and growling at one another. Once I came upon them standing each with his gun pointed directly at the other, and told them both in no uncertain terms how silly they looked. Of course, that's why we—why everyone— immediately thought it was old Norris who'd done it, as everyone knew about the feud. But I gather he has an alibi.'

'Yes, he has,' said Sergeant Primm.

'Then who killed him?' said Norman.

Inspector Jameson was just about to reply when he suddenly spied a pair of eyes peering at him from behind a tree. They seemed to belong to a boy of about eleven.

'Hallo,' he said. 'Who's this?'

'It's Peter,' said Norman, as Peter Montgomery stepped out and smiled shyly round at them all. 'What are you doing here, Peter? Run along home, now. This is not the place for little boys. I'm surprised your mother allowed it.'

'Oh, but she's here too,' said the boy, and Inspector Jameson looked up as a woman came into view. She was slim and fair, with bright blue eyes, and Jameson thought she was the prettiest woman he had ever seen.

'Hallo,' she said as she arrived. She did not wait for a reply, but immediately went across and took Margaret Tipping's hand kindly. 'How are you, Margaret?' she said. 'I hope you've managed to get some sleep. I was just coming to see you. I do wish you'd let me help you with something. There must be such a lot to do.'

'Thank you, Kathie,' said Mrs. Tipping with perfect equanimity. 'It's terribly kind of you, and of course you shall help, but it's all been such a shock and I'm not quite sure where to start.'

Norman introduced Kathie to Inspector Jameson with a proprietorial air, and she turned her smile on him and said how reassuring it was that the police could always be relied upon to work night and day when dreadful crimes of this nature came along, and never to rest until the criminal was caught. Without quite meaning to, Jameson immediately found himself resolving inwardly to do as she said and leave no stone unturned in his attempts to solve the mystery, even though the case was not strictly his.

'Are you really a detective?' said Peter suddenly. 'From Scotland Yard?'

'Now, Peter,' said Kathie. 'You're not to bother the police while they're working. This isn't a game. He'd like to be a detective when he grows up,' she explained to Jameson with another smile.

'Should you?' said Jameson to Peter, who blushed at being addressed directly by the great Scotland Yard inspector, and then nodded.

'It's not all fun and games, I'm afraid,' said Jameson. 'In fact, it's jolly hard work sometimes.'

'I don't mind hard work,' said Peter stoutly.

'Then perhaps we shall see you at the Yard one day,' said Jameson.

'I should like that,' said Peter, his eyes shining.

'Have you any other questions at present?' said Norman. Jameson gave a negative and he said, 'Then we shall go back, if you don't mind. I think Mother has been here long enough. Do come back with us,' he went on to Kathie. 'Mother would be glad of the company, I'm sure.'

Margaret Tipping nodded, and Kathie said, 'All right, then—but only if I can help in some way. Come along, Peter.'

The four of them went off. Angela said she had to get back to Two Tithes and excused herself too, leaving Inspector Jameson and Sergeant Primm alone.

'No surprises about what's going to happen there, I reckon,' said Primm, with a nod towards the departing group.

'What do you mean?' said Jameson.

'Tipping and Mrs. Montgomery. He's been courting her for months now,' said the sergeant.

'Oh?'

'Yes. The Cardews are keen on the match. Lady Cardew is her sister, you know. They've got plenty of money but they begrudge having to pay the boy's school fees. They want him off their hands. That's rich people all over for you.'

'Does she like him?' said Jameson.

Primm shrugged.

'Who knows with women?' he said. He glanced about and shivered. 'It's getting chilly, don't you think, sir? What do you say we go back to the station and talk over the case there?'

Jameson assented and the two of them went off, Jameson thinking what a pity it was that a woman like Kathie Montgomery should be thrown away on a man like Norman Tipping.

Chapter Nine

BACK AT THE little police station in Banford Green Sergeant Primm and Inspector Jameson sat at opposite sides of the sergeant's desk and consulted their notebooks.

'Tell me about this alibi,' said Jameson. 'This Norris chap looks like a perfect suspect if ever I saw one, but you say he couldn't have done it.'

'No,' said Primm. He flipped over a page and prodded at his notebook with a pencil. He cleared his throat and began. 'So, then, as you know, Saturday was the day of the church fête, and most people were there. This is what we know so far: early on Saturday morning Tom Tipping helped set up some of the stalls in Tithes Field. At eleven o'clock the fête was declared open, and Tipping stayed until about a quarter to twelve then left, as he had some things to see to on the farm. His wife was looking after the cake stall, and he promised to come back later and help clear up. He went home by his usual route, which was along Dead Man's Path. There he encountered Andrew Norris, and at about five to twelve, according to a number of witnesses from the village who were heading for the fête at that time, the two men had a loud argument in which Norris threatened to shoot Tom Tipping if he ever found him trespassing on his land again. This was a fairly frequent occurrence, by the way, so the witnesses didn't think much of it. At any rate, the argument subsided when the villagers arrived, and Tipping passed on. He arrived home and had a cold lunch, then at about twenty minutes to two took his shotgun and went out with his dog. This was his usual time to go out, and we know he did it on this day because he was met on Dead Man's Path by his son Norman Tipping and Mrs. Montgomery, who were heading to Tithes Field themselves. Mrs. Montgomery had been helping at the fête, but I gather she'd run home to fetch something and just happened to meet Norman Tipping on her way back. According to them, Tom Tipping said he would see them later and then passed out of sight. They hadn't gone more than a couple of hundred yards when they heard the sound of a shotgun going off. They were a bit puzzled but not particularly so, and they didn't bother turning back. A little farther on, they met Daniel Tyler from Burdett's going the other way, and it was he who discovered Tom Tipping's body a few minutes later, lying there with nobody near him except the dog. Tyler hared after Norman and Mrs. Montgomery in a great state, found them just going into the fête, and told them what had happened. They ran back with him and called the doctor, who called us. And a very pretty mess it is too,' he finished, sitting back.

'Yes,' said Jameson. 'Still, the presence of witnesses seems to narrow down the time of death nicely. He must have died at—what? A quarter to or perhaps ten to two?'

'Thereabouts,' agreed Primm. 'And at that time Andrew Norris was in the Red Lion, having a bite of lunch with his man Ben Shaw. Ben has sworn to it, as have the landlord and two of his regular customers, who were the only people there at the time, business being quiet on that day because of the fête. Norris and Shaw arrived at about a quarter past one, and went into the snug. They were brought some cold meat and cheese at half past one, and then left the place at ten past two. The landlord was in the tap-room with his eye on the door to the street all that time, and swears that Norris didn't leave. It's a great pity,' he went on. 'If it weren't for his cast-iron alibi then that would be that: we could lock him up and forget about it. The two of them have been fighting over that path for years, the silly old goats.'

'Does it really belong to Norris?' said Jameson.

'I couldn't tell you,' said Primm. 'He got the idea that it was his about twenty years ago, and went to law about it. It never got resolved, though, as there's just enough doubt in the deeds to his land to make it uncertain. What is certain is that everyone has used Dead Man's Path freely for centuries, and he's not going to stop them now. It's really just a convenient excuse for him to make things difficult for Tom Tipping.'

'Do you mean the feud came before the dispute over the path?'

Primm nodded.

'Yes,' he said. 'They haven't got on for years, ever since Tom married Margaret about forty years ago. Norris was sweet on her, you see, but Tipping stepped in, and they've been rowing ever since. 'Course, it's not so much the woman they're fighting over—it's more that old Norris is a bad loser and can't bear to be beaten. Tipping got what was his, you see, and now Norris wants to pay him back.'

'Goodness me,' said Jameson. He glanced at his watch. 'It'll be lunch-time soon, but if you don't mind I'd like to go back to Dead Man's Path first and look around more carefully, this time without interruptions.'

'Right you are, sir,' said Sergeant Primm.

Inspector Jameson looked about him as they came out of the police station. They were in the centre of the village, which was laid out around a large green. Many of the buildings were ancient and had thatched roofs, and the whole effect was very attractive and quaint. Of course, the signs of modernity had inevitably encroached upon even this quiet place, and on market days (for Banford Green, although now considered merely a village, had once been a thriving market town and still proudly held to that tradition), the cobbled streets that led off the green tended to be crowded with motor-cars and vans. Otherwise, there was little to disturb the peace, and as Jameson eyed the pretty cottages with their window-boxes full of flowers, he understood why people might choose to live here.

A few doors along from the police station was the Red Lion Inn, where Andrew Norris and Ben Shaw had had their lunch on the day of Tom Tipping's murder. It looked pleasant enough, and Jameson made a note to speak to the landlord. The two policemen crossed the green and walked down a narrow street, then turned left. This brought them to the entrance to Tithes Field and the start of Dead Man's Path. Tom Tipping's body had been found some way along it, and Jameson paused again to look about him.

'As you can see, sir,' observed Sergeant Primm, 'even if Andrew Norris did somehow manage to sneak out of the inn, he'd have been in full view of everyone in the street and couldn't possibly have run all the way here, shot Tipping and then come back without *someone* seeing him.'

'Is this the only way to Dead Man's Path from the Red Lion?' asked Jameson.

'Unless you can run through brick walls,' said Primm,

and pointed. Just past the entrance to Dead Man's Path was a lane. Jameson walked a little way down it and saw on the left farther down a row of tiny terrace cottages. Opposite them was the church, a pretty building of grey stone with a mossy roof, which sat within a quiet churchyard.

'The inn backs onto those houses,' said the sergeant, who had followed him. 'You'd have to jump over them to get here.'

'I see. That seems to settle it, then,' said Jameson.

They returned up the lane and entered Dead Man's Path. The sky was still gloomy and the path was even darker than it had been that morning. Nobody was about, and they reached the spot where Tom Tipping had died without meeting anybody. Sergeant Primm looked about him warily.

'I'm not one for believing in ghosts,' he said, 'but Margaret Tipping was right enough when she said this place was haunted. It's not the pleasantest of spots.'

'No,' agreed Inspector Jameson. 'Why is it called Dead Man's Path?'

'I don't know,' said the sergeant. 'But I've lived here all my life and my father used to call it by that name, *and* his father before him.'

'But where does it go? It's not a short-cut from the village to the fête, as far as I can tell. It starts at Tithes Field and leads—where?'

'There are farmhouses and cottages up that way,' said Primm. 'Mrs. Montgomery lives in one of them, and some of the farm-hands who work around here live in the others. And a little farther up still there are some newer houses, which were built when the river flooded about thirty years ago and washed away a street of old cottages on the lower land.'

'I see,' said Jameson.

A church bell rang out suddenly in the silence and made them both jump.

'I didn't realize we were so near the church,' said Jameson. He peered through the trees and saw the tumble-down wall of the churchyard. 'Hmm,' he went on. 'Whoever did it might have come here by any number of ways, it seems. He might have come from the fête in Tithes Field at that end, or from the houses at the other end.'

'Beyond those houses is open countryside,' said Primm helpfully, 'so anyone might have come from that way and done it. There's nothing to say it was someone from Banford. It might have been someone who just happened to be passing.'

'A random killing, you mean?' said the inspector. 'They're pretty rare. Was the motive robbery, perhaps?'

'No,' said the sergeant. 'That was our first thought, as a matter of fact. We've some troublesome gipsies hereabouts, but they're not that sort. They're more for the petty pilfering. They've never been known to attack anybody. We'll have a word with them, though.'

'Do,' said Jameson. 'Of course, with so many people out and about that day, whoever it was might have passed quite unnoticed. It would have been a matter of minutes to slip away from the fête and do the deed, for example.'

'That's true enough,' said Primm. 'There was a pretty large crowd there that day, and a lot of coming and going.'

'Whoever it was took quite a risk, though, since anyone might have turned up—and in fact there were three people nearby at the time that we know of,' said Inspector Jameson. 'He must have arrived, shot Tipping and then run off as quickly as he could before he was caught.' He turned his attention back to the path. 'So, then, our murderer might have arrived from either end of the path, or he might have come from the lane and through the churchyard, or he might have come from that house over there,' he indicated a large farmhouse that could just be glimpsed through the trees on the other side of the path, 'which I take it is the Tippings' house.' He paused. 'Where does Norman Tipping live?' he said after a moment.

'He has his own house on the edge of the village,' said Primm.

'Is he a wealthy man?'

'I couldn't say what he was before, sir,' said the sergeant, 'but I imagine he'll be rather wealthier now that his father is dead.'

The words hung significantly in the air, and the two men exchanged glances.

Chapter Ten

On her way back to Two Tithes, Angela decided to take a detour through the old orchard in which she had spent many a happy hour stealing fruit as a child. She crossed Tithes Field and climbed over a stile, beyond which was the orchard itself. The place looked much the same as it had twenty years ago, and she smiled to herself as she recognized a pear tree that she had been especially fond of as a girl, since she was convinced it produced the sweetest pears of all the trees in the place. She passed through quickly, for she was looking for something in particular, which she soon found. Just beyond the orchard, at the top of a slight incline, stood a stately oak tree of great age. From here it was possible to get a glimpse of Two Tithes house through the trees, and it was here that Joseph the footman—now Doggett the butler—with the help of the old gardener, long dead, had set up a swing for young Miss Angela at her special request. And there it still was, its wooden seat slightly cracked and its ropes greying and a little frayed, with a bare patch of ground below it which indicated that it was still used frequently—

presumably by local children. Angela smiled and for the first time felt something akin to a twinge of affection for the old place. She walked over to the swing and tested the ropes, then brushed off the seat and sat down gingerly. It was something of a squeeze, and her legs were rather too long for it these days, but still it was a swing and it was hers. She pushed off with her feet and then let go, enjoying the long-forgotten sensation and recalling how delighted she had been when Joseph had first brought her here and proudly but shyly shown off his handiwork. Of course, she had been much more daring then, and had liked nothing better than to push herself as high as she could, then at the very highest point launch herself into the air to see how far away she could land. The swing had been the cause of many bumps and grazes, she remembered.

She was still swinging gently back and forth, letting her thoughts drift pleasantly, when she suddenly became aware of someone approaching. It was the second of the two young men she had spotted that morning crossing the garden at Two Tithes, and he did not appear to have seen her, for he was scribbling in his notebook as he walked, stopping only occasionally to gaze into the air for a second and then resume writing. After proceeding slowly in this manner for some minutes he finally drew level with the oak tree, and stopped short as a particularly splendid idea seemed to strike him.

'Ha!' he exclaimed. 'That'll get 'em, see if it won't!'

He wrote down whatever it was, then closed his notebook with a snap and put it in his pocket. He took out a cigarette and inserted it into his mouth, then patted his jacket, looking for a light.

'Hallo, Freddy,' said Angela.

Freddy Pilkington-Soames started and whirled round.

'Good Lord, it's Mrs. M!' he said in astonishment. 'Whatever are you doing here?'

'Discovering that I'm rather wider these days than I was when I was twelve,' she replied regretfully. 'Still, I suppose I ought to be thankful that this branch appears to be holding my weight for now.'

'Are you here for the murder?' said Freddy. 'Don't tell me Scotland Yard have called you in specially.'

'Of course not,' said Angela. 'It's nothing to do with me. Did the *Clarion* send you? I saw you and your friend crossing the lawn this morning—and by the way, didn't you know it's very rude to walk through other people's gardens?'

'Nonsense,' said Freddy. 'It's not as though I was stealing the begonias. It serves them right, anyhow—if people will insist on putting a house in my way then they must expect me to walk through it.'

'A refreshing point of view, I admit,' said Angela. 'Still, though, you'd better watch out for Humphrey.'

'Humphrey? Is he the pompous old ass who caught me on the croquet lawn and told me it was young men such as I who had got the nation into the parlous state in which it presently finds itself?'

'That pompous old ass, as you call him, happens to be my brother,' said Angela.

'No!' said Freddy, and regarded her with some surprise. 'Really? Tell me you're joking. I can't believe you have a brother. In fact, I don't believe you were born in the normal way at all. I've always supposed that you emerged fully formed from a fountain, in a shower of jewels and rose-petals. Please don't shatter my illusions like that—I fear I shall never get over it.'

'Idiot,' she said good-humouredly. 'No, I'm afraid I came into being in the usual manner, and am presently showing what a dutiful sister I am by staying here and behaving with great sobriety and respectability.'

'Poor you,' he said. 'That sounds awfully dull. Still, I'm here now to shine a little light on things.'

'Yes, it's very kind of you,' said Angela. 'And how is the reporting business going?'

'Slow, very slow,' said Freddy. 'I expect it's the time of year.'

'But it's the middle of the season,' said Angela. 'Don't they send you to all the debutantes' dances?'

Freddy shuddered.

'They most certainly do,' he said, 'and I may never recover from the horror of it. I'm *supposed* to be there to observe and then find twenty different ways of describing pink tulle, but what actually happens is that I enter the room and a thousand beady eyes immediately regard me in the manner of a school of sharks contemplating a small and frightened herring. Then all at once I am pounced upon and plied with champagne, and someone says, "Of *course* you remember Bessie, don't you? She was at school with Evelyn Fox, *you* know, whose aunt ran off to Antibes with Harold Barker-White, who used to be the stepfather of Reggie Coverdale—now don't tell me you don't remember Reggie: he's doing *marvellously* well out in India now that he's recovered from the amputation," and then before I know it I'm smiling glassily and dancing with some trussed-up female who *might* be quite good-looking if one could only get a glimpse of her under all that silk and lace and rouge, and *might* even be rather good fun if only she hadn't been drilled to death in the proper behaviour and one could get a laugh out of her. I don't know what's wrong with the young men of today,' he finished, 'but I tell you this: it's coming to something when all the proud mamas of Mayfair are eyeing *me* up as a prospect.'

'Don't be silly—I'm sure you'll make some girl very happy one day,' said Angela kindly. 'So then, this murder must have been rather a godsend for you.'

'I'll say,' he said. 'As soon as it turned up I threw my dinner-suit on the fire and came down here like a shot.'

'And what is the *Clarion*'s position on the case?'

'I don't know yet,' said Freddy. 'I haven't thought of one. I've been scouting about all morning, but I've been rather hamstrung by the competition.'

'Ah, that would be the other man I saw. Is he a reporter too?'

At this, Freddy gave a sound expressive of utter disgust.

'A reporter?' he said. 'I beg you, please don't use that word in the same sentence as that—that—no, I won't flatter him by calling him a blister. As a matter of fact, to call him a blister would be an insult to right-thinking blisters everywhere. He's a weeping sore on the face of humanity, that's what he is.'

'Goodness,' said Angela. 'Who is he?'

'Corky Beckwith,' said Freddy. 'He works for the *Herald* —and I won't bore you with my opinions on that rag: suffice it to say that it's the sort of newspaper which employs people like Corky Beckwith, and *that* ought to tell you all you need to know about it.'

'How dreadful,' said Angela politely. 'I shall spit at his feet and turn my back on him if I happen to meet him accidentally.'

'Oh, I shouldn't bother,' said Freddy. 'The gesture would be quite lost on him. I say,' he went on more cheerfully, 'I haven't seen you in simply ages, have I? You're looking very well. Isn't that a sun-tan? Have you been abroad?'

'Yes, to Italy,' she said, and glanced down involuntarily at a rather pretty bracelet which she wore on her wrist. It was made of silver and inlaid with coloured glass in varying shades of green.

He saw it and said, 'And I see you bought yourself a new trinket while you were there. Murano glass, I should say—from which I deduce you have been to Venice.'

'Yes,' said Angela shortly, pushing the bracelet up her sleeve and out of sight.

'Aren't you impressed by my deductive powers?' said Freddy. 'Did you like the place?'

'Yes, thank you, it was very nice,' said Angela. She was keen to steer the conversation away from Venice, and so she said, 'Where are you staying while you're here?'

'At the Red Lion,' he said. 'It's not exactly the Ritz, but it was the only place I could find. I say, I don't suppose there's any chance of getting an invitation to stay at your house, is there?'

Angela was just about to say that she doubted it, when she caught sight of Elisabeth and Mrs. Randall walking up the little hill towards them.

'There you are,' said Elisabeth as they drew near. 'I wondered where you'd got to. Mother and I are just taking a little walk before lunch. It's a pity you disappeared, as I have a lot to do today and I did think you might have come out with her instead.'

'Freddy, this is my sister-in-law, Lady Cardew, and her mother, Mrs. Randall,' said Angela. 'This is Mr. Pilkington-Soames, Elisabeth. He's a reporter and the son of an old friend of mine.'

'Oh,' said Elisabeth, regarding Freddy down her nose. 'I suppose you're here about this dreadful murder business. Such a pity that people feel the need to read about goings-on of this sort. I suppose they must find it rather exciting, although I can't say I think it altogether in the best of taste.'

'Oh, I agree with you entirely,' said Freddy, who had sized up Elisabeth with a glance and judged it better to be respectful. 'Still, I'm afraid it must be reported. The public have the right to see the police at work and to know that something is being done. Otherwise they might come to believe that thieves and murderers can get away with anything they want, and that would never do.'

'I suppose you are right,' said Elisabeth with a sigh.

Mrs. Randall was observing Freddy through her lorgnette.

'Which newspaper do you work for, young man?' she said. 'The *Times*, I suppose?'

'The *Clarion*,' said Freddy, and had the grace to blush.

'Oh!' said Elisabeth haughtily. 'One of *those* papers. I'm afraid we don't—'

'The *Clarion*!' said Mrs. Randall with great interest. 'I don't take it myself, of course, but my cook does, and she lets me read it after she's finished with it. It's *most* interesting.'

'Come, Mother,' said Elisabeth in alarm. 'We had better be going.'

'Oh, very well,' said Mrs. Randall. 'When I see you next you shall tell me all about it,' she said to Freddy.

'It will be my pleasure,' said Freddy with a little bow.

'Hmp!' said Mrs. Randall, and was preparing to follow her daughter when a thought struck her and she turned to Angela and looked her up and down. 'Don't you think you're a little too old for him?' she said, and went off.

Freddy saw Angela glaring at him and coughed to hide his smirk. 'So that is the wife of brother Humphrey, is it?' he said. 'I should rather imagine they deserve one another.'

'They are a very respectable couple and do many good works,' said Angela carefully.

'Splendid,' he said. 'I'm glad you're making the best of

it. But never mind all that. Tell me what you know about this murder. Do you suppose the good people of Banford Green laid it on especially for you, knowing you were coming?'

'I do hope not,' said Angela. 'As a matter of fact, everyone rather thought it was a spur of the moment thing until the main suspect turned out to have an alibi.'

'Ah, yes, Andrew Norris,' said Freddy. 'I should like to speak to him—should have done it earlier, in fact, except that I understand he thinks nothing of waving his shotgun at anyone who happens to interrupt his after-dinner pipe or accidentally tread on his corns.'

'You understand correctly,' said Angela. 'I should try not to offend him if I were you.'

'Perhaps I'll send Corky to him, then, and kill two birds with one stone, so to speak,' said Freddy. 'Mr. Norris could work off his irritability and do society a favour at the same time. I'm certain that not a jury in the land would convict me.'

'Do I hear you taking my name in vain, Freddy?' said a voice, and they turned to find Mr. Beckwith himself in his regrettable jacket approaching at a most complacent saunter. He made a bee-line for Angela, gave her a ridiculous bow and a leer and said, 'Caulfield Beckwith at your service, madam.'

'Angela Marchmont,' said Mrs. Marchmont, eyeing him with some reserve.

'Ah, the famous Mrs. Marchmont!' cried Corky Beckwith sentimentally. 'Fair of face and unbending of purpose, the scourge of scoundrels and murderers everywhere. Why, I'll wager that every criminal quakes in his boots whenever he reads your name, and dreads the day when you will point the finger at him and intone, "That is the man, inspector; arrest him!" Meanwhile, Scotland Yard talks of you in hushed tones and hangs upon your every word, even as the society pages gush and chatter in excitement when you single-handedly establish orchid-mauve as the *only* colour to be seen in this season. Never before have such beauty and such fearsomeness been united in one slight frame. My lady, I lay myself at your feet, your devoted slave.'

He gestured magnificently at the ground before him.

'Do put a sock in it, Corky,' said Freddy.

'Oh, I don't know,' said Angela. 'I was rather enjoying it.'

'I hope my young friend here hasn't been bothering you *too* much,' said Corky. 'He's rather inexperienced in the ways of the world, I'm afraid, and hasn't quite mastered the art of—well, anything at all, to be perfectly honest. No matter, though, my lad,' he went on to Freddy. 'Give it a few more years and a few knocks here and there, and perhaps you'll be a *real* reporter one day. Remind me to lend you that old grammar of mine.'

'What do you want?' said Freddy, ignoring these aspersions. 'Can't a man have a private conversation without you butting in all over the place?'

'Oh, don't mind me,' said Corky. 'I just came up here for a cigarette and to enjoy the view. Do carry on.'

'He always does this when he thinks I'm going to beat him to a story,' explained Freddy. 'He can't just go and find his own ideas, you see; he has to steal mine.'

'I resent that remark,' said Corky, wholly unperturbed. 'To my knowledge you have never yet come close to beating me to a story.'

'Rubbish!' said Freddy. 'You know you're still smarting after I got the scoop on the Dollis Hill murders.'

'You may have got the scoop, but I got a far better

piece out of it,' said Corky, looking slightly nettled for the first time.

'Only because you made it up,' said Freddy.

'You wound me, sir,' said Corky with dignity. He was about to go on when he caught sight of Angela, who was showing signs of getting up and leaving them to it. 'I beg your pardon, madam,' he said. 'We shall save our little professional disagreement for later. Please don't go.'

'I don't wish to interrupt your shop,' said Angela.

'Not at all,' said Corky. 'It was terribly rude, and I apologize on behalf of both of us, since Freddy hasn't the wit to do it himself.'

Freddy scowled but said nothing, and the incorrigible Corky went on:

'Still, while I'm here, I don't suppose it can hurt to ask you whether there is anything you'd like to say on the subject of this shotgun murder, Mrs. Marchmont? I mean to say, since you are held in such high regard by the police, our readers would be tremendously excited to hear your opinion of the affair.'

'But I don't know any more about it than you do,' said Angela in surprise.

'That doesn't matter,' said Corky. 'Just say anything you like and I'll write it up.'

'I'd far rather you didn't,' said Angela.

But in his head Corky was already writing a story in which Mrs. Marchmont, resplendent in pale-blue organdie, vowed magnificently to bring to justice the man who had so cruelly deprived Thomas Tipping of his existence, leaving his wife a widow and his son an orphan.

'Not to worry,' he said vaguely, then took his leave politely and sauntered off.

'It's not like him to go without a fight,' said Freddy. 'I'd better go and find out what he's up to. Don't solve the case without me,' he said as he ran off.

Angela shook her head and wondered what nonsense would appear about her in the newspapers that evening. Whatever it was, she thanked her stars that her brother and sister-in-law did not read the *Herald*.

Chapter Eleven

ON TUESDAY MORNING an inquest was opened and immediately adjourned, since the police wanted to collect more evidence, much to the disappointment of the gaggle of locals who had turned up hoping for some excitement. That left Inspector Jameson and Sergeant Primm free to continue their investigation. Their first port of call was the Red Lion Inn, a pleasant-looking establishment which served as the village's main hotel and public house. They entered and found a wispy-looking woman sweeping the floor of the public bar. She gave them one glance, then went through a door and shouted, 'Bob!'

There was the sound of thumping, and after a few moments the head and shoulders of the landlord could be seen emerging from the trapdoor which led to the cellar. He was a tall, well-built man, and he had to duck his head in order to get through the door into the tap-room.

'Morning, Bert,' he said, nodding cheerfully at Primm. 'And this'll be the inspector I've been hearing about, I don't doubt.'

Jameson introduced himself and the landlord introduced himself in turn as Bob Sanderson.

'Have you come to ask me about old Norris again?' he said. 'I'd like to tell you different, but my story hasn't changed. I can't make things be what they aren't, however much I'd like to.'

'That's all right, Bob,' said Primm genially. 'I'd just like the inspector to hear the story from your own mouth, as it were. Just in case I've told it wrong.'

'Right you are, then,' said Bob. 'Where shall I start?'

Inspector Jameson glanced down at his notebook.

'I understand that Mr. Norris and his man Ben Shaw came in here at about a quarter past one last Saturday lunch-time,' he said. 'Is that correct?'

'As near as I can remember,' said the landlord. 'I don't say I've got it right to the last second, but I'm a careful man and I generally take note of times. It's a habit I've got into.'

'Did they have a drink in the public bar here?'

'No,' said Bob. 'They bought their drinks and said they wanted a bite to eat, and I told them things were quiet and they might as well go into the saloon where it was more comfortable, but Norris said he didn't fancy rattling around in there and he'd rather go into the snug. It was all the same to me, so that's where they went. A few minutes later —half past one or so, it was—I took them in some food and left them to it, and they stayed in there until they left at ten past two.'

'Are you quite certain of that?' said Jameson. 'Didn't they buy any more drinks?'

'Yes,' said Bob, 'Twice. Once a few minutes after I took them their food—let's say at twenty to two—and again at two o'clock or thereabouts.'

'Who bought them? And did he come in here to get them?'

'It was Norris, both times,' said Bob. 'And there was no need for him to come in here.' He indicated the little window through which drinks were served to patrons occupying the snug. 'He just called through from there.'

'And you didn't see either him or Ben Shaw at any other time until they left the place?' said Jameson.

'No,' said Bob. 'But like I told Bert here, they couldn't have got out without my seeing them, for I was here in the tap-room the whole time, as I had customers to serve. They're regulars and they like their beer and don't like having to wait for it, so that's where I was. As you can see, inspector,' he went on, 'the door to the snug is round *there*, and the door to the street is just *there*, and so if anyone wanted to leave they'd have had to come round by the bar, and I'd have seen them. And even if my back had been turned and I'd missed him, my regulars were sitting over there and they'd have seen him, but they didn't. And quite apart from everything else, neither of them was carrying a shotgun. If they had been I shouldn't have allowed them in.'

'Thank you. That seems clear enough,' said Jameson. He glanced towards the door of the snug. 'Might we have a look in there?' he said.

''Course you can,' replied the obliging Bob.

Jameson and Primm went into the snug and looked about them, and Jameson went and peered over the little bar back into the public room, where Bob Sanderson was now wiping a tap in desultory fashion.

'Hmm,' he said. 'You can't see into the snug from the tap-room unless you're standing right behind the bar, which means the landlord couldn't have glimpsed them by chance from anywhere except this spot.'

'That's right enough,' agreed the sergeant.

'Yes,' said Jameson. 'I was just thinking about the times. So, then, we have an interval of perhaps twenty minutes—that is, between twenty to two and two o'clock—in which nobody saw Norris.'

'Except Ben Shaw,' said Primm.

'Yes,' said Jameson. He looked around again and opened a door which led to a little corridor and a modern lavatory which looked to be of recent installation. 'Nothing there,' he said, and turned to another door. 'Now, where does this one go?'

'Only into the back yard,' said Primm.

Jameson opened it and stepped outside. As the sergeant had said, there was nothing here but a little yard enclosed by a brick wall a little less than six feet high. It was difficult to walk around it, being as it was full of piles of old rags, empty kegs, wooden crates, milk churns and what looked like the engine of a motor-car. Jameson picked his way gingerly across to the opposite wall. There was an old milking-stool there, and he stood on it and peered over the top. On the other side he could see a row of dilapidated-looking houses, each with its own tiny yard, most of which were strung across with lines of washing. Over the rooftops he could just see the church spire. As he looked at the house which backed directly onto the Red Lion, three or four small children ran out of it and into the yard. They were followed by a young woman carrying a basket of washing, who looked up at him suspiciously. He apologized hurriedly and jumped down. These, then, must be the houses he had seen yesterday which stood across the lane from the church.

'Nothing that way, as I told you, sir,' said Primm. 'Just houses.'

'No,' said Jameson. 'And I think I may have given one of the residents rather a shock just now.'

'That's Alice Hopwell,' said the sergeant. 'Poor woman. Her husband ran off and left her with no money and far too many children to look after. She's proud, though, and a hard worker. She takes in washing and does cleaning around the village, and the kids have to shift for themselves as best they can most of the time, the poor things.'

They went back indoors and through to the tap-room, where they thanked Bob Sanderson and left.

'Very well,' said Jameson as they stood outside the door. 'Let's be really thorough about this. I'm going to assume for argument's sake that in the twenty minute interval between twenty to two and two o'clock, during which Norris and Ben Shaw were in the snug by themselves, Bob Sanderson and his two customers were somehow struck temporarily deaf, dumb and blind, allowing Andrew Norris to sneak past them and into the street.'

'All right,' said Primm.

'Now, then,' continued the inspector. 'The question is, were those twenty minutes long enough for Norris to run all the way to Dead Man's Path, shoot Tom Tipping and then return to the snug?'

'Sneaking past the deaf, dumb and blind landlord again, I suppose,' said Primm. 'I don't know. Hallo there, young man.'

This last remark was to Peter Montgomery, who was hovering a little way away from them, watching them with great interest.

'Are you on the trail of the murderer?' he said breathlessly. 'May I come? I won't be any trouble, I promise.'

Jameson was just about to tell him to run along when Kathie Montgomery emerged from the butcher's shop and came over to them.

'Peter!' she said. 'What have I told you about bothering the police? You must come away at once. I'm terribly sorry, inspector,' she said, turning to Jameson, 'but he's so dreadfully enthusiastic about it.'

Jameson looked into Kathie's bright blue eyes and relented.

'Should you like to come with us?' he said to Peter. 'We're just looking at an alibi. I'm afraid it's not at all interesting, but you shall help us if you like.'

'May I?' said Peter, glancing up at his mother in great excitement.

'Are you sure he won't be in the way?' said Kathie, still looking at Jameson.

'Of course I'm sure,' he replied. 'He won't be any trouble, will you, Peter?'

'Oh, *no*, sir!' said the boy.

Kathie smiled gratefully, and Jameson suddenly felt like a hero.

'You idiot,' he thought uncomfortably.

'Now, mind, you must come away when they tell you to,' said Kathie, and with that she left them to it, slightly to Jameson's relief.

'Can you run?' he said to Peter.

'I should think so,' said Peter.

'Good. Now, I am going to walk to Dead Man's Path and stand in the spot in which Mr. Tipping died. We had better adjust our watches to the same time, Primm.'

They did so, and Jameson went on:

'Very well. I shall need fifteen minutes or so to get there. After that you, Peter, must run as fast as you possibly can to join me, pause for a few seconds and then run back here to Sergeant Primm. Do you think you can do that?'

'Yes, sir,' said Peter.

'I'm pleased to hear it,' said Jameson, 'for otherwise I should have to do it and I'm not sure I'm up to the task.'

He left Peter and Sergeant Primm and set off for Dead Man's path, and the experiment was duly carried out according to instructions.

'Just under eleven minutes on the way there, and nearly twelve minutes on the way back,' said Primm as the three of them stood together on the green some forty-five minutes later, Peter burying his face in an ice-cream which had been his reward. 'The shooting would have taken only seconds, of course, but still, that's twenty-three minutes altogether.'

'Yes, and of course we have to take into account the difference in physical condition between an eleven-year-old boy and a man in his sixties,' said Jameson.

'Then there's the fact that he didn't have a gun with him,' said Primm.

'He might have hidden it somewhere,' said Jameson, 'but still he would have had to stop to pick it up.'

'And someone would surely have seen him running down the street,' said the sergeant.

'Very well, then,' said Jameson, 'I think we can safely discount that theory and consider Norris's alibi to have been tested and found solid. Where does that leave us, then?'

'Back where we started,' said Primm.

'I hope not,' said Jameson. The church bell rang for a quarter to one, and he said, 'I hate to think on an empty stomach. Let's have something to eat and talk the case over in the meantime. How is the food at the Red Lion?'

'I've had worse,' said Primm. 'Bob's a good fellow, all told.'

'Then let's go there.'

Primm agreed and the two men said goodbye to Peter

and returned across the green. As they were about to enter the Red Lion a young man came out, and they stood back politely to let him pass. It was Freddy Pilkington-Soames. He greeted them with enthusiasm.

'So there you are, inspector,' he said. 'I've heard rumours of your presence since I got here yesterday, but so far you've remained determinedly elusive and I was beginning to think it was all a cruel hoax. But here you are, striding forth on your quest for justice as usual.'

'Hallo, Freddy,' said Jameson. 'Not so much striding forth as going for lunch. So the press have got wind of the thing, have they? I suppose it was only a matter of time. I do hope you're not going to make a nuisance of yourself.'

'I?' said Freddy. 'Certainly not. At least, no more than usual, and you can't say fairer than that. Things are quietish in London at the moment, though, and so a story like this is inevitably going to attract attention.'

'Just so long as you don't write any nonsense,' said Jameson, who was familiar with the sort of story commonly produced by publications such as Freddy's.

'Of course I won't,' said Freddy with dignity. 'I am bound by honour to speak and write only the truth, come what may.' He saw something over Jameson's shoulder and his face darkened. 'You'd better watch out for Corky, though. He's hot on the scent of who knows what—or at least, he thinks he is—and his pen produces only the purest, thrice-distilled fiction.'

The two policemen turned to see Corky Beckwith standing a few feet away, apparently engaged in conversation with a pretty, dark girl, who was regarding him contemptuously.

'Hallo, Marthe,' said Freddy, recognizing her. 'Did Angela send you out? Is this gentleman bothering you?'

'Gentleman? Which gentleman do you mean?' said

Marthe with magnificent disdain. 'There is a *person* here who insists on asking me questions of the greatest impertinence, but as for *gentlemen*—' here she gave a sniff, '—I see none before me but yourselves. Excuse me, for I am very busy and have no time to stay here. *Bonjour*, M. Pilkington-Soames, *bonjour, M. l'Inspecteur.*'

And with that she sailed off, her nose in the air.

'What did you interrupt for?' said Corky. 'That's Angela Marchmont's maid. We were getting along famously, and I had all but got her to agree to speak to me about her mistress. I had in mind a piece for the women's pages about Mrs. Marchmont's beauty secrets—how she does her hair, what she puts on her face—you know the kind of thing: "Our lady detective never goes to bed without first anointing her face with a generous amount of Calvert's Cold Cream, in order to ward off the arrival of those fine lines which *will* begin to encroach once a woman reaches a certain age." If you hadn't turned up I'd have had it all straight from the horse's mouth.'

'Don't talk rot,' said Freddy. 'Why, she squashed you neatly in about three words.'

'Nonsense,' said Corky. 'I am unsquashable.'

'Well, that's true enough,' said Freddy.

Corky, undaunted, now turned his attention to Jameson and Primm.

'Hallo, inspector,' he said. 'Are you going to give me the low-down on this story, then?'

'Sorry, Mr. Beckwith,' said Jameson, who knew Corky of old. 'We've got nothing for you at present, I'm afraid, but I'll let you know as soon as we have anything that's worth printing.'

'Never mind,' said Corky, who never let a lack of official information get in the way of a story. 'I shall think of something. I say, though, speaking of Mrs. Marchmont, when I talked to her yesterday she told me she would be helping you with the investigation.'

'Did she?' said Jameson in surprise, thinking it was most unlike Angela.

'She never said anything of the sort, you ass,' said Freddy.

Corky waved his hand.

'She may not have said it in so many words, but I could tell she was thinking it,' he said. 'I don't mind telling you, inspector, that the presence of Angela Marchmont on the scene raises this murder far above the plain, common or garden crime and puts it firmly at the forefront of the public interest. Very well, then, if you've nothing to say for the present I shall go and begin writing up my story. Goodbye.'

He strolled off with a smirk and a nod. Freddy glared after him.

'Poor Angela,' he said. 'What has she done to deserve Corky Beckwith? Perhaps I ought to have a word with her.'

He went off, and the two policemen exchanged glances then went into the inn.

Chapter Twelve

'So,' said Jameson, once they were fairly settled at a table in the corner and had ordered the veal and ham pie, which Bob Sanderson had recommended as being particularly good. 'Who murdered Tom Tipping, if not Andrew Norris?'

'Well, with Norris out of the picture—and always assuming it wasn't a random stranger who just happened to be passing and took a dislike to Tipping for some reason —the next most obvious suspects are his family, of course,' said Sergeant Primm. 'I should never have said it of them, but we can't ignore the possibility that they may have done it.'

'No,' agreed Jameson. 'Very well, then. I've met them both, but of course I don't know anything about them other than what they told me yesterday. Suppose you tell me more about the Tipping family—in fact, you'd better tell me something about Tom Tipping first, since he's the poor fellow who's come off worst in all this. Why would someone want to kill him? Was he a particularly unpleasant man?'

'No,' said Primm. 'Not as such. He was friendly enough to those who knew him, but I imagine he wasn't the easiest of men to get on with for those as had to live with him.'

'What do you mean?'

'Why, he could be a bit overbearing at times,' said Primm. 'You know—the sort who won't let you finish what you're saying before he jumps in with his own remarks, so you're never quite sure whether he's heard you. He didn't do it enough to irritate, though, so perhaps that doesn't mean anything. And he had a funny sense of humour—by which I mean to say peculiar, not to laugh at. He liked to bait people. You know how he provoked old Norris about Dead Man's Path. That was just like him. Once he knew your weakness you weren't safe from his jokes, even though he was the only one who found them funny. I think he liked to find people's weak spots and prod at them, if you catch my meaning. He was mightily pleased with himself for stealing Margaret from Norris years ago, and couldn't resist boasting about it. Of course, that irritated Norris, and then when this question of the path came up, Tom saw another opportunity to provoke him. He was always insisting to Norris's face that the path was common land, and when it turned out that Norris had gone to law about it, he wrote to the local newspaper to say that Norris was weak in the head—of course, he didn't quite put it like that, but that was what it sounded like.'

'Perhaps he really did believe that Dead Man's Path was common land,' said Jameson. 'From what I've heard here, the only person who really believes it belongs to Andrew Norris is Andrew Norris himself.'

'That's true enough,' said Primm, 'but Tom Tipping made a point of opposing Norris deliberately. Of course, in the end, what started out as a case of mild dislike turned into an out-and-out feud.'

'This Tipping doesn't sound the pleasantest of fellows,' observed Jameson.

'Oh, he was all right as long as you didn't take him too seriously,' said Primm. 'Of course, it might have been different for his family, since they had to live with him all the time.'

'Yes,' said Jameson. 'What you've told me about him might have been a good enough motive for murder. He might have unwittingly goaded someone into it. But who? Do you think Mrs. Tipping might have done it? What can you tell me about her?'

Sergeant Primm paused to collect his thoughts.

'She's a close one,' he said at length. 'I should call her a dark horse. You can never tell what she's thinking.'

'She didn't seem especially upset about her husband's death,' said Jameson, 'although that might have been shock, of course. I assume they'd been married a long time. Was it a happy marriage?'

'It's difficult to tell,' said the sergeant. 'He used to have little digs at her in front of other people. Sometimes you could take it as a joke but at other times it seemed a bit less than kind. Some people might not have minded it, but Margaret Tipping never struck me as having much of a sense of humour. I shouldn't be surprised if he'd worn her down over the years.'

'Enough for her to take a shotgun and kill him?'

'Well, that's the question, isn't it?' said Primm. 'When you put it like that it doesn't seem likely. I shouldn't have called her the type, but of course there's no saying what a woman might be driven to after forty years of marriage to a man who continually provokes her.'

'True enough,' said Jameson, glancing at his notes.

'And there's the question of how she did it, since she was supposedly helping at the fête all day. If she did do it she must have slipped away pretty quietly.'

'You'll have to speak to Lady Cardew about that. She organized the thing, and she and Margaret Tipping were on the cake stall together for most of the day, when she wasn't playing Lady Bountiful. She might be able to give you more information.'

'Yes, I shall certainly pay Lady Cardew a visit,' said Jameson.

'She'll probably try and send you away with a flea in your ear,' said Primm. 'They set great store by their respectability, the Cardews, and I don't suppose she'll relish being associated with murder.'

'Nobody is associating them with anything—unless, of course, Lady Cardew has a motive you haven't told me about.'

'No,' said Primm. 'She'd probably be scandalized if she caught Tom using a fish fork for the beef, but I don't suppose she'd go so far as to blow his brains out.'

'I'm pleased to hear it. Very well, then, let's move on to Norman Tipping. What can you tell me about him?'

'A bit overbearing like his father, but without Tom's sense of humour,' said Primm. 'Although, of course, that might be to his advantage. He's always struck me as a bit staid and dull—and pleased with himself for it.'

'Was he on good terms with his father?' said Jameson.

'I believe so,' said Primm. 'In fact, as far as I know, the three of them all got on perfectly well with each other, but of course you never know what goes on behind closed doors, do you?'

'What motive might he have had, then?' said Jameson. 'Money, presumably.'

'Yes,' said Primm. 'I don't know the exact state of

affairs, but I imagine the farm will go to him one day, and it may be that he gets some money now, too. Once we've heard from Tom's solicitor we'll know more, but he's away until tomorrow. Norman is certainly a likely suspect, since we know he was nearby at the time of his father's death. Who's to say he wasn't lying about what happened on Dead Man's Path that day?'

'He was with Mrs. Montgomery, though, wasn't he?' said Jameson.

'Of course,' said Primm, 'but there's nothing to say she wasn't in on it too. She's got a big enough motive to keep quiet if she's going to marry Norman Tipping. She's poor, you know—her husband died just after the war and left her with a little boy and not much money, and I'm sure she'd rather not have to rely on her sister and brother-in-law for the lad's support. She's got every reason to keep quiet if Norman *did* do it.'

Jameson did not like the thought of this one bit, but made no comment. Instead, he said:

'We must question this Daniel Tyler who passed them on Dead Man's Path. Perhaps you might speak to him, Primm. We need to know exactly when the shotgun blast was heard, and whether there was time for Norman Tipping to have done the deed before Tyler came on the scene.'

'Right you are, sir,' said the sergeant.

'In the meantime I shall go and have a word with Norman Tipping myself,' said Jameson. 'I'd like to know what he has to say about his father. I believe you said he lives on the edge of the village.'

'That's right,' said Primm. 'At the other end of Dead Man's Path, as a matter of fact.'

'Did Norris never take issue with him using the path?'

'Oh no,' said Primm. 'Norman's far too careful of himself to get caught up in someone else's row. He never let himself get drawn into it.'

'Sensible fellow,' said Jameson. 'Well, then, let's see what he has to say for himself.'

Chapter Thirteen

NORMAN TIPPING's house was situated on the very outskirts of Banford Green and was square and solid, rather like the man himself, with little decoration about its exterior. When Inspector Jameson rang the bell, the door was answered by a young woman brandishing a broom who informed him that Mr. Tipping was out and not expected back immediately. The woman looked familiar to Jameson, but it was not until she had shut the door that he remembered who she was: it was Alice Hopwell, who lived in the cottage that backed on to the Red Lion, although she had shown no sign that she recognized him.

He set off back into Banford with a sigh. It was a walk of only half a mile or so but the weather was pleasant and the countryside around him attractive, and so he decided to take a little detour past a cluster of pretty cottages that stood off to one side of where Dead Man's Path began. He was just regarding the first one and admiring its colourful window-boxes and neatly-painted fence, when he saw that someone was kneeling by a border in the front garden, weeding. It was Kathie Montgomery. She glanced up.

'Hallo, inspector,' she said, and smiled as though she were pleased to see him.

Jameson took a second to find his voice.

'Hallo, Mrs. Montgomery,' he replied. 'I didn't realize this was your house.'

'Yes,' she said.

'It's very pretty,' he said.

'It is, isn't it? I like it here. I know it's only small, but it's big enough for Peter and me—and he's away at school most of the time, anyway.'

'It's term-time now, though. Has he been ill?' said Jameson.

'Yes, with measles. Rather a bad attack, unfortunately. He's much better now, but I thought I'd better keep him at home for a few more days, just to be on the safe side. He won't stay in and rest, though. I don't suppose you've seen him, have you?'

'Not since we left him earlier. He said something about scouting about for footprints. I feel rather guilty now—I'm afraid we made him run this morning. I do hope he won't feel any ill effects from it.'

'Oh, no, I'm sure he won't,' she said. 'I dare say I'm just being a little over-anxious. He's all I have, you see.'

'Of course,' said Jameson.

'Have you been speaking to Norman?' she said, looking in the direction of Norman Tipping's house.

'That's why I came up here, but he's not in,' said Jameson. 'I wonder, might I speak to you instead?'

She stood up and brushed the earth off her hands.

'Certainly,' she said. 'Let's go inside. Everyone knows everyone else's business here, so if you want to say anything private it's best to do it indoors.'

He followed her into the cottage and found that the inside was just as neat and trim as the outside. Kathie showed him into a tiny parlour that looked out on to the front garden.

'I must just go and wash my hands,' she said. 'Would you like some tea? Weeding's thirsty work, and I should rather like a cup myself.'

Jameson usually said no to tea when it was offered to him by possible murder suspects, but instead he found himself accepting. He sat politely, looking around him and listening to the sound of her bustling about in the kitchen. She sang as she worked, and Jameson was just thinking to himself what a delightful voice she had when the song was broken off abruptly. She came into the parlour a minute or two later, carrying the tea tray, which he leapt up to take from her. She was a little pink in the face.

'I'm sorry, I was singing again, wasn't I?' she said. 'I do it without realizing, you see, but of course I oughtn't to inflict it on my visitors. My sister Elisabeth is always telling me off for it.'

'I'm sorry you stopped,' he said. 'I was rather enjoying it.'

'That's kind of you, but I don't suppose it's exactly appropriate anyway, given the purpose of your visit—at least, I assume you're here because of Tom.'

'I'm afraid so,' said Jameson. 'I understand you were one of the first people to find Mr. Tipping on Saturday after he had been shot.'

'Yes,' she said soberly. 'I was.'

She poured some tea and handed it to him.

'If it's not too upsetting for you, would you mind telling me what happened?' said Jameson.

'Certainly. Where would you like me to start?'

'I should like to have a general picture of what happened that day,' said Jameson. 'I understand you were helping at the fête.'

'Yes,' she said. 'I helped set it up in the morning, then when it opened I was in the tea tent for a little while with my mother, and after that I stood in for Angela Marchmont on the bric-à-brac stall while she went to get something to eat. When she came back I went back to the tea tent and found that Mother had overturned the tea urn and the tablecloth was sopping wet, so I said I'd run home to fetch another.'

'You came all the way home? Isn't that rather a long way?'

'Yes, it is,' said Kathie. 'It didn't occur to me until afterwards that it would have been much quicker to get one from the big house, but—well, Elisabeth's things are much nicer than mine and she's rather careful of them, and with Mother tending to spill tea all over the place I thought it made more sense to fetch one of my old ones instead.'

Jameson noted her tact, and said, 'What time was this?'

'I left the fête at about a quarter past one, I think. I don't know what time I got home but it can't have taken long as I ran most of the way. At any rate, I grabbed a couple of tablecloths and came out and saw Norman, who was just on his way to the fête, so we walked together along Dead Man's Path. I think we were about halfway there when we met Tom going the other way with his dog. He said he'd see us later and then passed on.'

'How did he seem to you?' said Jameson. 'Did you notice anything unusual in his manner?'

'No, nothing,' said Kathie. 'He seemed quite his normal self.'

'He didn't say he was going to meet someone, I suppose?'

'No, nothing like that. We didn't stop and chat, or anything like that, just said hello and went on our way. A minute or two later we heard a loud bang, but didn't think anything of it, and then shortly after that we passed Daniel Tyler going the other way. We'd just arrived at Tithes Field when Daniel came running after us and told Norman that his father had met with an accident. We raced back with him and found—' here she broke off. 'Well, you know what we found,' she finished sombrely. 'He was quite dead—we could see that straightaway. I ran to fetch the doctor, and the doctor called the police.'

'I'm sorry, I don't mean to upset you,' said Jameson.

'Not at all,' said Kathie. 'You have to ask these questions, I quite understand that.'

'Thank you. Very well, did you see anybody else at all other than Tyler on your way to the fête, either before or after you passed Mr. Tipping?'

'No,' said Kathie. 'There was no-one.'

Jameson paused. He wanted to ask the next question carefully.

'I'd like to know more about the shot you heard.' he said at length. 'You say you heard it shortly after you passed Mr. Tipping and before you met Daniel Tyler. Can you be absolutely certain of that? The three of you didn't hear it together, for example? Or had you perhaps even already passed Tyler when you heard it?'

She thought for a second.

'No,' she said. 'We heard it first and then saw Daniel afterwards. I know particularly because I remember thinking vaguely when he came into view, "Oh, that must be where the noise came from." But then I saw he wasn't carrying a gun and so the thing passed out of my mind.'

'Was Mrs. Tipping at the fête when it happened, as far as you know?' he said.

'Yes, I think so. Norman went to fetch her as soon as the doctor said it was all over. He took her home—

avoiding Dead Man's Path, of course—and I joined them at the farmhouse afterwards, once the police had arrived.'

'I see,' said Jameson. He was about to move on to delicate ground. 'Now, I shall understand if you don't wish to answer the next question, but I'm afraid I have to ask it all the same.'

He paused.

'Go on,' she said.

'Very well. Here it is: are the family on good terms? I mean to say, what were the relations between Mr. Tipping and his wife and son?'

She did not seem offended, and he was relieved.

'They got along well enough,' she replied after a second. 'Norman was fond of his father, I should say. He was certainly very shocked and upset when he died.'

'What about Mrs. Tipping?'

Kathie looked uncomfortable.

'Why, I couldn't say,' she said hesitantly. 'I *believe* they got along well. Norman—or better still, Margaret—will be able to tell you more about that than I can, though.'

She closed her mouth and Jameson said no more, but he was certain that Kathie knew or suspected something about the relationship between Margaret and Tom Tipping that she was unwilling to tell. It was not fair to press her, however—and indeed it would be useless to do so anyway, for experience told him that once a person had decided to withhold something, then nothing he could do would change their mind. It was best to let them come round of their own accord—and indeed, there were other people in the village who would be able to tell him what he wanted to know.

He thanked her, and she said he was quite welcome and offered him more tea. They chatted about other things, and it was not long before they discovered that she knew the sister of an old friend of his. They spent some time exclaiming over the fact, and then ended up talking at length about other people they both knew slightly but cared nothing about, purely—in Jameson's case, at least—in order to prolong the conversation. At last Jameson glanced at his watch and started, for he had been gone far longer than he intended. She laughed at his rueful face and said that he was welcome to blame his lateness on her, and he said of course he would do nothing of the sort. He stood up and she came to see him out, and there was an awkward moment and a pause when they accidentally brushed against each other in the narrow passageway. He apologized and she said, 'Oh!' and looked taken aback, but did not move away from him. They held each other's gaze for much longer than they ought to have, but then the moment passed and he took his leave and walked back into Banford, his head spinning slightly, wondering whether she had put something in his tea.

As he emerged from Dead Man's Path he pulled himself together with an effort. Sergeant Primm ought to be back at the station by now, and they could compare notes. Jameson wanted to know what Daniel Tyler had said. If Tyler's story agreed with Kathie's then that meant there were no witnesses to confirm that she and Norman had been nowhere near Tom Tipping when he was shot. There was no getting away from the fact that if Kathie was indeed engaged to Norman Tipping, then she had just as much motive as he did for wishing his father dead. But were they really engaged? Nobody seemed quite sure. Jameson wished he had had the courage to ask her. It was his duty as a policeman to ask personal questions in a cold and dispassionate manner, but he had been unable to bring himself to do it. And yet it was vital that they find out, for it meant the difference between a strong and a weak motive. If they were *not* engaged then Kathie was less likely to try and protect Norman, but if they *were*—well, that meant she had far more reason to do so.

Jameson paused outside the police station. He would speak to Primm and find out what Daniel Tyler had said. If he had heard the shot while Kathie and Norman were in view of him—or even after they had passed him—then they were in the clear. Otherwise, if he had heard it a few minutes before he met them, things looked much more suspicious. He hoped very much that Kathie had got it wrong.

Chapter Fourteen

DESPITE AN AFFECTATION OF IDLENESS, Freddy Pilkington-Soames was in actual fact a young man of great resourcefulness and determination who, once he had got an idea into his head, would not let go of it until he had brought it to fruition. At present, his two overriding goals in life were: 1) to put one over on Corky Beckwith, and 2) to ingratiate himself with the ladies of Two Tithes. The outcome of 1) was at present uncertain, for Corky had of late ceased to follow him around the village, and seemed bent on mysterious business of his own, but on 2) Freddy set himself to work, and by Wednesday afternoon had succeeded so far as to procure an invitation to tea, by the simple expedient of promising to include a paragraph about the church fête in his next piece about the Banford Green murder.

He duly presented himself and found, rather to his relief, that Sir Humphrey Cardew had gone to his office in London, and that the little party consisted of Lady Cardew, her mother Mrs. Randall, a large woman who was introduced to him as Mrs. Hunter the vicar's wife, and Angela. He therefore put on his best manner and set himself to exercising his not inconsiderable charm on the ladies. Lady Cardew, it was true, was still rather suspicious of him (it would clearly take some work to overcome her disdain for the popular papers), but Mrs. Hunter liked his apparent plain speaking, while Mrs. Randall regarded him through her lorgnette with distant interest. Angela, of course, was a sport and required no winning over at all.

'I say, this shortbread is simply delicious,' said Freddy. 'Who made it?'

He knew full well, having been primed earlier by Angela, that Elisabeth's was the fair hand which had baked the biscuits. Lady Cardew nodded graciously and admitted responsibility.

'It was meant for the fête,' she said, 'but there was too much so we kept this back. Rather a good thing, as it turned out, or it would have all gone down with the rest of the cake stall.'

Freddy raised his eyebrows in polite interest.

'There was an incident with an escaped pig. It was rather my fault,' said Angela in the dutiful but expressionless manner of one who has said the same thing many times.

Evidently there was much entertainment to be had from this incident, and Freddy was about to take full advantage of it when he happened to glance at Lady Cardew and saw a triumphant expression flash briefly across her face. There was nothing ill-natured about Freddy, so he decided to let the subject drop. He could always tease Angela about it later. Instead, he said after a moment:

'I understand you had a nasty accident on your bicycle the other day, Mrs. H. I hope it wasn't too serious. Still, though, I hope you've learned your lesson. I've always said those penny farthings are a menace. Far too high off the ground to be safe.'

Mrs. Hunter gave a shout of laughter and wagged her finger at him.

'You impudent boy,' she said. 'As a matter of fact, my bicycle is quite a modern one. I'm a great believer in getting plenty of fresh air, and there's no better way of doing that than by cycling everywhere.'

'You won't be able to do it for a while, though, will you?' observed Elisabeth.

'No,' said Mrs. Hunter. 'It's a great shame, but the doctor has advised me to stay off it for a week or two until my wrist is quite better. Just a sprain, you know,' she said to Freddy, 'but Dr. Rutherford says I was lucky not to break it. Thank goodness for Alice Hopwell, that's all I can say. I know she's let herself go rather, and of course she has far too many children, but she's kind-hearted enough with it. I was just outside her house when I fell, and she picked me up and took me home. I was worried about bicycle thieves, but she said she had a stout chain and a padlock and would lock it up for me by the church until I was ready to fetch it. We haven't had any rain since Saturday so I suppose it's all right where it is for now. Gipsies!' she said suddenly. 'Now there's a story for you, Mr. Pilkington-Soames.'

She was about to launch into a tirade on her favourite theme when Mrs. Randall leaned forward and spoke up.

'It must be tremendously exciting, being a reporter,' she said to Freddy. 'You must meet all kinds of people.'

'Oh, I do,' said Freddy. 'Most of them are quite dread-ful, though.'

'I wanted Angela to tell me all about her friends in the *criminal underworld*,' went on Mrs. Randall, pronouncing the words with great relish, 'but she's pretending to be respectable and won't. You needn't have such scruples, though.'

'Oh, no, I can tell you all about what Angela gets up to,' said Freddy slyly. 'Shall I tell her about the whisky in the cupboard incident, Angela?'

Angela shook her head quickly in alarm, and Freddy remembered himself.

'Oh, no, I'm terribly sorry, of course that was someone else,' he said hurriedly.

'We drink very little in this house, Mr. Pilkington-Soames,' said Lady Cardew grandly.

Mrs. Hunter beamed in approval.

'Quite right,' she said. 'I myself occasionally take a glass of blackcurrant wine after Harvest Festival, and a little sherry at Christmas, but other than that Stephen and I generally abstain. I have seen only too well the effects alcohol can have on people. They have the right idea in America, don't you think, Mrs. Marchmont?'

Angela made some polite reply and Freddy spent the rest of his visit entertaining them with anecdotes of his life as a reporter for the *Clarion*, although he was unable to tell his best stories for the benefit of Mrs. Randall, who seemed really bloodthirsty, since he was unwilling to upset Lady Cardew.

Eventually he took his leave, saying that he had to go and write up his story about the fête.

'Why don't you come with me, Angela?' he said. 'You can tell me all about it from the point of view of the lady detective. Don't you know you've got a celebrity here?' he said to the other ladies. 'If I mention her name in the story that will be a sure-fire guarantee of its being read. Why, the whole country will know of the wild success of the Banford Green church fête!'

With that he left, taking Angela with him.

'I say,' he said as they walked out, 'your sister-in-law is rather hard work, isn't she?'

'Perhaps a little,' admitted Angela.

'I wonder if she's ever had any fun in her life.'

'I rather think she has fun by not having fun,' said Angela. 'She's not a bad person, you know, just a little— inflexible, let's say.'

'She's nothing like her mother at any rate,' said Freddy. 'Or her sister.'

'Oh, you've met Kathie, have you?' said Angela.

'Yes. Lovely girl, isn't she? I gather she's engaged to the main suspect in the murder of Tom Tipping.'

'Is he the main suspect now? I wondered how long it would take before they fastened upon him.'

'It was bound to happen. Family members are always the most obvious suspects,' said Freddy. 'Of course, that puts Kathie in the picture as an accomplice.'

'Which is clearly nonsense,' said Angela with something like a snort. 'I should as soon believe I'd done it myself as suspect her.'

'But doesn't she have a motive if she's engaged to him?'

'She's not engaged to him. She told me so herself. And I'm pretty sure she's not in love with him either. Everyone thinks they're going to get married, but I don't think *she's* entirely convinced of the idea.'

'It's a shame she gives Norman Tipping an alibi, then, since he's such an obvious suspect,' said Freddy. 'I mean, if he did it, then she *must* have been in on it. Otherwise he can't have done it.'

'Unless the murder didn't happen in the way we think it did,' said Angela.

'What do you mean?'

'I don't know,' she said. 'I'm just wondering at random. I'm not supposed to be detecting, as Humphrey doesn't approve of it much, so I suppose I ought to stop thinking about it.'

They were now crossing Tithes Field. The weather was dull and chilly and Freddy shivered.

'What rotten weather for the middle of summer,' he said. 'If it's going to be cold it might at least go the whole hog and rain too. It must be rather a change from Italy, what? I say, I'm rather jealous of your holiday. I've always wanted to go there myself. Tell me about Venice. What was it like?'

Angela made some reply and tried to change the subject, but she was too hasty in doing it and he immediately became suspicious.

'That's twice you've done that to me,' he said. 'Why don't you want to talk about Italy? Were you fleeced of your life savings by a taxi driver or something?'

'Of course not,' she said with a laugh.

But Freddy was by no means stupid. He regarded her closely and understanding dawned on his face. He stopped.

'Oh, *I* see,' he said with something like triumph.

'What?' she said, stopping also.

'I thought I recognized that look of yours,' he said. 'I ought to have realized the other day.'

'Which look? I haven't got a look,' she said.

'Yes you have,' he said. 'I've seen it enough times before. It's one part sheepishness to two parts pure mischief, and it invariably means only one thing. Who is he?'

'What are you talking about?' said Angela fearfully.

'Come on, there's a man, isn't there?' said Freddy. 'So *that's* why you're looking so sleek and self-satisfied—you're in love! How thrilling! Tell me, would I approve? He has very good taste in jewellery, I must say.'

'Don't be ridiculous,' she said, trying to laugh, although

she was inwardly horrified at having been so easily seen through. She was struggling with very mixed feelings about her Italian adventure—not the least of which was guilt— and the last thing she wanted was an inquisitive reporter asking questions and digging the whole thing up.

'You can't deny it,' said Freddy. 'You know I'll find out one way or another.'

'But there's nothing to find out,' said Angela.

She was saved, much to her relief, by Corky Beckwith, who turned up just then looking exceedingly pleased with himself.

'What have you got to be so happy about?' said Freddy. 'Have you arranged for someone to be run over by a train in front of you, just so you can get the story?'

'Of course not,' said Corky. 'Although I shall make a note of that thought and save it for a slow day.'

'I wasn't trying to give you ideas,' said Freddy. 'Come on, what have you got?'

'Oh, I suppose it can't do any harm to tell you,' said Corky smugly, 'since I've already telephoned in my story and it's too late for you now. As a matter of fact, I have been questioning the farm-hands at the Tippings' farm.'

'Do you mean they were prepared to speak to you?' said Freddy. 'I should have thought they'd be more inter- ested in getting that jacket off you and putting it on a scarecrow. Goodness knows, it frightens me enough.'

Corky gave a little appreciative snicker.

'No, no, young Freddy,' he said. 'One day you, too, will learn the art of getting information out of people. It's easy enough if you've the wit. I was thinking of offering a corre- spondence course on the subject. Of course I'd give you a special rate, since we're old friends.'

'Oh, I see, you bribed them, did you?' said Freddy.

'But what have you found out?' said Angela impatiently, for it was evident that Freddy and Corky could spar for hours in this fashion if left to themselves.

Corky turned to her and gave her a mouthful of teeth.

'Madam, I live only to serve you,' he said. 'I have found out that Tom and Margaret Tipping were not on the best of terms. In fact, I might go so far as to say that the love had long gone from their marriage, and that they were living together on sufferance. It pains me to say it, but such is the case. I am going now to speak to someone who has promised to tell me all about it. I believe I am hot on the scent. Look out, young Freddy— I should say the *Herald* is about to steal a march on the *Clarion*.'

'You ass,' said Freddy. 'You're far more likely to ruin things. Why, you're the sort of fellow who'd go and gawp at a dead body just for the fun of it and trample on all the clues while you did it.'

Corky looked sulky.

'It's all very well for you,' he said. 'You've got an "in" with the inspector. How did you manage to get so pally with him, anyway?'

'Sheer, native charm,' said Freddy. 'I realize it's more difficult for you, being an imbecile and all that, but you never know—perhaps he'll take pity on you and throw you some scraps.'

Corky sniffed, then turned his full attention on Angela.

'Mrs. Marchmont, I don't suppose you've changed your mind about helping me with my story? I simply won't believe you aren't tempted by the prospect of seeing your thoughts on the case in print. Come, now, I shall write something anyhow, so you may as well do it. I have it on the word of my editor that we can give you two whole columns on page four. How can you refuse such an offer?'

'I don't know the answer to that any more than you do,

Mr. Beckwith,' said Angela, 'but it appears that somehow I can.'

'Oh, very well,' said Corky, unperturbed. 'Mind, I shall keep trying.'

He went off, and Freddy scowled.

'Bother,' he said. 'Now I shall have to solve the mystery before he does.'

'Can't you just leave it to the police?' said Angela.

'What, when my honour and reputation are at stake?' said Freddy. 'Never!'

He was about to hold forth at length on the utter unfitness of Corky Beckwith to be allowed anywhere near a pen and paper, when he felt a tug at his jacket and looked down.

'Hallo!' he said in surprise. Looking up at him was a small child of perhaps three. She had tangled hair and a very grubby face. 'Where did you spring from, young lady? What's your name?'

The child giggled.

'Dordina,' she said.

'Does your mother know you're here?' said Angela.

'Mama's gone out,' said the child.

'Well, Georgina,' said Freddy. 'I don't think you ought to be out by yourself, so you'd better show us where you live.'

The little girl took their hands quite happily and allowed them to swing her all the way to the bottom of the field and across the road. They appeared to be heading for Church Lane, but it took them a while, for each time Georgina spotted anyone she insisted on stopping and shouting, 'What's him?' and then laughing uproariously. Eventually they arrived at what was presumably her home, which Inspector Jameson would have recognized as Alice Hopwell's house. Georgina stopped.

'What's him?' she said, pointing at Angela.

'Him is a her,' said Freddy, amused. 'Is this your house?'

Just then Alice Hopwell came out, accompanied by two or three curious children.

'Georgina!' she snapped. 'What have I told you about not running out? Thank you,' she went on to Freddy and Angela. 'I just slipped out for a moment and when I got back she was gone. She will keep wandering off.'

'Mama! It's the nother man!' said Georgina, pointing at Freddy.

'Yes,' said Mrs. Hopwell. 'Now, come indoors.'

Georgina ran to her mother without a backward glance, and the Hopwells all went inside, leaving Angela and Freddy to continue their walk.

They returned up the lane and entered the village. Angela was anxious to prevent Freddy from resuming his tormenting of her, and so she said:

'Do you think Corky was telling the truth, then? I mean, about Tom and Margaret Tipping's not being on the best of terms?'

'I don't know,' said Freddy. 'Normally I should say that everything that comes out of his lips is a downright lie, but he seemed so jolly pleased with himself that I shouldn't be surprised if he was on to something.'

'But do you really think the farm-hands would talk for money?'

'You'd be surprised at what people will do for money,' said Freddy darkly. 'It never ceases to amaze me. Why, only last week I had one young lady offer to give me her views on her own parents' divorce so long as I was prepared to stump up the ready. Naturally I declined.'

'Goodness!' said Angela. 'Still, though, just because

people are prepared to talk, it doesn't mean that what they say is true, does it?'

'No,' said Freddy. 'In fact I should say that if money is concerned in the matter then one can't guarantee anything at all.'

'And even if it is true, and the Tippings didn't get on, it still doesn't mean she killed him. As far as I know, Margaret Tipping was helping at the fête all day, up until the moment Norman came and fetched her to tell her what had happened.'

'Ah,' said Freddy, 'but can we be sure she was there all the time?'

'Well, I haven't heard Elisabeth complaining, which I'm pretty sure she would have done if Mrs. Tipping had disappeared at any point,' said Angela.

'I imagine she would, yes,' conceded Freddy.

'Then of course there is the question of the weapon. It's all very well saying that Mrs. Tipping might have slipped away and shot her husband, but where did she get the gun?'

'Yes, I must admit the question of the weapon is something that has been bothering me,' said Freddy. 'Of course, people wander about with shotguns all the time around here, but the two people with the strongest motive don't seem to have been anywhere near a gun at the fatal moment.'

'No,' said Angela thoughtfully. 'And don't you think it's odd that there have been no reports of people with shotguns wandering around the place on Saturday?'

'Perhaps everyone is so used to seeing them that they don't think anything of it,' said Freddy.

'I dare say you're right,' said Angela.

They had now entered the village proper, and as they crossed the green they saw Inspector Jameson emerge from the police station. He approached them and greeted them cheerfully.

'Aha,' said Freddy. 'Our man on the inside. Come on then, inspector, tell us which of the Tippings did it.'

'I've no idea,' said Jameson, 'and I shouldn't tell you even if I did.'

'I thought as much,' said Freddy. 'I fear my scoop must wait.'

'Mrs. Marchmont, is your sister-in-law at home?' said the inspector. 'Is it too late to call on her, do you suppose? I should like to ask her one or two questions.'

'I shouldn't have thought so,' said Angela. 'She was entertaining the vicar's wife when we left. I'm sure she'll be delighted to see you.'

Freddy sniggered at this and Inspector Jameson looked at him suspiciously, but before he could remark they were joined by Kathie, who was carrying a basket of eggs.

'Hallo, Kathie,' said Freddy. 'Where are you taking those?'

'I said I'd take them to the vicarage,' replied Kathie, as Inspector Jameson wondered how Freddy had managed to get on first name terms with her already. She lowered her voice. 'As a matter of fact, I've had to come the long way round, because I saw Mr. Norris by the church, and I thought it better not to get caught up in conversation with him, given the circumstances.'

'Very wise,' said Freddy. 'I gather he's a difficult character at the best of times, but I expect things must be even more awkward at present. Is he still waving that shotgun of his around?'

'No, he didn't have it with him today,' said Kathie. 'I don't know why.'

'Perhaps the recent events have taught him a lesson,' said Angela.

'More likely he thinks he's won the war now that Tom Tipping is dead, and so he doesn't need to carry it any more,' said Freddy without thinking, then caught himself as he saw Kathie's face. 'Oh, I say, I am sorry, Kathie. That was dreadfully crass of me. Do forgive me.'

'It's quite all right,' said Kathie. 'I was rather thinking the same thing myself.'

'Still, if he had any finer feelings at all, he'd keep out of everybody's way for a while,' said Freddy. He glanced at his watch and gave an impatient click of the tongue. 'I hate to desert you all,' he said, 'but I promised I'd telephone old Bickerstaffe at six o'clock and let him know of developments. He likes to keep a sharp eye on what his reporters are doing. It's terribly provoking, but I'd better go. Angela, you might thank Lady C. for me. And don't think I've forgotten about the pig,' he said as an afterthought, as he sloped off.

'What was that about a pig?' said the inspector.

Angela sighed, while Kathie giggled delightedly and explained. As she did so, Angela noticed that Jameson was gazing at Kathie as though slightly stunned. For a moment she was puzzled, but then the truth dawned on her and she had a similar revelation to that experienced by Freddy a few minutes earlier with regard to herself. She raised her eyebrows.

'Well, well,' she thought.

Had she not been personally involved in the story of the pig she might have gone off there and then and left them to it, but of course it would have looked odd if she had, so she merely stood and observed them both covertly as they smiled and talked to one another as though she were not there. Jameson's feelings were evident enough, and although Kathie was more cautious, her glowing cheeks and sparkling eyes spoke volumes. Angela, who liked both Inspector Jameson and Kathie very much, hoped that something might come of it, but was determined to say nothing to either of them since it was quite clearly none of her business. In any case, the situation was rather delicate—firstly because of Norman, and secondly because of the murder. She would leave them to themselves, she thought.

At length, Kathie took leave of them and left. Inspector Jameson watched her go. Angela immediately forgot her resolution not to interfere and decided to give him a little encouragement.

'She's terribly sweet, isn't she?' she said.

'Hmm?' said Jameson, reluctantly tearing his attention away from Kathie's retreating figure.

'Kathie, I mean,' said Angela.

'Er—yes, I suppose she is,' he said uncomfortably.

'They're not engaged, you know,' went on Angela. 'Not yet, at any rate.'

He stared at her. He had not realized he was being so obvious.

'I see,' he said.

There was a short silence, then she smiled at him.

'You'd better hurry if you want to speak to Elisabeth,' she said. 'They dine early at Two Tithes. I'm going for a walk. I dare say I shall be late for dinner, as usual.'

And with that she walked off, leaving him standing there, deep in thought.

Chapter Fifteen

LADY CARDEW WAS FAR TOO impatient to have noticed whether Margaret Tipping had been at the fête all day. As Elisabeth informed Inspector Jameson, she had stood on the cake stall for *some* of the time, but of course as the main organizer of the fête she had had other things to see to as well, and had frequently had to hurry off to resolve some difficulty or other, leaving Margaret to hold the fort alone. Mrs. Tipping's exact whereabouts at the presumed time of the murder therefore remained a mystery—at least until someone else could be found to give her an alibi. The police had also spoken to Daniel Tyler, who swore on his oath that Norman Tipping and Kathie Montgomery had been telling the truth, and that he had met them only a matter of seconds after the gun was heard to go off. Since Tom Tipping's body had been found about two hundred yards farther along the path, it would have been almost impossible for them to have done it then. Nothing the police could say would shake Tyler in this story, and so they were reluctantly forced to conclude that either he had made a genuine mistake or he was telling the truth.

On Thursday morning, frowning over the latest entries in his notebook, Inspector Jameson set off along Dead Man's Path. He was going to speak to Norman Tipping—by arrangement this time. In the absence of any better theories Tipping was still the main suspect, even though Daniel Tyler's evidence seemed to let him out. Still, Jameson wanted to follow up every lead, and he was determined to find out more about the relationship between Norman and his father.

As Jameson walked, he mulled over the case. The timing of the gunshot was a stumbling-block, certainly, and seemed to throw the field wide open. Of course, there was *one* possibility, a certain interpretation of events, that would put Norman firmly back into the picture, but Jameson pushed it to the back of his mind and told himself that the absence of a weapon made that possibility highly unlikely. He was uncomfortably aware that he was willing Norman Tipping to be innocent—since Norman's guilt would, of course, implicate Kathie Montgomery in the murder—but even so, he was not prepared to investigate that particular avenue until he was forced to. Being as he was a man of the utmost integrity, Jameson was starting to think that he ought to withdraw from the case, since it was becoming abundantly clear to him that he could not be totally impartial. It would be difficult, however, since he had promised Sergeant Primm that he would do what he could, and he was not one to break a promise. Very well, he should go through the motions of the job as conscientiously as possible, present Primm with the evidence he had collected, and then retire to London and let Primm do what he would with it.

He arrived at Norman Tipping's house and was admitted by Alice Hopwell. Inside, the place was fitted out in accordance with the taste of a man who had no time for fripperies, and Jameson could not help wondering whether Kathie Montgomery would feel at home here. Mrs. Hopwell showed him into a large sitting-room, where he found Norman Tipping standing by the window, engaged in watching two dogs fighting outside. Tipping turned round and greeted him as he entered.

'Will there be anything else, Mr. Tipping?' said Alice Hopwell.

'No, thank you, Mrs. Hopwell,' he said distantly, and she nodded and went out. Jameson shortly afterwards heard the front door shut as she left.

'So then, inspector,' said Norman Tipping. 'I gather the police are no further forward in discovering who carried out this appalling crime.'

By the tone of his voice he might have been talking about some story he had read in the newspapers rather than his own father's murder, but Inspector Jameson had been a policeman for many years and had seen all kinds of reactions to death from bereaved families in that time, and so he knew that nothing could be inferred from it.

'I shouldn't quite say that,' he said, 'although of course the case does present a number of difficulties, such as the apparently short interval in which the murder must have been committed, and the fact that neither you, Mrs. Montgomery nor Daniel Tyler saw anybody else in the vicinity at the time.'

'Well, presumably that must mean that the killer was hiding, lying in wait,' said Norman. 'How terrible, to think that my father's murderer was probably within a few yards of us when we passed him. If only we had asked him to come to the fête with us, then this could not have happened!'

Jameson made no comment, but instead said:

'I should just like to be absolutely clear on this point.

Are you quite sure that you and Mrs. Montgomery were together the whole time? She didn't walk ahead of you at any point, for example? Were you out of sight of each other at any time?'

'No, we walked together all the way,' said Norman. 'And I don't quite like what you're suggesting. I assure you that Mrs. Montgomery had no motive at all to murder anyone.'

Jameson wondered whether he was being wilfully obtuse, but did not rise to this.

'I'm sorry, Mr. Tipping,' he said, 'but I have no choice but to ask questions of this kind. This is a murder investigation, and I'm afraid personal feelings must not be allowed to come into it.'

He was fully aware of his own failings in this respect, but ignored them.

'Very well, then,' said Norman reluctantly. 'I suppose you must do your duty, but I can't say I like it.'

Jameson smiled in acknowledgment, and went on, 'Apart from Andrew Norris, are you aware of anyone else who might have had a motive to kill your father? Did he have any other enemies that you know of?'

'No, none at all,' said Norman.

'I understand he had rather a particular sense of humour, which might not have gone down too well with some people,' said Jameson carefully.

'He had a robust sense of humour, certainly,' said Norman. 'I can't say it was always to my taste, but really, the occasional joke hardly constitutes a motive for murder, does it?'

'It depends,' said Jameson. 'Perhaps if someone had been the butt of his jokes for many years, they might be driven to desperate measures.'

'I don't quite understand what you're getting at,' said Norman.

Very well: it was time to bring the thing out into the open, thought Jameson.

'Did you and your mother get on with your father, Mr. Tipping?' he said.

Norman bridled.

'Ah, now I see your line of thinking,' he replied coldly. 'You are trying to imply that one of us might have done it. Well, I can assure you that what you are suggesting is utterly ridiculous. Quite apart from anything else, both of us have an alibi for the time in question.'

Jameson did not contradict him, but instead said:

'Do you own a shotgun?'

Norman was offended now, but was determined not to lose his temper.

'Of course I do,' he said. 'Everyone around here owns one.'

'Are there any at your father's house other than the one he carried?'

'Yes, yes, I dare say there are,' said Norman. 'And since it is clear the way your mind is working, I suggest you take mine and then go to the farm and have a look at those too. I can assure you that none of them was used to kill my father.'

'Thank you, I shall do that,' said Jameson. 'You do understand why I have to ask these questions, don't you?'

'Oh, I suppose so,' said Norman grudgingly. 'Very well, I shall go and fetch mine and you can have a look at it.'

He went out and came back with the article in question, which he handed to Jameson.

'It's not loaded,' said Norman. 'I should never dream of keeping a loaded shotgun in the house. It would be terribly dangerous.'

Jameson examined it closely. As Norman had said, it was not loaded. He handed it back with thanks.

'I understand you have been speaking to Mrs. Montgomery,' said Norman. 'I don't like her being mixed up in all this.'

'I don't suppose she likes it much either,' said Jameson. 'But I had to speak to her, too, since she is a witness.'

'You ought to have come to me first,' said Norman. 'I could have spoken for her and told you she had nothing to say.'

'Perhaps she preferred to speak for herself,' said Jameson.

'She ought to have refused to talk to you until she'd spoken to me. What did she tell you? I have a right to know.'

Jameson raised his eyebrows.

'I thought you were quite certain she had nothing to say,' he said.

'*She* had nothing to say,' said Norman. 'We were there together, and she ought to have let me do the talking for us both. What did she tell you?'

'I'm not at liberty to reveal that,' said Jameson, 'but I can't stop Mrs. Montgomery from telling you if she wishes. You will have to ask her, I'm afraid.'

'Don't worry, I shall,' said Norman pompously.

Inspector Jameson took his leave and walked back towards the village, feeling more conflicted than ever. He found Norman Tipping's high-handed manner very irritating, and in any other circumstances would have been quite happy to discover that the man was guilty—but if he was, then where did Kathie come in? She must be complicit, in that case. Of course, there was the question of the gun, and Jameson clung to that. Daniel Tyler was quite certain that neither Norman nor Kathie had been carrying a shotgun when he met them, but there was no doubt that that was what had killed Tom Tipping. Where was the weapon, then? Had the murderer killed Tipping and then run off, taking the gun with him? Or had he perhaps hidden it somewhere? Nobody had been seen with a gun on Saturday—or at least, no witnesses had come forward to say they had seen anybody carrying one. A shotgun was not something that could be shoved in a pocket and hidden, and the police had found no sign of it when they searched the area, so where was it? Until they found it, the case would not be solved, Jameson was certain of it.

Chapter Sixteen

'I SEEM to be hitting a brick wall on all sides,' said Inspector Jameson to Sergeant Primm once he had got back to the police station. 'Nobody is budging on the story of what happened on Dead Man's Path. Daniel Tyler has no particular reason to lie, as far as I can tell, and we have no witnesses to say that anybody else was in the area at the time. And of course, there's this damned shotgun. If one of our suspects did it, what did they do with the gun? Your men have scoured the place from top to bottom, and there's no sign of it.'

'No,' said Primm. 'That's not to say it's not there, but if it is it's pretty well hidden. Of course, whoever it was might have shot Tom Tipping, hidden the gun somewhere and then come back for it later before we'd had a chance to search the area properly.'

'True,' said Inspector Jameson. 'Norman Tipping's shotgun is safely at home now—but still, we have Tyler's word for it that Tipping couldn't possibly have done it. And of course Daniel Tyler couldn't have done it because the gunshot was heard before Tipping and Mrs. Mont-gomery met him coming the other way.'

'It's a pity about those two,' said Primm with regret. 'They're the ones with the motive.'

'I *had* heard that there's no engagement yet,' said Jameson cautiously. 'If so, then perhaps Mrs. Montgomery would have less of a motive for trying to protect him.'

'Pfft!' said Primm. 'Engagement or no engagement, she's sure of him. She's pretty and well-bred, and just the sort of wife he'd be looking for if I know anything about Norman Tipping. She'll make him look good, you see.'

'That's rather cynical of you, Primm,' said the inspec-tor. 'One would hope that there'd be at least *some* affection in the case.'

'Depends what you mean by affection, doesn't it?' said Primm. 'She's a nice girl, and she's been alone for a long time without much money. P'raps he came along and offered her a comfortable life and kind treatment and she was willing enough to accept it.'

'Then you don't think they are in love?'

'I can't imagine Norman Tipping falling in love, can you?' said Primm. 'He's far too much the careful sort. He probably likes her well enough. And she—well, she's a kind-hearted soul.'

'Would that be enough to make her lie for him, though? I could perhaps understand it if she loved him, but if she doesn't then it just makes her look horribly mercenary, and I shouldn't have thought she was the type.'

'No, I shouldn't have thought so either,' agreed Primm. 'But facts are facts.'

'And evidence is evidence,' said Jameson. 'And so far we have very little of that. Very well, let us see what Margaret Tipping has to say.'

'If you can get anything useful out of her then you're a

better man than I am, sir,' remarked Primm cheerfully. 'She's a close one, all right.'

'That may be so, but I must try, at least,' said Jameson, and went out.

The Tippings' farm stood to one side of Dead Man's Path, on the other side of a large field. The farmyard itself was much more clean and spruce than Jameson had expected, and he wondered whether Margaret Tipping was responsible. He knocked at the door and she answered it quickly. There was a mop in her hand.

'I'm cleaning,' she said unnecessarily, and stood back to let him in. The kitchen flags were still wet, and he stepped gingerly over them. 'Don't worry,' she said. 'I'll do it again after you've gone. There's to be a funeral, you see—when the police say we can have it, at any rate—and I want the house to be spotless.'

Jameson wondered whether she had been concentrating on the cleaning as a means to avoid thinking about what had happened. Sudden deaths could take people that way. Mrs. Tipping led him into the parlour, which was dark and silent, apart from a loudly ticking clock on the mantelpiece. After a moment she seemed to recall her manners, and invited him to sit. He did so, and she perched on the edge of a chair opposite. For a minute or two they sat, facing one another in the dim light, the sound of the clock the only thing breaking the silence. She was staring at him so dispassionately that he felt quite uncomfortable.

'Have you found out who did it yet?' she asked eventually.

'No,' said Jameson. 'That's why I am here. I should like to know more about your husband. I believe if I can find out more about him, then that might give us some idea of why he was killed and who killed him.'

'What do you want to know?'

He glanced at his notebook.

'Other than Mr. Norris, did your husband have any enemies?'

She stood up suddenly, then went over to the window and started wiping a duster along the window-sill, even though from where he was sitting it looked perfectly clean.

'No,' she said at last. 'Not that I know of. At least, none that would be prepared to put themselves out by killing him.'

This seemed a strange way of putting it, to say the least.

'Then everybody liked him?' said Jameson.

'That's not what I said, is it?' said Mrs. Tipping.

'What do you mean?' said Jameson. He was wondering whether he would have to drag every single piece of information out of her.

'Why, there were people who liked him and people who didn't. Those who didn't kept away from him as a rule.'

'Who were they?'

She looked at him as though he were slightly slow-witted.

'Nobody in particular,' she said. 'Everyone has *someone* who doesn't like them, but if we all went around murdering people we didn't like there'd be nobody left, would there? I dare say there are people who don't like you much, inspector, but you're still here.'

'Oh, I see,' said Jameson. 'I thought you were speaking about a particular person.'

She said nothing, and Jameson, who was getting rather impatient, decided to stop beating about the bush.

'Did *you* like him?' he said.

'Not especially,' she said, as though she were telling him the time. 'But again, I didn't kill him. Nor did I want to.'

'What about your son? Did he get on with his father?'

'They never understood each other,' said Margaret. 'Norman's a serious sort. But they rubbed along well enough.'

Jameson was finding her a puzzle. There was no animation in her face as she talked about her family, and in fact she seemed devoid of any feeling at all.

'You think I'm cold,' she said suddenly, as though reading his mind. 'I'm not. Or I never used to be, at any rate. But my life didn't turn out the way I expected so I had to make the best of it, and I discovered a long time ago that the best way to do that was not to feel too much. After all these years I think perhaps I've forgotten *how* to feel.'

'I'm sorry,' said Jameson, and meant it.

'Don't be,' said Margaret. 'I'm all right.'

She seemed determined to be unemotional, so Jameson went back to his questions.

'Tell me about the fête,' he said. 'You were on the cake stall that day, I understand.'

'Yes,' she said. 'I went to get something to eat at about one o'clock, I think, but apart from that I was on the stall all day, until Norman came to fetch me and tell me what had happened.'

'Is there anyone who can swear to that?' said Jameson. 'Lady Cardew says she saw you *some* of the time. Is there anyone else who might have seen you—especially around lunch-time or shortly afterwards?'

'Mrs. Randall, I suppose,' said Margaret, thinking. 'Except I don't think she saw very much at all.'

'Why not?'

'She drinks,' said Margaret flatly. 'I don't know why on earth they let her do the tea. She knocked the urn over.'

'Ah,' said Jameson, taken aback.

'I think I talked to Mrs. Hunter,' went on Mrs. Tipping.

'She might remember. There's bound to be someone, anyway. I was there all the time. But you know,' she went on, 'I couldn't have done it anyway. I don't know how to fire a gun.'

'What about your son?' said Jameson. 'He has a shotgun.'

She looked at him, but said nothing. Jameson was finding the whole conversation very odd. Usually it was difficult to ask such questions because people tended to get upset or angry, but in this particular case it was difficult because Margaret Tipping's coldness was making him distinctly uncomfortable. He pressed on doggedly.

'Do you think he might have done it?' he said.

She looked as though she were giving the matter serious consideration.

'It's possible,' she said. 'That is, if you're asking whether he'd be capable of it. He might be. But I don't think he did. He was with Kathie, wasn't he? She'd never put up with anything like that.'

When she spoke of Kathie her face became *almost* animated, and Jameson took heart from it. Still, he had more questions to ask.

'Who inherits this farm?' he said.

'Norman,' said Margaret. 'Although I'm allowed to stay here. That's what Tom told me, at any rate. I assume he was telling the truth, although I suppose it might have been one of his silly jokes.'

'What about money? Did your husband have any to leave?'

There was no point in asking it delicately.

'Yes, I think so,' she replied. 'He never told me how much, exactly, but I think Norman and I both get something. Norman will know. Or the solicitor.'

Jameson asked to see the shotguns, and she showed

him two, which he duly examined. He then took his leave. She showed him to the door and as he left he saw her wiping the doorstep with the mop. Primm had been right: there was little to be got out of her. It seemed that they were hardly any further forward.

Chapter Seventeen

WHILE INSPECTOR JAMESON was struggling to get Mrs. Tipping to talk, Angela had been having rather the opposite problem with Mrs. Hunter. She had been pressed into paying the vicar's wife another visit, but refused to go without Kathie, since she rather feared that without some assistance, after ten minutes of listening to Mrs. Hunter's pronunciations she might have to make an unseemly bolt for it. Kathie laughed at this and duly agreed to accompany her.

As it happened, the visit was not as bad as might have been expected—for Angela, at least—since Mrs. Hunter was still full of the murder and had little time for any other subject. This time, it was Kathie who had to suffer, as Mrs. Hunter had now heard some of the stories which were beginning to circulate.

'I feel you ought to know, dear,' she said to Kathie. 'Rumours will start, and I shouldn't like you to be taken by surprise.'

'Oh, I know exactly what people are saying,' said Kathie, 'and of course it's all nonsense. Poor Norman—it's bad enough that he's lost his father without people saying he did it.'

'And that you were an accessory,' added Mrs. Hunter helpfully.

'Now, you don't really believe that, do you?' said Kathie with a smile.

'Of course not,' said Mrs. Hunter. 'You're a dear, and I shall never say any different. But the police are stupid fellows in general, and so you must stand by Norman and make them see sense. I myself am quite certain it was those gipsies who did it. And even if it wasn't, why, anyone might have come along Dead Man's Path and killed him. There's nothing to say it was anyone who knew him, now, is there? Why, it could have been a passing escaped lunatic.'

'Are you troubled with many of those around here?' inquired Angela.

'Not especially,' said Mrs. Hunter, who took the question seriously. 'But such things can happen. Some of these old soldiers who wander about aren't quite right in the head, you know. Of course, they really ought to be locked up for their own safety and that of others, but they aren't, and we don't know that one of them mightn't have taken it into his head to go mad with a shotgun.'

'But nobody has seen anyone of that kind loitering about the place recently, have they?' said Angela.

'They know where to hide,' said Mrs. Hunter darkly.

There was no reply to this, and the visit ended soon afterwards, somewhat to the relief of the visitors.

'This whole thing does seem rather hard on you both,' said Angela to Kathie as they emerged. 'I hope not everybody has been as blunt as Mrs. Hunter.'

'Oh, no,' said Kathie. 'Most people are much more discreet than that—although I dare say they all talk about it when we're not there.' She paused. 'Do you think the police believe it?' she said.

'I've no idea,' said Angela.

'I thought you might know, since you're such great friends with Inspector Jameson,' said Kathie.

'I'm too friendly with you, so I don't suppose he'd tell me anything,' said Angela.

'I know it all looks very suspicious,' said Kathie hesitantly, 'but I should hate him to think badly of me.'

'Oh, I don't think you need worry about that,' said Angela, once again forgetting her resolution not to interfere.

'What do you mean?' said Kathie, glancing up.

'Don't you know?' said Angela with a smile.

Kathie's cheeks went slightly pink.

'I wasn't quite sure,' she said after a moment. 'I thought perhaps I was imagining things.'

'No, I'm pretty certain you're not,' said Angela. 'It's obvious enough to me, at any rate.'

'Oh,' said Kathie, and fell silent.

Angela could not help asking the next question.

'But what about you?' she said. 'How do you feel about it?'

Kathie let out a laugh that was half a sob.

'I simply couldn't tell you,' she said. 'The last few days have been so awfully confusing. I'd been trundling along quite contentedly, thinking that Norman would probably ask me to marry him sooner or later, just as everybody expected, but then Tom was killed and the police came, and Scotland Yard, and—' she paused. 'And now I'm wondering whether I'm quite as contented as I thought I was.'

'I see,' said Angela.

'Something has happened,' went on Kathie all in a

rush. 'To me, I mean. I don't know how to explain it, but it's the most peculiar feeling, and I'm not altogether certain I like it. Sometimes I'm terribly agitated and fidgety, and can't seem to settle to anything, but then at other times I find myself spending an hour staring out of the window as though I'm waiting for something—although I have no idea what. It's not like me at all. I thought at first it must be because of Tom's death, but if it is, then I must be a very bad person indeed, or why else should I feel so happy?'

'I'd have thought it was obvious,' said Angela.

'Yes, I'm rather afraid it is,' said Kathie quietly.

'Why afraid?' said Angela.

'Because of the murder, of course,' said Kathie. 'Tom is dead, and Norman and I are suspects, and everyone thinks we're engaged anyway, and it would look simply dreadful if I didn't stand by him while all this is going on. Don't you see?'

'Yes, I do,' said Angela.

'It's horrid of me to be thinking of someone else at such a time—especially the investigating policeman, of all people, but I don't seem to be able to help it,' said Kathie. 'I wish I could stop, and then we could all go back to the way we were before. But how *can* I stop?'

'I don't know,' said Angela, 'but I do know there's no use at all in trying to pretend you're in love with one man when in actual fact you're in love with another.'

'Am I, though?' said Kathie. 'My head is in such a whirl that I don't know whether it's real, or whether it's merely that I've gone a little mad because of the whole peculiar situation. Perhaps it's nothing at all and I'll get over it in a day or two—I simply don't know. It would certainly make things easier if that were the case. Still,' she went on wistfully, 'I do wish people wouldn't take my engagement to Norman *quite* so much for granted. That's the trouble with living in a small village, you see: there's nothing much to do except talk about the neighbours and arrange their lives for them.'

'Yes, that sort of thing can be rather tiresome,' said Angela. 'But Kathie, you wouldn't do something that made you unhappy just because people expected it of you, surely. Just as you wouldn't turn down the opportunity to be happy for the same reason.'

'No,' said Kathie. 'But nobody has offered me the opportunity to be anything—not Norman, and not anybody else, so until someone does I must go on as I have done. Listen to me,' she said impatiently. 'Here I am, talking a lot of nonsense about falling in love when someone I know has been murdered. I ought to be ashamed of myself. I won't think of it any more—at least, not until this is all over. By that time I dare say I'll have talked myself out of it and everything will return to normal.'

'By all means, talk yourself out of it if that is what you want,' said Angela. 'I'm sure you and Norman will be very happy together.'

Kathie threw her a suspicious look, but Angela had assumed her blandest expression, for she had reminded herself that it was none of her business, and that further interference might do more harm than good. These things had a way of working themselves out, and after all, Kathie was a grown woman who was quite capable of making her own decisions. Angela determined to say no more on the subject and to leave them to it.

The two ladies said goodbye and Kathie headed back towards her cottage, while Angela turned her steps homewards. As she passed the church she saw Mrs. Hunter's bicycle still chained up outside, and glanced up at the sky. There had been no rain since Saturday although the weather had been dull, and she was just wondering how much longer it would hold when she saw Andrew Norris just ahead of her—unarmed, this time, although his dog stood by his side and she eyed the creature warily.

'Oh, don't worry about him,' said Norris cheerfully. 'He won't bite—not unless I tell him to, at any rate.'

Angela was hardly reassured by this, but wished Mr. Norris a good day. He seemed inclined to talk.

'I see the police are just as puzzled as everyone else as to who shot Tom Tipping,' he said.

'Are they?' she said politely.

'I should say so,' he said. 'They tried to pin it on me, you know, but for once I had nothing to do with it. It'll be Norman and his girl next—you mark my words. And then when they can't prove *they* did it either, they'll probably arrest Bob Sanderson, Mrs. Goddard and the vicar in turn. And then when they've gone through everyone else they'll have no choice but to arrest themselves!'

He cackled with laughter at his own wit.

'I gather you don't think much of the police, then,' said Angela.

'No, I don't!' he said. 'Arresting a man before they've even looked into the matter properly. What were they thinking? They made me spend a night in the cells on a hard bed. I like to be comfortable at my age—not that I'm not fit and healthy, of course—never better—but still, it was chilly and I was all aches and pains by the time they released me. And how do you think it looked? You might not believe it, but I'm a respectable man. I've lived in Banford all my life and that sort of thing doesn't look good. I know people have been talking about me behind their hands. How am I supposed to get my reputation back?'

'But everyone knows you didn't do it,' said Angela. 'I don't think you need worry about your reputation too much. I'm sorry you had to spend a night in prison, but you must admit you were the most obvious suspect. You can't go around threatening to shoot a man and then expect not to be arrested when that same man is found shot, now, can you?'

He gave a short bark of laughter.

'I suppose you're right, when you put it like that,' he said. He gave her a leer. 'So, then, missy, I hear you're a famous detective these days. Why don't *you* set to and put the police right?'

Angela had the impression that there was something he wanted to say.

'Perhaps I shall,' she said. 'Where do you suggest I start?'

'Closest to home, that's where,' he said. 'Who had the biggest motive to kill Tom Tipping? Why, his family, of course. It's nearly always family in these cases, isn't it? Especially when there's money involved.'

'Is there money involved?' said Angela.

'Tom was near, very near,' said Norris. 'Margaret ought to have thought of that before she married him. He kept her short. Kept both of them short, as a matter of fact. It's poor form to make your wife ask for money—but there, she made her own bed and she had to lie in it. She chose him over me and had to live with the consequences. I'd have been generous, but she never thought of that. Still, though, there ought to be plenty of money now he's dead —if she gets to keep it, of course.'

'Are you suggesting that Mrs. Tipping killed her husband?' said Angela.

He shook his head.

'Hardly,' he said. 'She wouldn't bother with all that. But Norman, now: that's a different matter altogether. He tries to cut a fine figure, but he's in need—very much in need, if what I hear is true. That girl of his—she's used to the finer things, and she'll want more than he can give. From what I hear, he hasn't two pennies to rub together, and his father refused to advance him anything. But that's not a problem for him any more, is it? Not now his father is safely out of the way.'

'How do you know all this?' said Angela.

He cackled.

'Go and ask Jimmy,' he said.

'Who is Jimmy?'

But he wagged a finger at her and shook his head, then strolled off, leaving Angela in great perplexity. He evidently had no intention of saying anything more, so she set off for home and decided to stop in at the police station on the way to report what he had said. Inspector Jameson was out, but Sergeant Primm was there, and she told him of their conversation. Primm listened with interest.

'I wonder, now,' he said. 'Jimmy. I wonder whether he mightn't have been talking about—' He stopped. 'It would make sense,' he went on.

Angela waited, but he would say no more. He thanked her and she went out.

She returned to Two Tithes just before tea-time. Until now she had taken care to spend as little time there as was possible without actually being rude, since she assumed that Humphrey and Elisabeth would prefer it that way, but when she entered she found Humphrey waiting for her in the hall, and wondered for a second whether she was about to be accused of deserting them, for his expression was stiff and haughty.

'Ah, there you are, Angela,' he said. 'I wonder if I might have a word with you in private.'

'Certainly, Humphrey,' she said in surprise. She

followed him into his study, curious to know what it was all about.

They went in, and Humphrey sat himself carefully behind his desk. He did not invite her to sit, but instead picked up a copy of a newspaper that rested there, and looked at it significantly. Angela sensed trouble.

'What's that?' she said.

'It is a newspaper called the *Herald*,' said Humphrey. 'I use the word "newspaper" loosely, you understand. However, I am rather disturbed by an article I have found in it.'

'I didn't know you read that kind of rag,' she said. She assumed there was something in the paper that concerned her, and since she would not suffer being summoned to her own brother's study as though she were an unruly pupil called to the headmistress's office for a carpeting, she threw herself deliberately into the most comfortable chair in the room and crossed her legs. Had she had a cigarette about her she would have lit it, but instead she said:

'I take it from your face that there is some absurd nonsense about me in it.'

'Is it nonsense?' he said.

'I imagine so, but until you tell me what it says, I can't comment,' she replied.

He put on his glasses, then opened the newspaper and searched carefully for the right page. If he was hoping to intimidate her he was disappointed; in fact she was merely irritated, for she was sure it was all an act. At last he found what he was looking for and pushed the newspaper across to her. She reached for it in some trepidation, since she generally made it a rule not to read about herself.

'Oh, goodness,' she said, wincing slightly as she read. 'I see this is Corky's doing. He did rather threaten to write something of the kind, but he really has outdone himself, hasn't he?'

'I am sorry you take this so lightly, Angela,' said Humphrey. I thought you might at least have restrained yourself from seeking this sort of publicity while you were visiting us here at Two Tithes. In London I dare say things are very different, but here in the country we have appearances to maintain. People have long memories and they don't appreciate this kind of thing.'

'Why, you don't suppose for a second that I had anything to do with this drivel, do you?' she said.

'What else am I to think?' said Humphrey. 'The writer says he spoke to you directly and attributes several statements to you, most of which—and always allowing for the execrable grammar of a man who must submit a story in a hurry—I should never have supposed you capable of making.'

'That's because I didn't,' she said. 'I never said any of this stuff. I mean, look at this: "Let it be hereby proclaimed to the people of Great Britain that I shall never rest until this evil miscreant is caught and hanged—" oh, goodness me, the man makes me sound like a positive imbecile! Here, take the thing and burn it,' she said, thrusting the paper back at him, pink in the face. 'Listen, Humphrey,' she went on, 'I swear to you I had nothing to do with it— and really, I'm rather disappointed that you could believe it of me. I know you don't particularly approve of me, but I should have thought you'd know better than that. I'm not *quite* as vulgar as you seem to think.'

'But then why does it say he spoke to you?' he said.

'He did speak to me—at length,' said Angela. 'And I refused to talk to him about the murder, so he made something up. Look, I suffer from this sort of thing far more than you do, you know, since I'm the one who has to put up with the general public thinking me an idiot. You're only affected by association, so I don't know why it should bother *you* so much.'

'It's not only the publicity, though, is it?' said Humphrey. 'I am concerned, very concerned, Angela. You gave me your word that you would not involve yourself in any detective-work while you were here. The police have a difficult enough job as it is, without an amateur lady detective inveigling her way into the investigation and taking over.'

'I've done no such thing!' exclaimed Angela. 'I've never inveigled my way into anything in my life. I wouldn't even know how to inveigle. And as for taking over—why, that's simply nonsense! I assure you that I've kept well out of it, just as I promised. I won't deny that I've spoken to the police, but Inspector Jameson is an old friend of mine so I could hardly avoid him. Other than that, I've left them to it, and I'll continue to leave them to it—but only if you'll believe me. Quite frankly, if you're determined to be convinced that I'm secretly running about the countryside hunting down murderers, then I may as well actually do it.'

An uncertain expression began to dawn on Humphrey's face.

'I don't wish to cast doubt on your veracity,' he said, 'but you must admit it looks rather odd. And another thing: there hasn't been a murder in Banford Green for a hundred years or more, but as soon as you arrive someone is shot dead. Why is that, do you suppose?'

'Pure coincidence, of course,' said Angela. 'Unless you're suggesting I organized the thing for my own entertainment.'

'No-o,' said Humphrey, although he did not seem quite certain of it.

'That's a relief,' said Angela. 'I know you think we

society women are all irredeemably jaded and debauched, but I don't think I'm *quite* at that stage yet.'

'It is no joking matter,' said Humphrey.

'I know it's not,' said Angela. 'Someone has died and it's not funny at all. I should like the person who did it to be arrested, but I'm happy to leave that job to the police. And I promise you I didn't say any of that stuff in the *Herald*. Now, please, let's forget it and go in to tea.'

'Oh, very well,' said Humphrey. 'I apologize. I'm sorry I thought the worst of you. I ought to have known you would never have done anything of the kind.'

'Why, thank you, Humphrey,' said Angela in some surprise. 'That's very generous of you, and I'm quite happy to forget it was ever mentioned. But for goodness' sake, let's burn that newspaper.'

'That might be wise,' he agreed.

They went into the drawing-room, where there was a slightly frosty atmosphere. Mrs. Randall peered at Angela through her lorgnette and gave her a grimace that might have been interpreted as a smile, but Elisabeth was stony-faced.

'Angela informs me that she had nothing to do with the story in the *Herald*,' said Humphrey. 'Perhaps it will be better if we never speak of it again.'

'I'm glad to hear it,' said Elisabeth, although she looked unconvinced.

Mrs. Randall looked disappointed, but said nothing, and they all busied themselves with tea, Angela feeling relieved and surprised that Humphrey had believed her. Perhaps he was not such a bad old stick after all, she thought, and resolved to have a word with Freddy to see if anything could be done to keep Corky Beckwith under control in future.

Chapter Eighteen

ON FRIDAY MORNING Sergeant Primm entered Banford Green police station to find Inspector Jameson frowning over another story in the previous evening's *Herald*, which Angela had missed in all the furore over her own appearance in the paper.

'You've seen it, then, sir,' said Primm.

'Yes,' said Jameson. 'I shall have to speak to Corky Beckwith. We can't have this sort of thing being published when we're in the middle of a delicate investigation.'

The story to which he referred was based loosely on a conversation with Andrew Norris, who claimed to know the true state of relations within the Tipping household, and hinted at motives for Tom Tipping's murder which had yet to come to light, although much was made of a supposedly secret will. In the article, Norris was given free rein (with Corky's helpful additions) to criticise the police, the Tipping family, his neighbours, the Government, and the *Herald*'s rival newspaper, the *Clarion*. According to the story, the police were shortly expected to arrest the main suspect, and it did not take too much knowledge of the case to understand that the suspect in question was Norman Tipping.

'Corky only just stopped short of naming him,' said Jameson. 'The man's a menace. He ought to know that writing stuff like this can prejudice a trial.'

'Yes,' said Primm. 'Still, you might have to admit he's right when you hear what I've found out.'

Jameson looked up and saw that the sergeant had an air of suppressed triumph.

'Go on,' he said.

'Do you remember I mentioned that Mrs. Marchmont was here yesterday?' said Primm.

'Yes,' said Jameson. 'She'd been speaking to Andrew Norris. Have you talked to him to find out who this Jimmy is?'

'I didn't need to,' said Primm, looking even more pleased with himself, 'because I bumped into Jimmy himself this morning.'

'Who is he?'

'One James Cleary, known around these parts as Irish Jimmy. He's by way of being a bookmaker. We know him very well.'

'Oh, a cash operator, is he?'

'Exactly,' said Primm. 'Well, now, we don't trouble ourselves with him too much, but now and again we give him a warning or a fine and he goes off and promises to be a good boy—until the next time. At any rate, we and he rub along together nicely, generally speaking. Anyway, I'd been wondering whether he was the same Jimmy old Norris had been talking about, and as luck would have it I happened to see him this morning, so I just asked him, casual like, whether he'd had any dealings with a certain person lately. Now, Jimmy knows better than to clam up on me on a big race day, so he was happy to talk. More than happy, in fact, as it seems he's been foolish enough to give the certain person in question credit all this year and half of last.'

'And let me guess: that certain person has been avoiding him lately,' said Jameson.

'Why, how on earth did you guess that, sir?' said Primm, opening his eyes in mock surprise.

'I gather you are referring to Norman Tipping,' said Jameson. 'What sort of sum are we talking about?'

'The best part of a thousand pounds,' said Primm.

Jameson whistled.

'Exactly,' said Primm. 'Anyway, the last time Jimmy saw him he asked for the money, but Norman said he didn't have it at present. Jimmy caught him by surprise, it seems, for he got a bit flustered and let slip that his father had promised him a loan and that Jimmy could have the money next week. Two weeks later, there was still no sign of it so Jimmy went and spoke to Tom Tipping, who laughed as though he'd never heard such a joke and said that Norman had taken Jimmy for a fool, as Tom would never be stupid enough to throw good money after bad like that, even if he was disposed to give his son a loan—which he wasn't, as Norman was quite old enough to look after himself now without having to come to his father for help.'

'I see,' said Jameson. 'So Tom wasn't inclined to bail out his son. How did Jimmy take the news? These people don't take kindly to defaulting debtors, generally speaking. I suppose threats were made?'

'Perhaps,' conceded Primm. 'Jimmy's got a temper on him, and he's been in trouble in the past that way. I shouldn't be surprised if he put the fear of God into Norman, and that's a powerful driving force.'

'It is,' said Jameson.

'At any rate,' went on the sergeant, 'I was just on my

way back here when I happened to see Norman Tipping and thought I might as well speak to him as not, and so I told him what Jimmy had said.'

'And how did he take it?'

'As you might expect. He blustered and denied it for a bit, but then admitted it was true. I asked him if he had a gambling habit and he got very pompous and said absolutely not, and what did I take him for? He said it would never happen again, and that every man was entitled to make a mistake in life, surely?'

'That's fair enough,' observed Jameson.

'It would be if it was true,' said Primm, 'but I reckon it's all nonsense. If you ask me, he's got the habit badly. And all this, of course, gives him more of a motive than ever to have murdered his father. We know Norman owns a shotgun and that he had a good reason to do it; now all we need to do is break that alibi of his.'

Jameson picked up a pencil and toyed with it thoughtfully. His heart had been sinking all the time Primm was talking. He had been hoping to avoid the question—hoping somehow that an entirely different solution to the case would come to light before he had to face it—but now it could not be put off any longer, and so he said:

'The alibi is easy enough to break if you disregard the sound of the shotgun.'

'What do you mean?' said Primm in surprise.

'Why, that the noise is the only evidence we have that Tom Tipping was killed when everybody assumes he was,' said Jameson. 'If it weren't for that, then he might have been killed half an hour or even an hour earlier for all we know.'

Primm stared at the inspector as his words sank in.

'Do you mean to say that Tom wasn't killed in those

147

few minutes at all?' he said. 'Then who fired the shot that was heard?'

Jameson shrugged. He was suddenly sick of the case and wanted nothing more to do with it.

'It might have been anything or nothing,' he said. 'Perhaps it wasn't a shotgun at all, but a car backfiring.'

'Then Norman might have done it after all,' said Primm. He paused. 'But in that case, why did he walk along Dead Man's Path afterwards with Mrs. Montgomery? You'd have thought he'd take care not to go anywhere near it after the murder.'

'I don't know,' said Jameson. 'I don't know anything. All I can tell you is that we have every reason to arrest Norman Tipping for the murder of his father. He owns a shotgun, he was in the area at the time as far as we know, and by his father's death he inherits enough money to pay off his debts. That's quite enough to justify an arrest. There *is* no alibi as such. The sound of a shotgun going off is only circumstantial evidence that might easily be explained away.'

He waited while the sergeant thought about it some more.

'What about Mrs. Montgomery?' said Primm at length. 'If he did it an hour earlier, as you say, then she can't have been with him at the time, since she was at the fête.'

'No,' said Jameson, 'but it might not have been an hour earlier. It might have been only ten minutes earlier, in which case she might easily have been with him when he did it. And even if she wasn't with him at the time—even if she really did just walk back to the fête with him later, as she said, then she must have seen Tom's body lying there as they passed. She can't have avoided seeing it. In that case, why didn't she mention it?'

'I see,' said Primm. He looked sober. 'I don't like to

think of her being involved,' he said. 'There's that son of hers—what will happen to him?'

Jameson said nothing but his mouth was set in a thin line. He had done his duty and much good it had done him. He had presented Sergeant Primm with everything he needed to arrest Norman Tipping and Kathie Montgomery, and now he would have to try and live with himself for it. It was impossible for him to continue any further with the case, so there was nothing for him to do but to go back to London. There he could lick his wounds in private and try not to think too hard about what he had been responsible for. For perhaps the first time in his long career, Jameson found that he hated his job, and what it forced him to do. Perhaps when he got back to Scotland Yard he would request a few days off and go away somewhere for a little while to try and forget things. He showed nothing of this in his face, however, but merely said:

'You'd better get an arrest warrant. I doubt very much you'll have any difficulty.'

'I shouldn't have thought so,' agreed Primm. 'I reckon we'll have Norman Tipping in custody by the end of the day. I'd better take in Mrs. Montgomery too, although I don't like it. Won't the Cardews kick up a fuss!'

'I dare say they will,' said Jameson. 'And I'm sorry to leave you to it, Primm, but I'm wanted back in London today, so I won't be in at the finish, I'm afraid.'

'That's a shame, sir,' said Primm.

'Well, it wasn't my case in the first place,' said Jameson. He wanted nothing more than to get away as quickly as possible, and so he took a hasty leave of the sergeant and left the police station to walk to his car, which he had left at the top of Church Lane.

If he had been hoping to escape without seeing Kathie again, however, he was disappointed, for just as he reached the car he saw her emerging from Dead Man's Path on her way into the village. She approached him and greeted him cheerfully, but then her expression became one of concern as she saw his face.

'Why, what's the matter, inspector?' she said. 'Has something happened?'

'Good morning, Mrs. Montgomery,' he said. 'I'm just returning to London as I am needed at Scotland Yard.'

She looked puzzled at his stiff reply, which was quite unlike his normal manner to her.

'But what about Tom?' she said.

'It wasn't strictly my case,' he replied. 'I was only looking in on it, so to speak. I've left it in the hands of Sergeant Primm and his inspector, when he returns. If you have anything new to report, you can speak to them.'

She regarded him questioningly, and he found himself unable to meet her gaze.

'Something has happened, hasn't it?' she said after a pause. 'Why are you really leaving?'

He knew he ought not to answer this, but he could not help himself.

'Because I can't be impartial,' he said at last. She was silent, and he went on, 'When someone is murdered a detective has to put aside his personal feelings and ask all kinds of unpleasant questions of people. Normally it doesn't bother me, but in this case I'm finding it particularly distasteful, and I've realized I can't—I ought not to continue.'

'I see,' she said. 'Why are you finding it so distasteful?'

'Because every question I ask seems to return an answer I don't like,' he said, 'to the extent that I have been tempted to disregard vital evidence. I can't do that and do my job properly, and so I am withdrawing from the case.'

'I don't quite understand. What evidence do you

mean?' she said. She hesitated. 'Is it to do with Norman and—and me?'

He did not answer directly, but he did not need to, for his look was confirmation enough.

He said, 'You know, of course, that Norman Tipping is the chief suspect in the case.'

'Yes,' said Kathie. 'And I also know that everyone thinks we were in it together. I can quite see why they would. But you know we weren't. You have Daniel Tyler's word for it that we couldn't have done it.'

'It's not quite as simple as that,' he said. 'Unfortunately, Tyler's word counts for very little in this instance, and I knew it but said nothing. I ought to have spoken up days ago, but I didn't.'

'Why not?' she said.

'Because then I should have had to arrest you,' he said quietly.

There was a silence as she digested what he had and had not said.

'So you see, I've already compromised myself,' went on Jameson. 'I've withheld information and betrayed everything I stand for as a policeman, and that being so, I'm hardly fit to remain on the case. I'm doing wrong even by telling you all this.'

'Norman didn't do it,' said Kathie suddenly. 'And neither did I. Everything I've told you is true, I promise you. I haven't lied, or kept anything from you. I simply couldn't—not when you've been so kind to me and Peter. I would never lie to you, of all people. Please say you believe me, inspector. I can bear to be arrested, but I couldn't bear it if you thought I'd been lying. Do you believe me?' It was almost a whisper.

He looked into those bright blue eyes of hers.

'Yes,' he said eventually. 'But I can't ignore the

evidence any longer, and that is why I am going back to London. I'm sorry.'

'Of course you have to go,' she said. 'You're right: you mustn't compromise your integrity—I quite understand that. I should think the worse of you if you did.'

'Thank you,' he said.

She gazed at him steadily and he wished he could tell what she was thinking, but her expression was unreadable. Whether by accident or design they were standing very close together and he knew he ought to step away from her and get into the car now, but somehow he was unable to do it. Just then, a slight breeze blew a strand of hair across her cheek and before he knew what he was doing or could stop himself he had reached up and brushed it gently away. She caught her breath and they both froze, his hand still suspended in mid-air. For a long moment all he could hear was the rushing of blood in his ears and the pounding of his own heart, then suddenly he was leaning closer to her and she was raising her face to his, and they would certainly have disgraced themselves there and then had they not been interrupted by a voice which hailed them at that moment from the head of the lane. They started guiltily and moved apart, and turned to see Norman Tipping approaching from the direction of the village. He looked cross and bothered—which was entirely under-standable if he had spent the morning speaking to Sergeant Primm about his gambling debts—and he looked at Jameson resentfully when he reached them.

'There you are, Kathie,' he said. 'I've been looking for you everywhere.'

'I'm sorry,' she replied, sounding flustered. 'I was speaking to the inspector and got distracted.'

'Shall we go?' said Norman. 'Mother is expecting us, and we are already late.'

'All right,' said Kathie. She threw Inspector Jameson a last startled glance but had no chance to say anything before she was urged away by Norman, and they walked off together. Jameson stood for a moment, attempting to recover himself, but without much success. He then got into his car and drove away, cursing his own stupidity. Had Norman Tipping not turned up just at that moment then who knew what might have happened? Or rather, he corrected himself, it was perfectly obvious what would have happened. He would have kissed Kathie Montgomery and then all would have been lost: the case would have been ruined and with it most likely his own reputation as a detective. His head and his heart were in a tumult. Of all the ridiculous things he had ever done, falling head over ears for a suspect in a murder case had to be the most idiotic. Whether she were innocent or guilty made no difference: she could never be his. Primm would get his warrant and arrest the two of them later today. If she was guilty she would go to gaol; if innocent then presumably she would marry Norman Tipping one day and be happy. Either way, it was nothing to do with him. All that was left for him to do now was to go home and get over her—if he could.

Chapter Nineteen

ON FRIDAY AFTERNOON the sun came out, and so Angela went into the garden to admire the flowers and to think. She had been reflecting a good deal about the case and was beginning to get somewhat apprehensive about it. The point about the gunshot had occurred to her a few days ago, but since nothing had come of it she assumed the police must have had good reason to cling to Norman and Kathie's supposed alibi. Still, several days had now passed without anything happening, and she was surprised at the inaction of Inspector Jameson, for whom she had the greatest respect. He had shown his feelings for Kathie Montgomery plainly enough, and Angela wondered whether they might not perhaps be affecting his ability to act. Until recently, she should have said that he would never compromise his own integrity, but when she thought of her own recent romantic entanglement, she was forced to admit that even the most upright of people—among whom she generally counted herself—might have their weaknesses on occasion. Here, her mind drifted back to Venice, and she had to check herself. Drat the man! Why did the thought of him always make her smile so? He did not deserve her, that was certain enough. She had told him as much and he had laughed and quite agreed with her, but said it should never stop him trying. Still, she was back in England now, safe from his nonsense, and with a murder investigation going on all around her to prevent her thoughts from straying *too* much, at least.

Who had killed Tom Tipping? Secretly, although she would never have admitted it aloud, she wanted Norman Tipping to have done it alone and without assistance—for of course, Kathie could not possibly be involved in any way, Angela was quite certain of that. But could Norman have done it without Kathie's involvement? He had the motive, if what Andrew Norris had said was true, and he had been in the area at the time. Supposing the gunshot was a red herring, and that the murder had been committed by Norman earlier: why, then, had he walked along Dead Man's Path afterwards and drawn attention to himself? And was there any way in which Kathie might have walked with him without seeing Tom Tipping's body lying there? Had Norman hidden the body, perhaps, for some reason of his own? No, she recalled, of course not, for Daniel Tyler had found it lying there quite in the open. Might Norman have somehow distracted Kathie's attention away from the body as they passed it? Angela shook her head. No—that was a ridiculous idea, and supposed that Kathie was not only half-blind but also an idiot.

What if the gunshot *was* the sound of the murder, then? In that case they were back where they started, and anybody might have done it. Angela could not help wondering about Margaret Tipping and her cold, unemotional demeanour. Had her alibi been checked? Angela supposed it must have. She tried to think back to the fête, but it had been such a day of confusion that she feared her memory could not be relied upon. She had certainly seen Margaret on the cake stall earlier in the day, but as to the time of the murder (when was it? About a quarter to two, she seemed to remember)—why, she could not say what had been happening, for then she had been occupied with trying to sell everything on her bric-à-brac stall.

She wandered through the garden and under the pergola, and as she did so her thoughts were driven back to the other day, when they had watched through the window as Freddy and Corky sauntered across the lawn without so much as a by your leave. How offended Elisabeth had been! Poor Elisabeth; it must be such a bore to be so stiff in all things. It was a great tragedy to be born without a sense of humour, thought Angela. She frowned. An idea had come fleetingly into her head, but had then disappeared. What was it? Was it something about Italy (in which case it could be safely disregarded), or was it about the murder? Angela was almost certain it was the latter. She retraced her thoughts as far as she could, but was unable to pin the idea down, and eventually decided that the best thing would be to stop worrying about it. No doubt it would come back soon enough if it was important.

She had drifted out of the flower garden as she reflected, and was now wandering through the shrubbery, out of sight of the house. Here it was pleasant and shady, for it was rather a hot afternoon, and she was tempted to remain a while. She paused to admire a particularly large and luxuriant japonica, and was just starting to think that perhaps she had been out long enough, and that she ought to go back in and make more of an effort with Elisabeth, when she suddenly heard a noise that sounded like 'Psst!'

She looked about her, but saw nothing. She must have imagined it. She was about to move on when she heard it again: 'Psst!'

'Odd,' thought Angela. She went towards where she thought the sound had come from, rounded an enormous rhododendron and there, in a sheltered nook, discovered Freddy Pilkington-Soames and—to her astonishment—Mrs. Randall, sitting on a wrought-iron bench and wearing identical looks of mischief. Each held a drinking-glass filled with something, and between them on the bench were a little silver flask and a bottle of some dark liquid.

'Hallo,' said Angela, somewhat taken aback. 'What's all this?'

'We're having a little celebration,' said Freddy.

'Oh?' said Angela. 'What are you celebrating?'

Freddy looked at Mrs. Randall.

'I don't know,' he said. 'What *are* we celebrating?'

His voice was slightly slurred.

'I have no idea,' said Mrs. Randall. 'I'm sure we'll think of something.'

She cackled and gave a hiccup.

'Well then, we're probably celebrating the joy of life and the beauty of the day,' said Freddy.

'That ought to do it,' said Mrs. Randall. 'It is a very fine afternoon, you must admit. The sunshine is simply glorious.'

Angela might have pointed out that they were sitting in the shadiest part of the garden and could hardly even see the sky, let alone the sun, but she sensed that logical debate was not the order of the day, and so merely agreed that the weather was indeed splendid.

'But since you're here, let's have a toast!' said Freddy, as though struck by a sudden idea. 'I should like to propose a toast to the divine Mrs. M. May the light of your detectoring eye never grow dim.'

He held up his glass and took a drink.

'What about me?' said Mrs. Randall. 'You ought to toast me. I am the oldest lady here.'

Angela noticed that she had stuck her lorgnette in her hat, where it bobbed about merrily like a large, pearl butterfly.

'But we've already toasted you,' said Freddy. 'Four times at the last count. Or was it five?'

'Freddy,' said Angela reproachfully. 'What on earth do you think you're doing? What is Elisabeth going to say when she finds out you've been plying her mother with drink?'

'What do you mean *I* have been plying *her* with drink?' said Freddy, drawing himself up indignantly. 'Tell her, Mrs. R: whose idea was it?'

'Mine,' admitted Mrs. Randall, hanging her head sorrowfully. A wicked look came across her face and she cackled again. 'Although if you were any sort of gentleman you'd take the blame,' she said.

'Alas! I am of the younger generation, and I fear this kind of etiquette has been sadly lacking in my upbringing,' said Freddy. 'Humphrey was right: it's young men like me —or do I mean young men such as I?—who have plunged the country into the disarray in which it presently finds itself.'

'But it's three o'clock,' said Angela. 'It's far too early for this sort of thing.'

'Nonsense,' said Mrs. Randall. 'Now, are you going to stand there gaping like a fish or are you going to come and join us? Do have a drink. I've been wanting to have a nice, cosy chat with you for simply days, but Elisabeth would never let me.'

Freddy had been rummaging in his pocket and now produced another glass, which he wiped clean with great ceremony.

'Courtesy of the Red Lion,' he announced. 'It's not exactly Baccarat, but it possesses the requisite concavity and thus serves our purpose admirably for the present.'

Angela sat down with some trepidation, and Freddy poured her a large measure each from the flask and the bottle. She took a sip and coughed.

'Goodness me,' she said, wiping her eyes. 'That's rather intriguing. What is it?'

'Dubonnet and gin,' said Freddy. 'Mrs. R. is instructing me in the secrets of the cocktail bar. Or corrupting an innocent youth, if you prefer.'

'Naughty boy,' said Mrs. Randall.

'Rubbish,' said Angela. 'You are entirely incorruptible, Freddy.'

'You flatter me,' said Freddy.

'Not at all,' said Angela. 'I meant you were corrupted long ago and the job is quite complete. There is nothing left to be done.'

'I suspected as much,' said Mrs. Randall.

Angela took another sip. The drink was a strong one and she was beginning to feel a pleasant fuzziness in her head.

'So, then, I expect you've been out hunting down criminals while we've been idling the afternoon away,' said Freddy.

'No, I haven't, as a matter of fact,' said Angela. 'I promised not to do any detecting, so this morning I helped Elisabeth arrange some flowers in vases and placed them to advantage in the various rooms of the house. After that I wound wool until lunch-time, and this afternoon I have been taking a gentle stroll in the garden. I have been polite, considerate and helpful. I have not smoked, used unladylike language or told off-colour jokes—even though I had rather a good one from William yesterday. My behaviour, in short, has been impeccable. I fear, however, that this state of affairs is not destined to continue for the rest of the day—look here, are you sure this is only gin?'

'It's marvellous stuff, isn't it?' said Freddy. 'I must say, I've never subscribed to the theory that we youngsters are the only ones who know how to enjoy ourselves. I have always been quite certain that those of statelier age and greater experience than I must know how to shake it about a bit—or must have known at one time, at any rate—and this afternoon I have been proved right in my theory. Mrs. R, I salute you.'

He raised his glass and drank. Mrs. Randall accepted her due with a gracious bow of the head.

'By the way, I see Corky has produced another of his *magna opera*,' went on Freddy. 'Or didn't you read his story? I rather hope you didn't.'

'I most certainly did,' said Angela with a shudder. 'Can't you do something about him, Freddy? Humphrey really believed I'd said all that rot.'

'Don't you think that says more about Humphrey than it does about Corky, though?' said Freddy.

'Perhaps it does,' said Angela. 'I hadn't thought of it like that.'

'How on earth can you and Humphrey be part of the same family?' said Freddy. 'I still can't quite believe it. Are you sure your mother didn't—'

'Freddy!' said Angela.

'I was *going* to say adopt you from an orphanage,' said Freddy, while Mrs. Randall sniggered.

'Of course you were. As a matter of fact, though, I might ask the same question of Elisabeth,' said Angela boldly.

'Don't look at me,' said Mrs. Randall. 'She takes after her father. I never got on with him and I don't get on much better with her. She's such a bore, don't you think? I can see why she married your brother. They deserve one another, I should say. Have you met those boys of theirs? Dreadful little beasts. I know Elisabeth thinks they're the most gifted creatures ever to grace the earth, but quite frankly, whenever I see them I get the most awful urge to slap them. Horrid brats.'

'They're just like Humphrey was as a boy,' said Angela. 'Awfully cold and calculating.'

'Ah, now it all comes out,' said Freddy, who was enjoying the conversation immensely. 'But what about you, Angela? Are you going to tell me you were a paragon of virtue and obedience as a child?'

'Of course not,' said Angela. 'As a matter of fact I was rather a terror. But then, I was very bored most of the time because Humphrey wouldn't play with me, so I think I ought to be excused for getting up to mischief.'

'But why are you being so virtuous now?' said Freddy. 'I mean to say, on this visit? And, by the way, why exactly *doesn't* brother Humphrey want you to do any detecting?'

'Because it is unseemly in a woman,' said Angela. 'Especially one of my position and respectability.'

Freddy snorted.

'Respectability, indeed,' he said. 'Here, your glass is empty—you'd better have some more.'

'Yes, respectability,' said Angela with dignity, and took another drink.

'Respectability is overrated,' said Mrs. Randall sadly. 'If you'll take my advice, you won't bother with it. Look at me: I went all out for respectability in my youth, but after a while the reputation sticks and you can't shake it off, so now I have to skulk in the rhododendrons whenever I want to have fun. "We drink very little in this house, Mr. Pilking-ton-Soames,"' she said, in such an accurate imitation of

Elisabeth that Angela put her hand over her mouth to suppress a giggle. 'Hmp,' she went on, and subsided into silence.

'Well, then, Angela, if you have promised not to detect any murderers, presumably you can't give me any inside information on the case either,' said Freddy, who was never entirely off duty, although given his present state it was somewhat doubtful whether he would be able to remember tomorrow anything that he was told today.

'No,' said Angela. 'Everyone thinks Norman Tipping did it and Kathie helped him, though. Even Andrew Norris said as much. And I'm fairly sure the police believe it too.'

Too late she remembered that Kathie's mother was there and might be shocked to hear the news. But Mrs. Randall was made of stern stuff.

'Pfft!' she said. 'It serves her right for thinking of marrying him. Silly girl. I could have told her he was no good, but girls never listen to their mothers. I wish I'd had sons,' she said wistfully. 'They're so much easier.'

'Never mind,' said Freddy. 'I'll be your son, if you like. My mother wanted a daughter so it's a fair exchange. She can have Kathie and you can have me.'

'What an excellent idea,' said Mrs. Randall. 'You shall be a credit to me, I'm quite sure of it.'

They beamed at each other fondly, and more drinks were poured, and then of course they all had to make another toast to Freddy and his new mother. By this time Angela was starting to feel slightly dizzy, and she decided that she had had quite enough.

'So, then, this off-colour joke you mentioned, Angela,' said Freddy after a short pause in which they all stared glassily in different directions. 'I think it's only fair that you share it with the company, don't you agree, Mrs. R?'

Mrs. Randall nodded vigorously.

'Oh, I don't know that I ought,' said Angela primly.

'Of course you ought,' said Freddy. 'We have provided the cocktails, and now you must provide the entertainment —pay your way, so to speak.'

'Oh, very well,' said Angela, and prepared to oblige. She had barely started, however, when to her surprise Freddy suddenly shot out of his seat and bolted into the bushes. She had hardly time to register the terrified look on Mrs. Randall's face before she heard a voice say loudly:

'What on *earth* is going on?'

It was Elisabeth, who had come upon them unexpectedly and was standing there, a look of horror on her face. Angela glanced down at the glass in her hand, and at the flask and the bottle which stood on the seat between her and Mrs. Randall, and then back at Elisabeth, whose expression had now changed from shock to haughty fury.

'Er—hallo, Elisabeth,' she began, uncomfortably aware that she was not in the fullest possession of her faculties. 'We were just—'

'Mother,' said Elisabeth, ignoring Angela. '*What* are you doing?'

'Why, I don't quite know, dear,' said Mrs. Randall. 'I was just passing when Angela offered me a glass of this cordial, but I don't think I like it very much.'

'Cordial?' snapped Elisabeth as Angela stared in astonishment at Mrs. Randall, whose manner had altered completely, for she spoke in the gentle and puzzled tones of one who, while taking an afternoon stroll through the flower garden, had been lured unwittingly away from the path of pure and virtuous innocence and into a den of vice and debauchery. 'That's not a cordial—it's alcohol! Have you been drinking? Angela, what have you given my mother?'

'Alcohol?' said Mrs. Randall in tones of the greatest dismay. 'Are you sure? Angela, you never said it was alcoholic. But now you come to mention it, I must confess I am feeling a little dizzy.'

'Of course you're feeling dizzy,' said Elisabeth. She drew herself up. 'Angela, I'm *surprised* at you.' Words could not express the depth of her reproach.

'But I didn't—' began Angela. It was no use, however, for Elisabeth was not listening.

'Mother, you must come back to the house at once,' she said. 'Here, take my arm. You're not in any fit state to walk by yourself.'

Mrs. Randall struggled obediently to her feet and clutched at her daughter's arm.

'Thank you, dear,' she said. 'I'm so sorry to be such an inconvenience.'

'Of course you're not an inconvenience,' said Elisabeth. 'We'll get you back to the house and you can have a lie down until you're feeling better. I shall see *you* later, Angela. And don't think I didn't hear that shocking language you were using just now,' she added. 'I must say, I thought better of you.'

The two of them sailed off in great state, leaving Angela sitting open-mouthed in outrage, which was not helped by the look of pure malice that Mrs. Randall threw back at her as they left.

Chapter Twenty

WHEN ANGELA GOT BACK to the house she crept as quietly as she could up to her room and summoned her maid. Marthe took one look at her and made her lie down on the bed with a cold compress to the head while she went to the kitchen to prepare something which, she assured Angela, would restore her to the full use of all her senses within an hour. She returned a few minutes later with a glass containing something brownish and unidentifiable.

'Here, *madame*, drink this,' she commanded.

Angela took a sip and shuddered.

'Heavens!' she said. 'What on earth is it? It's quite foul. Marthe, I do believe you've given me this deliberately to teach me a lesson.'

'Finish it,' said Marthe. 'It will make you better. Here is a drink of water to take the taste away, and now you must lie on the bed for a little while.'

'Oh, very well,' said Angela, and did as she was told, for her head was still spinning and she wanted to be fully recovered by dinner-time. She put the compress back over her forehead and sighed. 'I think I've rather ruined any chance I ever had of convincing Elisabeth that I'm not a disgrace,' she said.

'But why try?' said Marthe. 'I have seen her. I know the type. She already has a fixed idea about you and it will not make her happy to persuade her otherwise. Better, surely, not to disarrange yourself by trying to be something you are not.'

'Normally I should agree with you,' said Angela, 'but I do have *some* pride, and I don't think it's unreasonable to let her know that, unlike her mother, I am not generally in the habit of drinking in the bushes like a tramp. Just wait till I see Freddy, though—I shall give him a jolly good piece of my mind. He ran off before Elisabeth saw him, but if he thinks he's going to get away scot-free he is very much mistaken.'

'Ah, M. Pilkington-Soames,' said Marthe, who at last saw an opportunity to find out what she wanted to know and was determined to seize it. 'He is an artful one—or he thinks he is. This morning he offered me money in return for some information.'

'Did he? What information?' said Angela in surprise.

Marthe began folding some clothes.

'He said you met a man in Venice,' she said with apparent indifference, 'and he wanted to know about it.'

Angela sat bolt upright.

'He didn't!' she exclaimed. 'Why, that—I shall—'

Marthe made her lie down again, which she did with some reluctance.

'Of course, I did not tell him anything,' went on Marthe, and then proceeded to attack. 'How *could* I tell him anything, when I do not know anything? I did not think you would keep such news from me, *madame*. Is it that you no longer trust me?'

Her tone held just the right amount of injured dignity,

and she wore an expression of the utmost disappointment.

'Of course I trust you,' said Angela.

'Then why did you not tell me about it? You have always told me such things in the past.'

'But I don't have anything to tell,' said Angela feebly.

Marthe sniffed and looked offended.

'It is not my place to contradict you, *madame*,' she said, and subsided into frosty silence.

Angela was no match for Marthe in a huff.

'Look, I don't know what Freddy was talking about,' she said. 'He made some silly accusation the other day, and I told him it was nonsense, but obviously he didn't believe me.'

Marthe tossed her head and went on folding clothes with scientific precision.

'Why should you think there was anything to tell, anyway?' said Angela. 'Can't a person go on holiday without being accused of—things?'

There was no reply. Angela tried to assert her authority.

'I won't have you making suppositions about me without permission,' she said. 'It's highly improper.'

The silence grew louder if possible. Angela quailed.

'And anyway, even if there were—things to tell, it's not fair of you to try and get them out of me when I'm d— under the weather,' she said pleadingly.

But Marthe had no scruples on that head, and she scented victory. She allowed herself to thaw a little then proceeded to press her advantage ruthlessly, and by dint of alternate coaxing and feigned hurt pride drew Angela's secret out of her and reigned triumphant.

'Ah! He is *très charmant*, that one,' she said, looking pleased, for she had liked Edgar Valencourt.

'Yes,' said Angela dryly. 'And very persuasive, too, or I

should never have gone with him.'

'But why not?' said Marthe. 'If he likes you and you like him, what is to stop you?'

'Apart from the fact that he's wanted for theft in about ten countries, do you mean? Why, nothing at all,' said Angela, trying to ignore the headache that was beginning to throb at her temples.

'Pfft!' said Marthe, who cared not what a man did for a living provided he made her mistress happy. 'He will give it up for you. Does he love you?'

'I doubt it very much,' said Angela. 'He's far too wrapped up in his own cleverness to think about anyone but himself for more than about ten minutes.'

'But did he *tell* you he loved you?' persisted Marthe.

'He said many pretty things, and I should have been a fool to believe any of them,' said Angela, trying not to smile, for she was as foolish as the next woman in that regard.

'And what about you? Do you love him?'

'Of course not!' said Angela indignantly. 'I told you, the man's a criminal. I should hope I had more sense than to fall in love with him.'

'But—'

'But nothing,' said Angela. 'I've told you everything now, and you shall have to be satisfied with that. It was very wrong of me to go away with him, and the best thing to do will be to forget it ever happened.'

'Then you did not enjoy it?' said Marthe. 'He was not good company?'

Angela blinked. She was reluctant to admit, even to herself, how well they had got along together for those few days.

'Let us say I've satisfied my curiosity, and I won't do anything of the sort again,' she said after a pause. She saw

Marthe's disbelieving look, and went on sharply, 'I said goodbye to him and I meant it.'

Marthe did not reply, but as she turned to put the clothes in a drawer she happened to glance in the glass that stood above the dressing-table, and saw reflected in it Angela gazing at the pretty bracelet she had brought back from Italy. Marthe smiled to herself.

'Anyway,' went on Angela, 'you don't really suppose I don't trust you, do you, Marthe? You know I rely on you absolutely.'

'Of course I know it, *madame*,' said Marthe. 'And I will never betray your trust.'

'What a provoking infant Freddy is,' said Angela. 'I hope you took the money.'

'*Mais oui*,' said Marthe complacently. 'I am not stupid.'

They both laughed, the best of friends once more.

There was a stiff atmosphere at the dinner-table that evening. Marthe's concoction had done a good deal to restore sobriety and remove the headache, but still Angela would have preferred to spend the evening lying down in a dimly-lit room. Instead, she sat under the full glare of the Cardews' chandeliers, feigning an appetite and pretending to be completely unaffected by the events of the afternoon. To her annoyance, Mrs. Randall was absent—indisposed, as Elisabeth, ever mindful of appearances, told the servants —and dinner proceeded in a frigid silence. Humphrey, indeed, looked once or twice as though he were on the point of beginning a lecture, but each time he glanced at his wife and changed his mind. Angela was sorry for it, for she thought any kind of conversation would have been preferable to the cold shoulder. She took a sip of the water which had been pointedly served to her, and looked about her idly. After a few minutes, she became aware that Doggett, the butler, was trying to catch her eye, and raised her eyebrows inquiringly. He glanced at Sir Humphrey and Lady Cardew to make quite sure they could not see him, then looked significantly at Mrs. Randall's empty place and cast his eyes briefly upwards to indicate her present location. Angela nodded almost imperceptibly, trying not to smile. He glanced about him again then made a surreptitious motion as of one raising a glass to his mouth. Angela had to look down at her plate so as not to giggle.

'Are you quite all right, Angela?' said Elisabeth, catching sight of her. 'You're not feeling *ill*, are you?'

'No, I'm perfectly well, thank you, Elisabeth,' said Angela cheerfully. 'The fish is delicious, by the way. There's nothing quite like a hearty dinner after a day spent in the pursuit of health-giving activities out of doors, don't you agree?'

Elisabeth pursed her lips but said nothing. Angela cast a sly glance at Doggett, who was staring determinedly at the ceiling, and was just resolving that she should make him laugh by hook or by crook when the sound of the doorbell was heard.

'Who on earth could that be at this time?' said Humphrey. 'I had better go and see.'

He got up and went out, and was gone for some time.

'Where can he have got to?' said Elisabeth eventually, forgetting for the moment that she was not meant to be speaking to Angela. She was just about to rise from her seat and go after him when he returned, followed, to their surprise, by young Peter Montgomery, who was white-faced and frightened-looking.

'Peter! What are you doing here?' said Elisabeth. 'Where is your mother?'

'I'm afraid there's bad news, my dear,' said Humphrey. He looked as though he did not quite know where he was. 'The police have arrested Kathie.'

Chapter Twenty-One

IF SERGEANT PRIMM had hoped to deliver the boy to his aunt and uncle and then return straight to duty, he was disappointed, for of course they would not let him go until he had explained himself fully—and even then that was not enough to satisfy them, for the police could not simply go about arresting the sister-in-law of a Sir Humphrey without giving a satisfactory reason for it, and so they interrogated him at length and with great outrage and dignity, and Primm did the best he could to answer their questions without losing his temper.

Angela, meanwhile, had been the only one among the adults with the presence of mind to ask Peter whether he had had anything to eat, and when he replied in the negative had handed him into the care of the servants and instructed them to give the boy some dinner. When she returned to the drawing-room, she found Humphrey and Elisabeth in a great state, while Sergeant Primm was showing signs of trying to edge towards the door.

'But it's quite absurd,' Humphrey was saying. 'Surely

you can't possibly think that my wife's sister had anything to do with this matter.'

'I'm afraid we had no choice but to arrest her, sir,' said Sergeant Primm. 'We arrested Mr. Norman Tipping earlier this evening on suspicion of murdering his father, and since Mrs. Montgomery was with him at around the time the murder is thought to have been committed, we had to arrest her too on suspicion of being an accessory.'

'But you can't put her in prison!' said Elisabeth.

'Don't worry—she'll be well treated,' said the sergeant, 'and she may be allowed out on bail if someone is willing to stand for her, although that won't be until early next week now.'

'How much is that likely to cost?' said Humphrey.

'Of course we will stand for her,' said Elisabeth, casting an impatient glance at her husband.

'May we see her?' said Angela.

'Not tonight,' said Sergeant Primm. 'She may see a solicitor tomorrow, though.'

'We'll arrange that,' said Humphrey. 'I shall speak to Mr. Prendeville this evening.'

'I suggest you do so,' said Primm.

'Where is Inspector Jameson?' said Angela suddenly. 'May we speak to him?'

'Inspector Jameson returned to London this morning,' replied the sergeant. 'The case is now back in the hands of the Surrey police. And now I'm afraid I must go. I shall tell Mrs. Montgomery that young Peter is in safe hands. She was very anxious about him.'

He went off, leaving the three of them staring at each other in consternation.

'What is to be done now?' said Elisabeth at last. 'How could they possibly suspect Kathie of murder? I knew nothing of this. Why didn't she tell me?'

'They don't suspect her of murder,' said Angela. 'They think Norman Tipping did it and that she's lying to protect him. Unfortunately, they were the only people seen in the area at the time Tom Tipping died—and of course, it's always family who are the first ones to be suspected when someone is killed.'

'But I don't understand,' said Humphrey. 'How are they supposed to have done it?'

He and Elisabeth seemed to have forgotten their opposition to Angela's investigative activities, and they now looked to her for information. Angela explained her supposition about the clue of the gunshot, and how it had initially seemed to exonerate Norman and Kathie, although in actual fact it was not conclusive evidence at all.

'Then Daniel Tyler's story counts for nothing and they have no alibi?' said Elisabeth.

Angela admitted that was pretty much the case.

'But then what was the sound that was heard?' said Humphrey.

'I don't know,' said Angela. 'Perhaps it was something else entirely—a car backfiring, or something. Of course, if the defence can convince the jury that the sound *was* the shot that killed Tom Tipping, then that will go very much in Norman and Kathie's favour, but a determined prosecution will certainly try to plant a doubt in their minds.'

Elisabeth and Humphrey stared at each other. This talk of defence and prosecution made it all real, somehow.

'What will Mother say when I tell her?' said Elisabeth suddenly. 'She'll be terribly upset. How on earth am I to break the news?'

'Leave it until tomorrow,' said Humphrey. 'Don't worry yourself about it now. Perhaps we can even keep it from her for a while if you think she is too delicate to bear it.'

Angela raised her eyebrows but kept her thoughts to

herself. Her mind was busy. She very much wanted to know why Inspector Jameson had returned to London. Had he known that Kathie was about to be arrested? He must have done, she supposed. Perhaps that was why he had withdrawn from the case. If that was so, then there would be no help to be had from that quarter. It must have been terribly difficult for him to leave Kathie to her fate, but Angela knew him to be a man of integrity and was certain he would not shirk his duty. Still, there was nothing she could do about that. The most important thing now was to prove somehow that Norman Tipping and Kathie Montgomery had had nothing to do with the murder of Tom Tipping. But how was that to be done? Angela supposed everything would now be in the hands of the lawyers, and hoped that Humphrey was prepared to pay for a good one.

Just then, Peter sidled into the room and went across to Angela.

'Have you eaten?' she said.

'Not much,' he said.

'You had better go to bed, Peter,' said Elisabeth. 'Angela is sleeping in your room at the moment, so you must go in the blue room.'

'Come on, I'll take you,' said Angela, who saw that the boy needed comfort but was unlikely to get it from his aunt and uncle.

'Why did Aunt Elisabeth put you in the children's room?' said Peter as they climbed the stairs.

'It was my room when I was a girl,' replied Angela. 'I think she thought I would like it.'

'Oh,' he said. 'Then the horse must be yours.'

'Which horse?' said Angela.

The little wooden one with a chipped hoof. I found it

in the cupboard. I thought it didn't belong to anyone, so I took it.'

Just then a little flash of memory came back to Angela and she recalled the toy in question, which she had been given for her birthday one year. She had called it Dancer, and for a while it had been her favourite plaything.

'Do you still have it?' she said.

'Yes,' said Peter. 'It's at home. I'll give it back to you tomorrow, I promise. I'm sorry I took it.'

'Not at all,' said Angela. 'You shall keep it if you like. I was very fond of that horse but I have no use for it any more, and I am only glad that someone else has found it and is looking after it for me.'

They had now arrived at the door of the blue room.

'Are they going to hang Mother?' said Peter suddenly. He looked frightened.

'Why, of course not,' said Angela. 'You mustn't think like that. The police are doing their best to find the person who killed Mr. Tipping, and they've made a little mistake, but it will all be resolved very soon. Now, your mother is probably terribly worried about you, so you must be very brave for her sake while you are here. Your aunt and uncle will look after you, and you must help them all you can.'

He nodded.

'Tomorrow we shall think about what is to be done,' she went on, 'but in the meantime you must get a good night's sleep, or you'll be no use to anyone.'

'I will,' he promised. He turned to enter the room. 'Goodnight, Mrs. Marchmont,' he said.

'You must call me Angela,' she said. 'And if you feel frightened in the night, or anything like that, you may come to me, since I'm the one who stole your room.'

He smiled and went in, and Angela returned to the

drawing-room. When she entered, she immediately had the impression that Humphrey and Elisabeth had been talking about her in her absence, and this impression was shortly afterwards confirmed when Humphrey coughed and said:

'Ah, Angela.'

He fell silent.

'Yes, Humphrey?' she returned politely.

He tried again.

'This dreadful business,' he said. 'Of course, there's no question of Kathie's guilt. The police have obviously made a terrible mistake.'

'They have acted on the evidence they have, and so to that extent they've done exactly what they ought to have done,' said Angela.

'Still, we can't have innocent people being put in prison,' said Humphrey. He paused. 'You are by way of being an expert in these matters. I don't suppose you have any idea of who really committed the crime?'

'No, I don't. As you may remember, I promised at your specific request not to do any investigating,' said Angela, who after all was only human and could not resist a dig.

'Yes, you did,' said Humphrey, bowing his head. 'And now I am asking you to break that promise and look into it for us. The police have evidently decided they have the right people in custody, and so we cannot expect any further help from them. Please, Angela. If you won't do it for us, then at least do it for Kathie.'

Angela looked at her brother and sister-in-law and pitied them. They were so constrained by self-imposed custom and manners that they were completely at a loss when presented with a situation such as this one. She relented.

'Why, of course I'll look into it,' she said. 'I don't like seeing Kathie in gaol any more than you do. Now, I don't say I can solve the thing, but I'll do what I can. I know,' she said, as a sudden thought struck her. 'I'll get Freddy to help me.'

'Freddy Pilkington-Soames?' said Elisabeth. 'Wasn't he meant to be writing a story on the fête? I haven't seen any sign of it so far. Can he be relied upon, do you suppose?'

'He has his uses on occasion,' said Angela.

'What, that young man who trespassed in our garden?' said Humphrey.

Angela stared at him.

'Yes,' she said thoughtfully. 'He did, didn't he? How interesting.' She looked as though she were about to go on, but then changed her mind. Instead she stood up. 'It's been rather a long day and I do believe I'm tired,' she said. 'I shall start tomorrow, but now I'm going to bed. Goodnight.'

And she left the room abruptly, leaving Humphrey and Elisabeth staring after her in perplexity.

Chapter Twenty-Two

THE NEXT MORNING Angela was up bright and early, and by eight o'clock was walking briskly across Tithes Field in the direction of the village. She crossed the green and headed purposefully towards the Red Lion, then knocked and put her head round the door. Nobody was about so she entered and said, 'Hallo?'

The place seemed deserted. Angela passed through the public bar and tried a door. On the other side of it was a slightly more salubrious room which Angela supposed was the saloon. There was nobody there, so Angela came out and looked about her. To her left was another door, which was slightly ajar. She went through it and found herself in the snug. Opposite her was yet another door, standing wide open. Through it she could see the back yard, and beyond that some cottages and the very tip of the church spire. Angela went and stood in the doorway and saw Bob Sanderson busy moving things about for no particular purpose that she could see.

'Hallo,' she said, and made him start. He looked

surprised to see such a visitor, but came inside immediately and asked how he could help her.

'I have a message for Mr. Pilkington-Soames,' said Angela. 'It's rather urgent. Please tell him his mother telephoned.' She scribbled something on a scrap of paper as she spoke, and handed it to the landlord, who took it doubtfully.

'I'll take it to him, but he won't thank me for it,' he said. 'He was up late last night.'

'It's rather urgent,' said Angela again, 'and I'm afraid it won't wait.'

Sanderson nodded and disappeared. Angela returned to the public bar and took a seat. Five minutes later there was a thundering of feet and Freddy came hurtling down the stairs, his jacket half on and his tie unfastened. His eyes were bloodshot and his hair was standing up all over the place, and he looked ghastly. It was quite evident that he had kept on drinking after he had left them the day before, and was now suffering the consequences.

'Hallo, Angela,' he said breathlessly. 'Can't stop. I must telephone my mother.'

'Yes,' said Angela. 'I don't suppose you speak to her nearly as often as you ought.'

He was halfway out of the door as she spoke but something in her tone arrested him, and he stopped and came back in.

'All right, what's all this?' he said suspiciously.

'What's all what?' said Angela, opening her eyes wide.

'Why are you here? Did you bring this?' He flapped the note at her.

'That?'

'Yes, this,' he said.

'The telephone message, do you mean?'

'Yes, the telephone message,' said Freddy. 'You know very well what I'm talking about.'

'That would be the telephone message that says your mother has just found out what you got up to in Southend last February and is stopping your allowance, yes?' said Angela.

'Yes, that one,' he said, the truth starting to dawn. 'You seem to know rather a lot about it.'

'That's because I wrote it,' she said sweetly.

He drew himself up, aghast.

'Why, of all the—you—' he said. He regarded her reproachfully. 'That's a low trick to play, to drag a man up from his bed of pain and throw him into a panic like that. I thought better of you, Angela.'

'A fatal mistake on your part,' said Angela. 'You didn't really think I'd let you get away with running off and leaving me to face Elisabeth yesterday, did you? Quid pro quo and all that.'

'You're a wicked woman, Mrs. M,' he said.

'I have my moments,' she said modestly. 'Anyway, now you're up we can get down to business.'

'What business?' he said, sitting down. 'I can't get down to any business until I've had at least four more hours' sleep, followed by a decent lunch and a short nap.'

'There's no time for that,' said Angela. 'I need your help.'

'Why?'

'Because the police have arrested Norman and Kathie, and we need to find out who really did kill Tom Tipping before the whole thing gets completely out of hand.'

'I say,' he said seriously. 'That's bad news. Poor Kathie.'

'Yes, it is bad news,' said Angela. 'So you see, this is no time for you to be lolling in bed.' She dug in her pocket and handed him the little silver flask out of which they had been drinking the day before. 'Here, this ought to do the trick.'

'A touch of hair of the dog, eh?' said Freddy. 'Well, it's worth a shot, I suppose.'

Angela watched with malicious pleasure as he took a large gulp from the flask and then nearly spat it out in horror.

'Good God!' he exclaimed, glaring at her. 'Are you trying to poison me?'

'Drink it,' said Angela. 'I had to suffer the stuff yesterday, so I don't see why you should escape it. It's a concoction of Marthe's, and I promise it'll make you feel better.'

'But I can't finish it. I'll be sick,' said Freddy.

'Do it for Kathie,' said Angela. She watched as he held his nose and tossed the rest of the stuff down with a shudder. 'Now, go and smarten yourself up and have some breakfast, and I'll see you on the green in half an hour.'

'All right, then,' he said. 'I say, I feel a little better already.'

'Splendid,' said Angela. She stood up. 'By the way, what *did* you get up to in Southend?' she said as she prepared to leave. 'It must have been fun, whatever it was.'

'Oh, it was,' he said complacently, 'but a gentleman never kisses and tells.'

'I should think not. Nor does a lady,' said Angela. '*Or* a lady's maid,' she added pointedly, and went out.

'Ah,' said Freddy to himself.

Thirty-five minutes later, he joined her on the green, looking and feeling rather better after a wash and a hasty breakfast.

'We'd better hurry up before Corky gets up and spots us,' he said. 'He's been rather quiet for the last couple of days, and that gives me nothing but nervous feelings, as it invariably means he's plotting something.'

'Well, I hope it's not another story about me,' said Angela. 'I'm not sure I can stand the humiliation twice in one week.'

'More likely he's back to his old trick of following me about until I get a scent and then trying to get in before me,' said Freddy. 'Still, we appear to be safe for now. Where are we going?'

'Dead Man's Path,' said Angela. 'I'm not certain it will help much, but I want to take another look at the murder scene.'

They walked in silence until they reached the spot where Tom Tipping had been found, then stopped to look around them. The place looked exactly as it had the first time Angela had passed along it and encountered Mr. Norris and his dog, the sun shining through the leaves and dappling the path with greens and yellows. One would never have supposed that something so violent could have happened here.

'Odd how different it looks when the sun is out,' she said. 'When I came here two days after the murder, the weather was grey and overcast, and we all thought the place seemed haunted.'

Freddy was tramping about, swiping at the undergrowth with a stick.

'What are we looking for?' he said.

'I'm just trying to picture what happened that day,' said Angela. 'Tom Tipping was found just here, I think. He'd been walking in this direction when someone came up behind him and shot him in the back of the head.'

'Whoever it was must have sneaked up pretty quietly,' observed Freddy. 'Do you think he was lying in wait for him? And how did the murderer know Tipping would pass this way?'

'He came along here at the same time every day,' said

Angela absently. 'Everybody knew it.' She was thinking. 'Now, which way did the murderer come? The police have been assuming that he came along the main path.'

She left Dead Man's Path and picked her way through some nettles to a grey stone wall that could just be glimpsed beyond the trees. Here, the moss and ivy had weakened the stones and the wall had collapsed.

'The church,' said Freddy. 'Do you suppose he came this way?'

Angela did not reply but stepped carefully over the fallen stones and into the churchyard. It was cool and peaceful here, and she stood for a moment and gazed about her. Freddy stopped by a grave which looked clean and well-tended, and read the inscription on it.

'Oh,' he said, taken aback. 'It says here Lillian Cardew.'

'My mother,' said Angela in a matter-of-fact voice. She came and stood next to him. 'The flowers are starting to die. I shall have to get some new ones.'

Freddy removed his hat.

'She must have been a remarkable woman to have had you,' he said.

'She was, rather,' said Angela. 'Nothing to do with me, though. She was a far better person than I am.' She stood for a moment in reflection, and then turned away. 'Now,' she said briskly. 'This is the shortest way around to the front, I believe.'

They skirted the outer wall of the little church until they reached the front door. To one side of it stood a bicycle.

'Is that Mrs. Hunter's bicycle?' said Freddy. 'Her wrist must be taking longer to heal than she expected.'

'Yes,' said Angela. 'I shouldn't be at all surprised if it

turned out to be a fracture rather than a sprain. The bones in the wrist are delicate and it's easily done.'

'What's that tall thing it's chained to?' said Freddy.

'It's the old poor box,' said Angela. 'I don't think it's used any more.'

'Aren't poor boxes usually rather smaller than that?' said Freddy. 'They must have been pretty optimistic when they installed this one if they thought they could fill it. Are the good people of Banford Green generous enough to fill a box with money to a height of three feet or more?'

'Not as far as I know,' said Angela. 'I seem to recall from somewhere back in the mists of time that this particular one was donated by a local worthy who had been a sea-captain. He carved it out of the hull of his ship or something, and they hadn't the heart to ask him for a smaller one instead.'

'Well, then, all I can say is I hope he patched the hole it left before he put out to sea again,' said Freddy.

They emerged through the church gate and found themselves on Church Lane, standing opposite Alice Hopwell's cottage. Angela gazed at it with some interest, and as she did so the front door burst open and two of the Hopwell children came racing out. They began chasing each other up and down the lane, laughing uproariously. Freddy watched indulgently.

'It's the man,' said a voice next to them, and they turned to see Georgina Hopwell standing in the open doorway. At the end of the narrow passage behind the girl, Angela could just glimpse two more children playing quietly in the house's tiny back yard.

'Hallo, Georgina,' said Freddy. 'I hope you're being a good girl.'

Georgina inserted a finger firmly into one nostril and stared at him.

'You'd better be careful, or you'll dislodge your brain and push it out through the other one,' Freddy told her.

'Good girl,' said Georgina. 'Mama's gone out.'

The other two children ran back into the house, then the front door slammed and Angela and Freddy were alone again in the lane.

'Hmm,' said Angela.

'I see you're having one of your ideas,' said Freddy. 'I hope it's a good one.'

'As a matter of fact, it was you who put me on to it,' she replied.

'Ah, my usual stroke of genius,' he said. 'Tell me.'

She did so, and he whistled.

'I see,' he said. 'How can we prove it?'

'We're going to need William,' said Angela. 'I think he may be rather useful in this instance. Would you be a darling and fetch him for me? I want to scout about here a bit more.'

'Certainly,' he said. 'I'll bring him back here as soon as I can.'

'In the meantime I shall have a chat with the little Hopwells,' said Angela.

'But Mrs. Hopwell is out. Georgina said so,' said Freddy.

'All the better,' said Angela.

Freddy ran off, and Angela turned to knock on the door of the tiny cottage. There was the sound of scuffling and shouting, then the door opened and a grubby face peered out suspiciously.

'Hallo,' said Angela.

Chapter Twenty-Three

A FEW MINUTES later Angela crossed the lane and entered the churchyard through the gate. She walked briskly back up the church path, glancing back occasionally at the Hopwells' cottage, then crossed the fallen wall and returned to Dead Man's Path. She intended to search methodically in the undergrowth at the edges—although she did not really expect to succeed where the police had failed—and she was about to begin when she was brought to a halt by a strange sound. She whirled around and to her surprise saw Margaret Tipping, standing in the spot where Tom Tipping had died and sobbing.

Angela stood in surprise, not quite sure what to do at first. She did not wish to intrude on Mrs. Tipping's private grief, yet it would have been cold-hearted of her to abandon the woman without at least ascertaining whether there were anything she could do. She was still wondering when Margaret looked up and saw her.

'I suppose you think I'm crying for him,' she said.

'Aren't you?' said Angela.

'I know everyone thinks I ought to,' said Mrs. Tipping.

'I know what everyone is saying about me. You all think I'm cold and heartless—that I haven't even the common decency to weep for my dead husband. Well, now I'm weeping, but it's not for him.'

'What is it for, then?' said Angela.

'For myself,' she said. 'And if that makes me selfish, then so be it.'

Angela did not know what to say, so said nothing.

'Look at you,' went on Margaret. 'All smartly dressed and well cared-for. You probably don't remember me, but I knew you when you were small.'

'Oh,' said Angela. 'No, I'm afraid I don't remember.'

'Your mother and I were friends as girls, you see,' said Margaret, 'although we drifted apart as we got older. I was full of spirit, then. I wanted to know everything—wanted to go out and see the world. I was going to be a doctor, or a great explorer, or a professor. I wanted to study and learn everything. I was clever, you see.' She looked down at the ground. 'Of course, I never did any of that. Girls can't, can they? We have to stay at home and do as we're bid, and quite rightly, most would say. So I stayed here and got married and had Norman, and that was that. Nobody seemed to think I might want something more. Nobody seemed to care. Life goes on here, doesn't it? Just like it has for five hundred years or more.'

She glanced up again and looked directly at Angela as though defying her to utter a contradiction.

'I'm sorry,' said Angela inadequately.

But Margaret seemed not to need any sympathy. She had a listener, and that was all that mattered.

'I remember thinking when you were born that you were doomed like me—doomed to spend your life stifling in this place,' she said. 'You had spirit, just like I'd had, but I was certain you'd soon have it knocked out of you. You'd marry some respectable local man, as I did, and then waste away with the dullness of it all. The cake sales, and the church flowers, and the endless nothingness. But you grew up and went away, and I was so terribly envious of you. For a while I was tempted to run away myself, but where could I have gone? I had no money—Tom saw to that—and no education to speak of. I ought to have done it when I was young if I was going to do it at all. So I stayed here and read books about people who had adventures and screamed silently in my head as women do. You never had to do that, though, did you?'

'I suppose not,' said Angela.

'And look at you now,' said Margaret. 'You've done well for yourself, it's clear enough to see. I wonder how I'd have turned out if I'd done the same as you instead of wasting my life here.'

Angela wanted to say that her own life had not been exactly plain sailing either, but she stayed silent, for she knew that, given the choice, she would far rather have her own life than Margaret's—and in fact, it was fear of an existence like that which had prompted her to leave Banford in the first place.

'It's not too late, you know,' she said. 'It seems hard that it should take a death to set you free, but now you can do whatever you want. There is nothing to stop you.'

Margaret shook her head. Her tears had quite dried now, and she had reverted to her old, expressionless manner.

'I couldn't do it now,' she said. 'I'm too set in my ways —too old to change. And besides, there's still Norman to think about. You know they've arrested him, don't you?'

'Yes,' said Angela.

'I don't suppose for a moment he really killed his father, but it'll take all our money to prove it if it goes to trial, so

I'll be back where I started. I shouldn't mind, but it's not as though Tom was ever worth all this effort.'

Angela raised her eyebrows.

'That's another thing you got right and I got wrong,' said Margaret. 'You had a husband too, but you didn't hesitate to get rid of him when he didn't suit your purpose.'

'I shouldn't quite put it like that,' said Angela, taken aback. 'It's not as though I didn't have good reasons for it.'

'Well, and so did I, only I never acted. Tom was a cruel man, and I bore it for forty years—should have had to bear it for twenty more, perhaps, had someone not come and rid me of him.'

'Cruel, was he?' said Angela.

'Yes, cruel,' said Margaret. It was as though the walls had come down and now years of pent-up acrimony and resentment were at last finding utterance. 'I don't mean he beat me or anything like that—oh, no, he was far too clever to do anything so obvious. But he was never kind to me, like a husband ought to be to his wife. He treated me with disrespect in public and private, and belittled me when I was doing my best to be a dutiful wife. I knew shortly after I married him that I'd made a mistake. If there had ever been any love between us, it disappeared quickly.' She paused. 'I don't know why I'm telling *you* all this,' she said. 'Why, we hardly know each other.'

'Perhaps because we have a number of things in common,' said Angela. At that moment she pitied Margaret Tipping greatly. Despite her unprepossessing manner, her rancour and her evident bitterness, there was a certain tragedy about her grief over her wasted life, as she saw it.

'Perhaps,' said Margaret. 'Still, you know what it's like to be unhappy in marriage, so you don't want to hear all about my sorrows. But perhaps I oughtn't to have made them quite so obvious, and then the police wouldn't have come round and accused me of killing Tom.'

'You didn't have anything to do with it, did you?' Angela was almost certain she knew the answer, but wanted to hear it from Margaret herself.

'No,' said Margaret. 'But I might have had I known how to use a gun. On the day he died I was more angry with him than I'd ever been in my life.'

'Why?' said Angela.

Margaret again looked at the ground.

'It's hard to talk about such things,' she said finally. 'I don't know that it can do any good. Perhaps I ought to let it all lie, and forget about it.'

Angela said nothing.

'It was the humiliation of it,' said Margaret finally. 'Forty years I lived with him, and his spiteful ways, and his cruel sense of humour. But at least I thought it had been my own decision—my own mistake—the product of my own free will.'

'What do you mean?' said Angela. 'Surely nobody forced you to marry him?'

'No, of course not,' said Margaret. 'I married him because I thought I loved him. That was my fault, but I thought at least he was sincere too. Then last week I found out it was all a lie, and that I was nothing but the prize in a card game.'

She almost spat out the last few words.

'*What?*' said Angela, in the greatest astonishment.

'That's right,' said Margaret. 'He told me so the day before he died—out of spite, of course.'

'But how?' said Angela.

'Oh, it was all because of Andrew, of course,' said Margaret. 'The two of them had been rivals for years—

long before this dispute about Dead Man's Path came up. Andrew was sweet on me, once, and I liked him well enough, but I was in no rush to marry—I was still dreaming of another life, you see. As Tom told the story, he had seen me first and had told Andrew so. Tom thought that meant he had a claim on me, although there was nothing between us then. I don't know what went on, exactly, but I suppose it all happened while they were in drink. Tom could never bear to be beaten by Andrew in anything, and they agreed to fight it out over a game of cards. The loser was to withdraw and give the other a chance to win me. Win me!' she said bitterly. 'As though I were a trophy, or a rosette, or a prize cow, instead of a human being with feelings and wants and rights of my own.'

She fell silent, and her breast heaved with the indignity of it all, but her face was as expressionless as ever.

'And Tom won the game,' said Angela.

'Yes,' said Margaret. 'He won, and I don't suppose he cared two straws for me, but he was determined to have his prize and flaunt it before Andrew Norris, so he set himself to winning me over. He could be charming when he liked, and I was upset that Andrew had stopped seeking me out —although of course I didn't know why—and so I let myself be flattered into marrying Tom. I suppose he thought one wife was as good as another. It didn't take him long to find out his mistake, and I suffered from it for the next forty years.'

'And you never knew about it? Didn't Andrew Norris ever say anything?'

'No,' said Margaret. 'I suppose he didn't want to admit to having lost to Tom. I expect that's why he made such a fuss about Dead Man's Path: he was determined not to lose to him again.'

'But why did Tom suddenly decide to tell you what had happened after so many years?'

'I don't know. But we'd been angry with each other over something, and it turned into a row and he accidentally let it slip. I still hadn't quite taken it in when he started taunting me about it, even though he must have known how shocked I was. He said how did it feel to know that he'd only wanted me as a prize in a game? *And* he'd cheated at that. Then he looked at me as though he despised me and said if he'd known then what I was really like, he should never have bothered. Still, though, he thought it must be some consolation to me to know that Andrew had been furious when he had told him about the cheating.'

'Oh, he told Andrew, did he?' said Angela.

'That's what he said,' said Margaret. She paused. 'So, now you know it all, I suppose you'll go and tell the police. Tell them of the humiliation I've suffered. After all, it makes my motive stronger, doesn't it?'

'I think they will have to be told, yes,' said Angela gently. Mrs. Tipping was right: if ever there was a motive for murder, then this was it.

'I ought to have told them myself,' said Margaret, 'but I couldn't bring myself to do it—and besides, I knew I hadn't killed Tom, so what was the sense?'

'I'm sorry about all this,' said Angela, 'and I don't know what to suggest. Perhaps you could go away somewhere until all the fuss has died down. As it happens, I don't believe the lawyers *will* get all the money, as I'm pretty certain your son didn't do it, and I mean to see to it that he and Kathie are released as soon as possible. Once they are free, there's no reason you couldn't leave for a while. Perhaps you could go abroad.'

'I've always wanted to travel,' said Margaret wistfully. 'I

should love to go to Egypt.' She shook her head. 'I wish I could believe what you say, but I've been disappointed too many times in my life to rely on it. And I will spend the money on Norman if I have to—after all, he is my son.'

'I'm almost certain you won't have to,' said Angela.

'Well, you're the clever lady detective,' said Margaret. 'I hope you're right.' She seemed to realize where she was and looked surprised. 'I'd better get back,' she said. 'There's work to be done.'

She walked off abruptly, and Angela was left alone to reflect on their extraordinary conversation. Poor Margaret Tipping! How awful it must be to feel buried alive for forty years, and then find out that one's whole life had been founded on a lie. There was little wonder the woman felt so bitter. Angela hoped very much that she would be able to make good on her promise to secure Norman's release before long—otherwise she feared that Margaret was right, and all the money would disappear on solicitors' fees.

Chapter Twenty-Four

ANGELA HAD BEEN GOING to spend a little longer looking around the area for clues, but on reflection she decided that it was now a matter of urgency to speak to the police. Accordingly, she walked back into the village and entered the police station. There she found only a constable on duty, who informed her that Sergeant Primm had been called away to another village on a burglary case, and was not expected back until later that afternoon. She was about to explain what she had discovered, when it occurred to her that perhaps it would be of more interest to Inspector Jameson. She thanked the constable and said she would come back later, then went across to the telephone box that stood on the edge of the village green and made a call to Scotland Yard. After explaining herself patiently several times and using up most of her money she was finally put through to Inspector Jameson, who was not strictly on duty but had come in to catch up on some report-writing.

'Oh, inspector, I'm so glad you're there!' said Angela, cutting short his salutation. 'I need to speak to you about the Tipping case. I think I may have found the evidence you're looking for.'

'Do you mean you have proof that Norman Tipping did it?' said Jameson. 'You must give it to Primm, if so. He is in charge now.'

'Sergeant Primm is out,' said Angela. 'And in any case, it's quite the opposite. I know Norman didn't do it and I think I can prove it.'

'Are you sure?' said Jameson, sounding suddenly alert.

'Yes. I've spoken to—oh, bother,' she said, as the operator asked if she wanted any more time, 'I haven't any more change. Listen, Freddy and I are looking about for more evidence, but we need your help. Please come.'

'I'll be there as soon as I can,' said Jameson with decision, and rang off.

Angela came out of the telephone box and paused for thought. It would be at least a couple of hours before Inspector Jameson arrived. If they were lucky, that ought to be enough time for William to do what she wanted him to do. She hurried back towards Dead Man's Path and was just in time to meet Freddy and William at the bottom of Tithes Field.

'Here he is,' said Freddy unnecessarily. 'I haven't told him anything.'

William expressed the strongest curiosity to know what was wanted of him, and Angela explained as best she could. He listened and nodded in understanding.

'Do you think you can do it?' said Angela.

'I guess so, always assuming I can find him,' he said.

'That ought to be easy enough,' said Freddy. 'He's in the Red Lion every day from twelve o'clock.'

'How do you know that?' said Angela, impressed.

'I make it my business to know,' said Freddy loftily. 'I do

occasionally do some work in return for the five bob a week they pay me at the *Clarion*, you know.'

'I should never have guessed it,' said Angela. 'Very well, William, I shall leave it in your capable hands. You know what we want to find out, but you may have to ply him with a certain amount of drink before you can get it out of him.'

'What if he won't admit to it?' said William.

'I hope he will,' said Angela. 'We do have other witnesses, but they're children and I don't know whether the police will take their word for it. You shall just have to do what you can.'

'All right,' said William. 'I'll do my best.'

'If you can manage it you're a better man than I am,' said Freddy. 'I've spoken to him several times but he's as close-mouthed as an oyster and won't say a word to me.'

'Ah, but William has a particular advantage over you,' said Angela. She looked at her watch. 'It's a quarter past eleven now,' she said. 'You'd better go and wander about the village until the Red Lion opens. We shall see you later.'

'Very well, ma'am,' said William, and went off.

'What shall we do now?' said Freddy.

'I don't know,' said Angela. 'I've telephoned Inspector Jameson. He won't be here for another hour or two, though, and in the meantime I don't suppose there's much we *can* do.'

'We might go and have another look around by the church, or along Dead Man's Path,' suggested Freddy.

Angela wrinkled her nose doubtfully.

'I don't think there's anything to see,' she said. 'The police have searched the place thoroughly, and I seem to have spent half my time on Dead Man's Path since I got here. I'm starting to wonder whether I'm not a little more ghoulish than I care to admit.'

'I don't think you are,' said Freddy. 'You have a healthy curiosity, that's all. And someone has to do something to get Kathie out of gaol. The police aren't interested any more—as far as they're concerned, they've got their man and they can think about something else now.'

'I expect you're right,' said Angela. 'By the way, while you were fetching William I happened to meet Margaret Tipping and we had a very interesting conversation.'

She told him briefly what Margaret had said and he raised his eyebrows.

'I say,' he said. 'Poor Mrs. Tipping. Rather rotten luck for her to end up with a fellow like that, don't you think? I mean, I'm hardly a shining beacon of morality myself, but even I should never stoop to that sort of thing.'

'Of course you wouldn't,' said Angela. 'I think it takes a certain sort of person to do something so ill-natured. Still, he had to live with the consequences himself, too. I don't suppose the marriage was particularly happy for him either.'

'It serves him right,' said Freddy. 'I've no sympathy. I don't say he deserved to be shot in the head for it, but I don't suppose he'll be much missed.'

'No,' agreed Angela. 'However, you must admit it makes for a very strong motive.'

'Yes, it does rather, doesn't it?' he agreed thoughtfully.

They had been walking down Church Lane as they spoke, and just then they saw a familiar figure hurrying towards them up the road. It was Mrs. Hunter, the vicar's wife.

'Good morning, Mrs. H,' said Freddy as she joined them.

She did not return the greeting and they saw immediately that something was wrong, for her expression was shocked and indignant.

'Gipsies!' she exclaimed without preamble. 'I told you, didn't I? I said they were shameless and that they'd stop at nothing, but nobody listened to me. I don't know what Sergeant Primm thinks he's been doing lately, but I told him he ought to arrest them, and he didn't, and now look what they've done!'

'What have they done?' said Angela.

'What have they done? Only stolen my bicycle, that's what!' said Mrs. Hunter.

'Goodness me!' said Angela. 'Are you sure? But we saw it only a little while ago, chained up by the church. They must have done it in the past few minutes.'

'Well, not to say *stolen*, exactly,' said Mrs. Hunter, calming down a little. 'But they have most certainly made an attempt. Look, come and see. You two shall be witnesses.'

She turned and headed back down the lane, and they followed her into the churchyard and up the path.

'There!' she said dramatically, extending a finger.

The bicycle was still there, chained up, as it had been before. Angela had only glanced at it earlier, but now she looked at it more closely and saw what she had not noticed before.

'Oh!' she said.

'You see?' said Mrs. Hunter.

'Someone has tried to cut it away,' said Freddy. He bent and peered at it. The chain was a thick one, and had been wound around the frame of the bicycle and through the metal hasp on the lid of the old poor box. The whole was fastened by a padlock. Someone had evidently taken a saw or other cutting tool to the hasp, for it was buckled and ragged at its edge, although it was still in one piece.

'Yes, and look,' said Angela, pointing. 'Whoever it was has also tried to cut through the chain.'

'He must have had a good go at it,' observed Freddy. 'Why, there are marks all over it. He didn't get far, though. It's a stout chain, and that hasp looks as though it's made of stern stuff too.'

'I've said it before,' said Mrs. Hunter indignantly. 'I've tried to warn everybody, but nobody ever listens to me. These thieves must be stopped!'

'Perhaps you ought to take your bicycle home,' said Angela.

'I shall indeed,' said Mrs. Hunter. 'It's already been here far longer than I intended, but I thought it would be safe while my wrist recovered. Evidently I was wrong.'

'I'll take it back for you,' said Freddy. 'Do you have the key to the padlock?'

'Unfortunately not,' said Mrs. Hunter. 'Alice Hopwell has it.'

'I think she's out,' said Angela.

'Perhaps the children know where it is,' said Freddy. He ran off and returned a few minutes later with the key.

'Enterprising young souls,' he remarked. 'They made me give them sixpence apiece before they'd let me have it.'

'Yes,' said Angela. 'They certainly seem to have made a little money for themselves recently.'

The bicycle was unlocked and they wheeled it down the lane to the vicarage, where it was delivered safely into the custody of the Hunters' garden shed and locked up.

'There!' said Mrs. Hunter. 'I shall report it to the police as soon as I can. We can't simply let these people go on rampaging around the countryside, plundering and looting wherever they go. Now, you mustn't leave just yet, for I want to talk to you both about this ridiculous Tipping business. Why on earth have the police taken it into their heads to arrest Kathie Montgomery? I know we all joked that he did it and she helped him, but really, nobody could possibly have taken the idea seriously, could they? Do you suppose the police were listening to all the rumours and acted on them? If that's the case I shall have a very strong word with Sergeant Primm when I see him. Listening to gossip is no way to conduct an investigation. I never gossip myself, of course, but I have had occasion several times lately to speak to the parishioners on the subject. Thou shalt not be a talebearer among thy people, and neither shalt thou stand against the blood of thy neighbour. That's what I say. It's not right to speak ill of people before we know the facts. Or even after we know them,' she added.

'I don't think the police acted on rumours,' said Angela. 'Unfortunately, there is strong circumstantial evidence to suggest that Norman and Kathie were involved in Mr. Tipping's death.'

'Nonsense,' said Mrs. Hunter. 'Why, everybody knows Daniel Tyler has sworn they were nowhere near Tom when the shotgun went off.'

'There's no proof that the bang they heard was the shot that killed him,' said Angela. 'Everyone just assumed that was the case. For all we know, Mr. Tipping might have been killed some time earlier.'

'But of course it was the shot that killed him,' said Mrs. Hunter. 'What else could it have been? If it wasn't, and he died earlier, then they couldn't have passed along the path when they did without stepping over Tom.'

'Exactly,' said Angela, 'and that's what looks so suspicious. As things stand, there are no other suspects to speak of, and the two of them were on the spot at more or less the right time. You can't blame the police for leaping to the obvious conclusion.'

'Rubbish,' said Mrs. Hunter. 'Are you telling me they

shot him before everyone thinks he was shot, and then deliberately walked along the path later, ignoring the dead body as they passed and not caring who saw them? And how are they meant to have arranged the convenient gunshot noise and the meeting with Tyler?'

'It's not the police's job to explain that,' said Freddy. 'All they have to do is arrest the most likely suspect and then hand him over to the courts.'

'Well, it's a disgrace,' said Mrs. Hunter, 'and I can't see your brother and sister-in-law standing for it, Mrs. Marchmont. If I were in their position I should complain to the chief constable.'

'Oh, I've no doubt they will,' said Angela.

'And they must write to the newspapers too,' added Mrs. Hunter. 'Mr. Pilkington-Soames, you ought to take up the cause. This is a splendid opportunity for you to write something decent for a change. It will be a good way to get your name known. Perhaps you might even be offered a job with a proper newspaper on the strength of it.'

'I think that's a splendid idea,' said Angela maliciously. 'Don't you agree, Freddy? Shouldn't you like to work for a *proper* newspaper?'

Freddy ignored her and said, 'The newspapers can't do much in the case of an arrest, and there's nothing to say the two of them will be charged anyway.'

'But if the police think they have the right people then who is going to find the real culprit?' said Mrs. Hunter.

'Why, Angela, of course,' said Freddy, who was not going to let the earlier dig pass. 'Didn't you read the article about her in the *Herald* this week? She's by way of being a detective, you know, and according to the story she's sworn to bring the murderer to justice.'

'Really? I don't take the *Herald* myself,' said Mrs. Hunter, 'but Esther does. Perhaps she still has it.'

'Then I suggest you look it out,' said Freddy. 'It's a *marvellous* piece, and really shows Angela to best advantage.'

'Well, I shall certainly go and look for it if what you say is true,' said Mrs. Hunter. 'Now, can I offer you some tea?'

'We'd love to,' said Angela, 'but I'm afraid we must go. I have a murderer to bring to justice,' she added, glaring at Freddy.

'Well, I wish you the best of luck, my dear,' said Mrs. Hunter. 'And if there's anything I can do to help I shall be more than willing.'

Out in the lane, Freddy said, 'How long before Inspector Jameson gets here, do you suppose? Is there anything more we can do?'

'We'll have to see whether William has had any success,' replied Angela. 'Until then, I think we shall just have to wait.'

'Well, at least we appear to be on the right track at last,' said Freddy.

'I do hope so,' said Angela. 'I should very much like to know how the murderer managed about the gun, though. It's possible we may never find out.'

They were passing the church as she spoke, and as they did she glanced towards the spot where Mrs. Hunter's bicycle had stood.

'Oh!' she said. She stopped and began to laugh.

'What?' said Freddy.

She did not reply, but turned and hurried through the church gate and up the path.

'What are you doing?' said Freddy, following her.

Angela stopped next to the old poor box.

'What do you think?' she said.

He looked puzzled, then comprehension dawned on his face.

'Do you mean—' he said.

'It would explain the gipsies, wouldn't it?' said Angela.

'It certainly would. Go on, then,' said Freddy.

She tried to lift the lid of the box.

'It's stuck,' she said. 'Look, the thief bent the staple when he tried to saw through it and now the hasp won't lift over it.'

'Let me have a go,' said Freddy.

He tried to bend the staple back with his hands, but had to give up.

'What we need is a hammer,' said Angela.

'I don't suppose you thought to put one in your pocket before you came out this morning?' said Freddy.

'I carry many odd things in my pockets, much to Marthe's despair, but I have yet to resort to ironmongery,' replied Angela.

'Well, in the absence of that, a hobnailed boot will have to do,' said Freddy, removing the article in question from his own foot. He lifted the boot and gave the staple several sharp blows with the heel.

'Try it now,' he said.

With a little struggle, Angela managed to open the hasp, and lifted the lid. They peered inside, then their eyes met and they both smiled in triumph, for standing upright and leaning against the inside of the box was a shotgun.

Chapter Twenty-Five

'I DO like it when I get things right,' said Angela. 'It doesn't happen nearly often enough.'

'You're too modest,' said Freddy. 'Well, well—so this is where the gun was hidden. No wonder the police couldn't find it—it was locked up in here all the time.'

'Yes. The murderer presumably intended to come back and fetch it once the fuss had died down,' said Angela. 'But then Mrs. Hunter fell off her bicycle and Alice Hopwell chained it to the box for her. The gun's been here all week, under our very noses.'

'Whoever put it there must have been itching to get at it,' said Freddy. 'What a stroke of bad luck to carry out the perfect murder and then be unable to dispose of the weapon! The killer must have been terrified it would be found at any moment.'

'Terrified enough to try and break into the box, in fact,' said Angela.

'It's a good thing for us that our worthy sea captain gave it a lock made out of a ship's anchor,' said Freddy. 'Of course, all this makes it look very much as though the whole thing were premeditated.'

'Oh, yes,' said Angela. 'It was premeditated, all right. There's no doubt about that. Look—the barrel has been sawn off to make sure the gun fits exactly into the box.'

'And to make it twice as deadly,' said Freddy soberly.

'Yes,' said Angela. 'I don't suppose the murderer wanted to take any chances.'

'I take it this *is* the murder weapon?' said Freddy. 'I mean, I don't suppose the gun was just shoved in here as a donation to the poor. Let's see, now—we don't want to wipe any finger-prints off.'

He dropped his boot and fished in his pocket for a handkerchief, which he wrapped around his hand. Then he lifted the gun out of the box and broke it open carefully. Inside was a spent cartridge.

'It's been fired, right enough,' he said. 'I imagine Jameson will be very interested to see this when he arrives.'

'Well, good *morning*,' came a bright voice behind them just then, and they whirled round to see Corky Beckwith, wearing the ecstatic expression of one who had just been presented with an enormous birthday cake and a gold watch for good measure. 'I see the detecting duo have turned up something delicious for the pot.'

'What do you want, Corky?' said Freddy.

Corky affected a look of innocence.

'Why must you always assume I want something?' he said. 'Perhaps I come to give you moral support. For are we not colleagues, comrades, bosom bedfellows in our chosen profession?'

'Bosom bedfellows? What a ghastly thought,' said Freddy. 'Now, do scoot off, there's a good chap. Angela and I have important things to do.'

'Oh, it's *Angela and I*, is it?' said Corky. 'I see—so this is how you get your stories, yes? By seducing decaying gentle-women, and taking advantage of their vanity and joy at having ensnared a young man in their declining years to induce them to tell you everything.'

'Freddy, if you wanted to whack him one on the nose with that boot, I shouldn't do a thing to stop you,' said Angela with some energy.

'Just my joke, madam—although who am I to say whether it mayn't have just a *soupçon* of truth to it? Naturally, I should never *dream* of suggesting such a thing in print, however,' said Corky with a leer.

'I'm pleased to hear it,' said Angela, drawing herself up magnificently and taking a step towards him. 'Because if you did, I should be forced to sue firstly you, then that loathsome rag of yours for employing you, and finally your mother for giving birth to you in the first place. I have lots of money and a solicitor who has nothing better to do at present, so don't think it's an idle threat.'

Her voice came out as a hiss, and for the briefest of moments she looked like a mythical and terrifying creature poised to tear the eyes from the head of a poor innocent soul lying bound to a rock. Corky flinched.

'I suggest you apologize to the lady,' said Freddy.

Corky looked sulky and muttered an apology.

'Now then, as I said, the best thing you can do is to leave us alone,' said Freddy. 'The police will be arriving shortly, and as you can see we've some new evidence to show them.'

'So I gather,' said Corky. 'But why waste it on the police? I mean to say, by all means give it to them later, but can't you see that you hold in your hands this very minute a most sensational story in itself?' His face assumed a pitying look. 'Freddy, Freddy, you can't expect to make a success of this business if you fail to think of the business first and foremost. Justice is all very well, but the most important thing is that it be *seen* to be done. The general public have a right to know all that concerns them, and this shotgun is vital evidence. Think of the dramatic impact a photograph of this weapon would have, when splashed across half a page with below it the caption, "This is the gun that killed an innocent man and sent a guilty one to hang."' For a moment, his expression held a touch of the sublime. 'Why, such a scoop would be the making of us both!'

'Don't be ridiculous,' said Freddy. 'It's simply not done to interfere with a police investigation. You can't just go running off with evidence because you think it might make a pretty picture for the evening edition. This gun is probably covered with finger-prints and you'll ruin them.'

'Pshaw!' said Corky. 'Does anyone care about finger-prints these days? I thought they were old hat.'

'Sorry, Corky,' said Freddy. 'We're giving this to the police and that's that.'

'Oh, very well,' said Corky. 'You have me once again. But you can't blame me for trying.'

He sniffed and turned to walk away. Freddy set the gun down and bent to put on his boot, and quick as lightning Corky turned back and made a dart for it.

'A-ha!' he exclaimed in triumph, and made off at a run, the gun under his arm. Freddy, still wearing only one boot, immediately set off after him and the two young men disappeared around the back of the church.

'Oh dear,' said Angela. She picked up the boot and hurried after them.

In the churchyard, she found Corky weaving in and out of the headstones, pursued by Freddy, who was a fast enough runner but somewhat hampered by being only semi-shod. In and out they dodged, Corky giggling maniacally all the while, until they had run all the way around the church and were once more at the front. By this time Corky, who was not the fittest of men, was starting to flag slightly. He paused for an instant to decide which way to go, and in that instant Freddy took an enormous leap and brought him down to the ground. For the next few moments all that could be seen was a mass of flailing arms and legs as Freddy tried to wrestle the shotgun out from under Corky. Meanwhile, Angela stood at a safe distance and glanced about her, wondering whether she ought to go for help, for the fight seemed evenly matched and looked as though it might go on for hours.

'Get off me!' cried Corky. 'I'll have you for assault.'

But Freddy was not listening. He had managed to turn Corky over and had a knee on his chest as he tried to wrench the gun out of his hands. There was a struggle and then Corky somehow managed to bring the gun up. It clipped Freddy on the side of the head and he yelled and loosened his hold. In a trice, Corky was on his feet, and before anyone could say anything pointed the gun at Freddy, who was panting on the ground, and pulled the trigger. There was a loud click. Freddy gasped in outrage and called Corky an unrepeatable name.

'Ouch!' exclaimed Corky, and dropped the gun, for Angela had just stepped up and rapped him smartly on the knuckles with Freddy's boot.

'What on earth do you think you're doing?' she said severely, as Corky sucked his hand and regarded her balefully. 'You idiot,' she went on, as Freddy picked up the shotgun and got to his feet. 'If that had been loaded *you'd* be the one with your photograph in the paper tonight. You can't possibly be *that* keen on getting a story, surely.'

'It was an accident,' said Corky feebly.

'Rot,' said Freddy. 'You did it deliberately. Why, you

might have killed me! And not only that, but if there were any finger-prints on it before, then you've rubbed them all off. You ass, Corky. What do you think the police are going to say when they find out?'

'Oh, and of course you're going to tell them,' said Corky. His voice had become a whine. 'Not exactly honourable, is it, to squeak on a fellow reporter.'

'You hardly deserve the title,' said Freddy with dignity. 'And that's beside the point, anyway. This is a murder weapon, and people will be asking questions about it in court. For all we know, someone's life may have depended on those finger-prints.'

'Ah, yes, the murder,' said Corky, looking suddenly thoughtful. 'Did I hear you say you'd called the police?'

'Yes, and we're expecting them at any minute,' said Freddy.

'I see,' said Corky. 'Very well, then, I shall leave you to it. I'm awfully sorry about firing the gun at you, old thing. It was just in the heat of the moment and all that. Of course I knew it wasn't loaded.'

He smiled genially then turned on his heel and walked off.

'What is he up to?' said Angela. 'I can't believe he's just going to leave us and miss out on the fun.'

'I expect he's remembered some kittens he forgot to drown earlier,' said Freddy, rubbing his head. 'Let's just be thankful that he's gone for now. He's given me a ringing headache.'

'Perhaps I oughtn't to have threatened to sue him,' said Angela. 'I suppose it might have provoked him slightly.'

'Oh, no. He doesn't need to be provoked to act like an imbecile,' said Freddy. 'He can do that wholly off his own bat. You were rather marvellous in your fury, though. I've never seen you in a temper before.'

'Yes, well, he is quite extraordinarily irritating,' said Angela. 'I don't wonder he annoys you. Now, then, I think we ought to do something with this shotgun, just in case he comes back. Let's go back to the vicarage and ask Mrs. Hunter to look after it, shall we?'

'An excellent idea,' said Freddy. 'She will no doubt keep us talking for another hour and that will fill the time nicely until Inspector Jameson gets here.'

Chapter Twenty-Six

INSPECTOR JAMESON finally arrived in Banford Green at about half past two, later than he intended. His superintendent had caught him as he was about to leave, and had kept him in conversation about a blackmail case which the super insisted required delicate handling, for it involved a minor politician. Jameson listened politely and agreed that everything possible ought to be done to keep the case out of the public eye, but all the while he was fighting the urge to tap his feet and glance at his watch. Finally, the super let him go, and he hurried down the stairs and out of the building. Once in his car and safely on the Surrey road, he turned his mind to the matter at hand. Mrs. Marchmont's hurried telephone-call had given him little information but had lifted his spirits more than he dared to admit to himself. Could she really have found the evidence necessary to exonerate Norman Tipping—and by extension, Kathie Montgomery—from the charge of murder? Sergeant Primm had telephoned the night before to inform him of their arrest, and Jameson had congratulated him, outwardly pleased at the progress that had been made on the case. Inwardly, however, he had hated himself for the part he had played in putting Kathie in gaol, and he had spent a sleepless night trying to convince himself that he had done the right thing. He hoped very much that Angela's evidence could be relied upon. She was not the type to exaggerate the importance of a thing, but on the other hand she was not of the police, and therefore could not be expected to know what sort of evidence would stand up in court and what would not. Still, she had never let him down in the past. Perhaps she had succeeded in finding something that the police had missed.

The first thing he saw as he parked the car by the green was William, Angela's chauffeur, who was just then emerging from the Red Lion Inn in company with an old man. They seemed to be on very friendly terms, and Jameson raised his eyebrows—first, because it seemed an odd sort of thing for Angela's driver to be doing at that time of day, and second, because the man did not look to Jameson like the sort of person with whom William would normally keep company.

The old man went away, and William saluted the inspector cheerfully.

'Hallo inspector,' he said. 'I guess you're expected.'

'I think so,' said Jameson. 'Am I to understand that you know what this is all about?'

'Not the whole story,' said William, 'but I do know that Mrs. Marchmont and Mr. Pilkington-Soames have been doing some investigating this morning, and have found out one or two mighty interesting things.'

'Where are they now?' said Jameson.

'Why, I don't know,' said William. 'They set me on to finding something out for them, and I was just going to look for them.'

'Is that what you were doing in the Red Lion?' said Jameson.

William nodded and grinned widely. He looked very pleased with himself.

'Come on,' he said. 'Let's go and find them, and you shall hear all about it when I tell them.'

They left the bustling centre of the village and walked towards the head of Church Lane. They had not gone far down the lane when they saw Angela and Freddy walking towards them.

'Oh, inspector, I'm so glad you've come,' said Angela as they approached. She wore the brightest smile. 'We've just had rather an eventful morning, and I'm dying to tell someone about it. And you're here too, William. Have you had any luck?'

'I should say so,' replied William.

'Splendid,' said Angela. 'Suppose we convene some-where more comfortable to discuss it.'

'Where do you have in mind?' said Jameson.

'Why, I don't know,' said Angela. 'You don't think they'd let us use the police station, do you?'

In the end they all went back to the Red Lion and sat in the snug.

'This is rather appropriate, as it happens,' said Angela. 'Now then, where shall we begin? First of all, inspector, I suppose I ought to mention that Freddy and I have found the shotgun that was used to kill Tom Tipping.'

Inspector Jameson sat up at once at this news.

'Are you sure?' he said.

'Reasonably so,' said Angela. 'Unfortunately, I must also tell you that Corky Beckwith happened upon us just after we found it and made himself rather tiresome, and so any finger-prints there may have been to start with have been smudged or lost. Still, I think it may not matter in the end once you've heard the circumstances.'

She related the story of how they had found the gun, and Jameson whistled.

'So it was there all along, chained up in the poor box,' he said. 'Rather remiss of us not to have looked there. Of course, we had rather assumed that the murderer took the gun away with him, but that's no excuse for us not to be thorough.'

'Oh, but if the murderer's plan was to work then he *couldn't* take the gun away with him,' said Angela. 'Not then, anyway. 'I imagine he planned to come back for it later, but by that time Mrs. Hunter had had her accident and it was locked away.'

'Where is it now?' asked Jameson.

'Mrs. Hunter is looking after it for us. She's tremendously excited about it and has promised to defend it with her life, so I think it's probably safe for now.'

'Whose is it?'

'That's the question, isn't it?' said Angela. 'And I think we can answer that too. Or perhaps William can. He's been finding things out for us.'

'Who was that old man you were talking to?' said Jameson.

'His name is Ben Shaw,' said Angela. 'Didn't you meet him when you were here before? He works at Low Meadow Farm for Andrew Norris.'

'Ah, yes,' said Jameson. 'The one who was eating lunch with Norris in this room when the murder took place. No, I hadn't met him.'

'That's the one,' agreed Angela. 'He swore that Norris was with him all the time, and I wanted to find out whether that was true, so I asked William to find out for me. Ben herded cattle in the Chicago stockyards for a while in his youth, you see, and he took a great fancy to William when he found out he was American, so it struck me that we might take advantage of that fact. Did you have to get him *very* drunk, William?'

'Not overly,' said William with a grin. 'He was only too happy to talk to me. He's an old man and doesn't care too much one way or the other what his boss gets up to, and he's not too keen on the police, so I guess he wasn't particularly interested in helping them.'

'Then he was lying?' said Freddy.

'No,' said William. 'He told the truth. The police just asked him the wrong question. According to him, they told him they wanted to know whether Mr. Norris had left the inn at any time while they were having their lunch—or dinner, as he called it. As far as Ben was concerned, Mr. Norris hadn't left the inn at all. Of course, what they ought to have asked him was whether Mr. Norris had left the *room*, and then the answer might have been different.'

'Then Norris *did* leave the room?' said Jameson. 'Why didn't Shaw mention that?'

William coughed.

'I guess the police pressed the point about leaving the inn a little too hard,' he said. 'Old Ben's kind of stubborn. He thought they were accusing him of lying, and that made him plant his feet even more firmly. They ought to have asked him the question as though the answer didn't matter, and then he might have told them.'

'So where *did* Norris go?' said Jameson.

'Out there,' said William, nodding towards the back door.

'Ah,' said Jameson, beginning to understand. 'And how long was he outside?'

'Old Ben wasn't too clear on that. I guess he was absorbed in his own lunch and wasn't really paying much attention. He just said Norris told him that Bob Sanderson had said there were some bits of wood in the back yard that he might have if he liked, and he was going to look at them, and that Ben was to stay where he was. Norris was gone a little while, and Ben never thought anything of it, because he had his pint of mild and his pipe, and then Norris came back in without saying anything, and they had another drink and then left. I don't think Ben was deliberately trying to protect his boss—he just answered the questions that were asked of him.'

'Naturally,' said Jameson. He got up and opened the back door, and went into the yard, followed by the others. Freddy put the old milking-stool next to the wall and stood on it to peer over.

'Nobody there,' he remarked, and jumped down. 'They must all be in the house. The Hopwell children, I mean,' he explained to Inspector Jameson. 'Their mother is out most of the day so they're left alone to get up to tricks.'

'And so they do,' said Angela. 'I spoke to them this morning, inspector. They told me a rather interesting story about an incident which occurred last Saturday.'

'I think I'm starting to guess what it was,' said Jameson.

'Oh, I'm sure you can,' said Angela. 'According to the two oldest, who are seven and six respectively, they were all outside in Church Lane that morning, waiting for their mother to return, as she had promised them twopence each for the fête, when they were approached by a tall man with a dog, who asked them if they wanted to earn a little money. Naturally, they were all ears and asked him what they should have to do. The man said they didn't have to do anything except keep a secret. He told them he was playing a sort of game with a friend of his—it was a bet, he said, if they understood that. He said that he and his friend were going to have a race from the Red Lion to the church and back, and whoever got back first would win the bet. The man said he thought his friend would probably run through the village and around to Church Lane that way, but the man was determined to beat him, and had had the bright idea of taking a short-cut through the children's house. He said it would be very easy—all he had to do was to jump over the back wall of the Red Lion and into their yard, then run through the house and into the lane. Then a few minutes later he would come back the same way. He made it sound as though it were a tremendous joke, and the children agreed to it, so he gave them a shilling each and said to expect him in about an hour and reminded them not to say a word. They stayed outside in the lane to play, and sure enough, a little while later, they saw the man come out of their house and run towards the church. He was gone a few minutes, and then he came back and disappeared into the house again.'

'I don't suppose they heard a loud bang shortly after the man came out of their house?' said Jameson.

'I did ask them, but they didn't remember,' said Angela. 'Does it matter?'

'No, but it would tie everything up neatly,' said Jameson. He stood on the milking-stool and looked over the wall. 'Then it really was as simple as that?' he said. 'Andrew Norris did it after all, but took a short-cut to make it look as though he had an alibi. Why on earth didn't I spot it myself?'

'You weren't here long,' said Angela fairly. 'If the case had been properly yours and you'd stayed, then of course you'd have worked it out—and probably more quickly than I did.'

'So the sound that was heard *was* the gunshot which killed Tom Tipping, and I've been complicating matters unnecessarily,' said Jameson. He shook his head. 'Not my best work, I'm afraid. Mrs. Marchmont, I take my hat off to you.'

'You must thank Freddy, too, for trespassing,' said Angela. 'Had it not been for that, I might not have realized the answer myself.'

'I don't quite understand,' said Jameson.

'Oh, it was a silly thing,' said Angela. 'Hardly anything, really. He just said that if people would put a house in his way then they must expect him to walk through it.'

'And I maintain my position on the matter,' said Freddy. 'Especially if it leads to this sort of thing. By the way, Angela, how did you get the children to tell you all? I thought they'd been given a shilling each to keep quiet.'

'Why, I merely raised my offer to half a crown,' said Angela, as though the answer were obvious.

'He must have hidden the shotgun by the church in preparation,' said Jameson, who was still thinking. 'That's why nobody saw him with a gun that day.'

'Yes,' said Angela. 'He sawed the barrel off, too. He ran past the church, collected the gun, shot Tom Tipping then returned, dropping the gun back in the box as he passed. I gather he's been loitering around in Church Lane all week, waiting for Mrs. Hunter to take her bicycle away. I saw him myself.'

'I wonder why he suddenly decided to kill Tipping now, after having threatened him about five times a day for years,' said Jameson.

'Ah, I think I know the answer to that too,' said Angela, and told him the story of Margaret Tipping and the card game. 'I think the news that Tom Tipping had cheated during the game, and had thus cheated Norris out of his wife as he saw it, must have been the final straw.'

'That's certainly possible,' agreed Jameson. He glanced

at his watch. 'Well, we are building up a very pretty case, but I think that in order to be perfectly sure of ourselves we ought to test the theory before we go arresting anybody else. We need to make certain that it is in fact possible to run from here to Dead Man's Path and back, through Alice Hopwell's house, in less than twenty minutes. One person must remain here and another go and wait on the path itself, and a record be kept of the times. Now, who is going to do the running?'

'Angela,' said Freddy promptly.

'As soon as fashion allows me to wear trousers in the daytime, I shall be more than happy to climb over walls in the pursuit of justice,' said Angela. 'Until then, you'll forgive me if I refuse. I vote William.'

William agreed at once, but Freddy said maliciously, 'As a matter of fact, I think it ought to be the person nearest in age to the suspect to do it. That's you, isn't it, inspector? We want to imitate the physical condition of the murderer as nearly as possible.'

'How old do you suppose I am, exactly?' said Jameson with some dignity.

'Not much older than I am,' said Angela, 'but at least no-one has described *you* as a decaying gentlewoman.'

'I *knew* that annoyed you more than the other suggestion,' said Freddy with a smirk.

'Freddy is right,' went on Angela, ignoring the last remark. 'We may as well be as precise as we can. I'm sure you're much fitter than Mr. Norris, inspector, but it can't hurt to do it this way.'

Jameson saw the truth of this.

'Very well, then,' he said. 'William, you stay here and time things at this end. I shall go and see if Mrs. Hopwell has returned. I don't want to frighten her out of her wits by running through her house unexpectedly. Mrs. Marchmont, perhaps you and Freddy might go and record the time at the other end.'

They all set their watches to the same time, and then Jameson, Angela and Freddy left the Red Lion and walked around to Church Lane. The two last carried on towards Dead Man's Path, and Jameson knocked at the Hopwells' door. It was answered by Alice Hopwell, who looked surprised.

'Is someone in trouble?' she said after Jameson had introduced himself. 'The children have been saying something about a man running through our house, but I don't know what they're talking about.'

Jameson explained merely that they had received new information about the Tipping case, and that he wanted to test out a theory. She was so surprised that she readily agreed to allow him to pass through her house. He thanked her and said to expect him in a few minutes, then went off.

Meanwhile, Angela and Freddy had arrived at Dead Man's Path and were preparing to wait for Jameson's arrival.

'I don't wonder Jameson wants to try this out for himself,' said Freddy. 'After all, they've already arrested three people and had to let one of them go. It doesn't exactly reflect well on the police to keep on arresting people at random until they hit on the right one, does it?'

'No,' agreed Angela. 'I do hope they will release Kathie quickly, though. I have never seen Elisabeth so worried.'

'Then she does have a heart in there somewhere,' said Freddy. 'I was starting to doubt it. By the way, do you suppose Norris—'

He stopped suddenly, and his expression turned to a frown. Angela turned around to see what he was looking at, and to her dismay saw Andrew Norris and Corky Beckwith strolling towards them along Dead Man's Path as though they were the best of friends.

'So that's what he was up to,' muttered Freddy.

Angela had no time to reply before the two newcomers joined them.

'Ah, Mr. Norris, have you met Freddy Pilkington-Soames? He's a great pal of mine,' said Corky with a complete lack of shame. 'As a matter of fact, you might say that I taught him everything he knows about the newspaper reporting business. We have our occasional disagreements, but I don't think it's too much to say that Freddy would quite happily lay down his life for me if necessary, such is his gratitude for my tutelage.'

'What are you doing here?' said Freddy with a scowl. 'Why must you keep turning up and bothering us?'

'That's hardly polite,' said Corky. 'I merely told Mr. Norris that I believed some vital evidence had been uncovered in the matter of this rather unpleasant murder, which implicated Norman Tipping even more strongly than before—'

'Implicated—' began Freddy, his eyes opening wide, but Corky went on imperturbably:

'—and since Mr. Norris is so closely involved with events, having been unceremoniously arrested in the early stages of the investigation, I thought it only fair to invite him to come along and watch the proceedings.'

'Well, as you can see, there's nothing doing here,' said Freddy, wisely deciding to keep his thoughts to himself so as not to frighten Norris into some desperate action.

'So it appears,' said Corky, although his eyes were darting suspiciously from Angela to Freddy.

'I told you, didn't I?' said Norris to Angela. He seemed most pleased with himself. 'I said there was more to Norman Tipping than met the eye. It's not for me to spread rumours, but I wasn't a bit surprised when they arrested him. And now Mr. Beckwith here says they've found a clue that proves the case, although I don't know what it is.'

'It's just through this way,' said Corky, indicating the fallen wall of the churchyard. 'Shall we go?'

'This way? What is it, exactly?' said Norris. 'I wish you'd tell me. It seems an odd sort of way of going about things. Come on, Skipper,' he said to his dog. 'Drat the animal,' he said as Skipper ran off, having scented a rabbit, and began sniffing around a little farther along where the wall was whole. Norris whistled, but the dog refused to come to heel, and he muttered an imprecation and started forward.

As luck would have it, he had just bent over to grab the dog by its collar when Inspector Jameson turned up, out of breath. He did not see Andrew Norris or Corky Beckwith, who had spotted the inspector approaching and stepped smartly behind a tree, and before Angela or Freddy could warn him, said:

'I say, that back wall's not exactly easy to climb over. This Norris chap must be pretty agile for his age.'

Too late he saw their horrified expressions and whirled around to see Norris, who had heard every word. An expression of doubt and fear began to spread across Norris's face, and he straightened up and walked off quickly, leaving the others there, momentarily frozen to the spot. Corky just then stepped out from behind his tree, a delighted smile on his face, and Jameson took in the situation at a glance.

'I'm going to kill you, Corky,' said Freddy.

'You can do it later,' said Jameson. 'And I may just give you a hand. Come on, before he gets away.'

He ran off in the direction Norris had taken, and

Angela and Freddy followed him, with Corky tagging along behind. They need not have worried that Norris was planning to try and escape, however, for they found him in front of the church, peering into the poor box. He saw them and let the lid fall.

'Where have you put it?' he said.

'Put what?' said Jameson.

A smile crossed Norris's face. It was a defiant sort of smile and it said as clearly as anything could that he felt no remorse for what he had done.

'It's all up then, I suppose,' he said. 'And it was such a beautiful idea. It's just a shame that stupid woman had to go and fall off her bicycle when she did. The gun would be at the bottom of the river by now if she hadn't.' He paused, and looked at Corky, who was scribbling busily in his notebook. 'I suppose this was some trick of yours, was it? Well, it's one way to get a story, I suppose. Very well, then, take this down: I did it and I'd do it again tomorrow. He was a thorn in my side for forty years or more and I've felt nothing but relief since he died. There—that ought to look good in your newspaper, don't you think?' He glared round at the others. 'And I don't know why the rest of you are looking at me like that. Nobody will miss him, nobody will mourn him. I'll bet Margaret will be grateful to me when she finds out I did it, although she'll never say it. Go on, then, what are you waiting for? Arrest me. I'm an old man and I'm past caring what happens to me.'

Inspector Jameson stepped forward.

'Mr. Norris, I am arresting you on suspicion of the murder of Thomas Tipping,' he said. 'I must inform you that anything you say may be taken down and used as evidence.'

'Yes, yes,' said Norris impatiently. 'Shall we go?'

Chapter Twenty-Seven

AFTER HIS TRIUMPH in single-handedly bringing Andrew Norris to justice for murder (as set out at length in ornamental and self-congratulatory prose on pages four and five of Monday's edition of the *Herald*), Corky Beckwith had the presence of mind to slip back to London before Freddy could carry out his threat to commit violence upon him, there to bask insufferably in his own glory and dine out on his success in the Banford Green case. To listen to him, no-one would have supposed that he had by mere good fortune avoided causing a disaster by interfering in the investigation and forewarning the accused of the police's suspicions; on the contrary, according to Corky he had pretty much solved the whole mystery himself and performed the arrest without the police's actually being present. His stories for the subsequent week or so contained many heavy hints as to the incompetence of the police and certain well-known lady detectives, and from his pen much rhetorical oratory issued forth, furthermore, on the parlous state of some sections of the popular press (the

Herald excluded, naturally) and their inability to report the news that *really* mattered.

After the arrest, Freddy was rather grumpy for a few days, since he felt bound to stick to the truth—or at least some semblance of it, always allowing for the demands of his editor and his readers. Since he could with some justification claim to have helped solve the murder, it stuck in his throat to see Corky taking the credit, even though it was hardly the first time he had done it. Still, Freddy consoled himself with the thought that, unlike Corky, at least *he* had the advantage of a friend in the police, and that *his* stories at least contained solid facts rather than mere vainglorious boasting. And, of course, there was the ever-present and tremendously comforting knowledge that, however many scrapes Freddy might get into, he could never possibly be quite such an ass as Corky. He very soon returned to his normal cheerful self, therefore, and went back up to town to retrieve his dinner-suit from the fire and resume his duties as detached observer of the London season with no more than a slight shudder.

The police, meanwhile, who were somewhat embarrassed at having arrested the real murderer immediately only to let him go again, lost no time in releasing Norman Tipping and Kathie Montgomery. Kathie was overjoyed to be reunited with Peter, for she had been far more worried for him than for herself, and their reunion was most affecting. She took him home immediately and promised him another week off school, and Humphrey valiantly kept his mouth shut on this occasion and made no mention of school fees. Norman Tipping, on the other hand, was in a less cheerful frame of mind following his release. He had been most indignant at his arrest, and said one or two things about taking action of some sort against the police. In the end, he did

nothing, perhaps realizing what a lucky escape he had had—
and perhaps also taking into consideration the fact that,
following his father's death, he was now set to inherit enough
money to pay his debt to Irish Jimmy. Resolving to learn his
lesson, Norman vowed to himself that he should give up
gambling altogether, and was half-minded to cancel delivery
of the *Sporting Life*—but after giving it some thought, he
decided that there was no need to take such desperate
measures, and that he was perfectly capable of betting on a
horse now and again without getting into trouble. Norman's
mother Margaret welcomed him home with her usual lack of
emotion, and—as at any time—nobody could have said what
she was feeling on the occasion. Many in the village
wondered how she would get on without her husband, but
this question was very shortly answered when it was reported
that she had been to Cook's and taken herself off on an organized tour of Egypt for a month. As Andrew Norris had fore-
told, she said not a word about her thoughts on the subject of
Norris's guilt—or indeed her thoughts on anything to do
with the case, and so these can only be surmised.

The day after Kathie's return home, she and Angela
went to visit Mrs. Hunter at that lady's invitation. The
vicar's wife was tremendously excited at the events of the
past few days, and was eager to hear all the latest news and
dispense her own words of wisdom on the subject.

'And so I need not come and visit you in gaol after all,'
she said to Kathie. 'I had quite begun to think that I should
have to adopt you as one of my charity cases. You ought to
be thankful, my dear: prison would have done nothing for
those pretty looks of yours, and of course nobody would
have wanted to marry you after you came out. You'd have
been doomed to spend the rest of your life alone and
unwanted. Now things are quite as they were—and if
you'll take my advice, I'd set the wedding date as soon as

possible, before Norman spends all his father's money and becomes a poor prospect—for, let us be frank about it, he has little enough to recommend him besides his financial standing, now, does he?' Having carelessly dealt this devastating blow to the appearance, personality and rectitude of Norman Tipping, as well as to the motives and sincerity of Kathie with respect to the institution of matrimony, she beamed. 'Oh, but I *am* glad you're out,' she said. She then turned to Angela. 'And so you really did solve the mystery! I thought that young man was joking when he said you were known for your detective abilities. Well, I must say, if it's all true then you are *much* cleverer than you look. I should never have thought it myself. Tell me, are you staying here much longer? I imagine you and Lady Cardew must be quite sick of each other by now.'

'I am going back to London tomorrow,' said Angela.

'Ah, then I've no doubt we'll see you again for the wedding,' said Mrs. Hunter, with all the satisfaction of one who had arranged the thing herself.

'Is there going to be a wedding?' said Angela to Kathie as they walked up Church Lane afterwards on the way to Two Tithes.

'No, there isn't,' said Kathie firmly. 'I've had plenty of time to think lately, what with one thing and another, and I've come to the conclusion that I was rather letting other people make my decisions for me—I don't know why. Perhaps because it was easier, and saved me from having to face the truth myself.'

'You don't love Norman,' said Angela.

'Not in the least,' said Kathie. 'I know everyone would like to see me settled again, and for a while I half-thought it wouldn't matter that I didn't love him, but—' she paused and looked down. 'Now I realize it does.'

'I see,' said Angela.

'Peter and I will do perfectly well on our own,' said Kathie more cheerfully. 'After all, we've managed up to now. And why does everyone think I ought to have a husband?'

'Why indeed?' said Angela.

'I don't believe I need one at all. You do well enough without yours, don't you?' said Kathie.

'Oh, yes,' said Angela with some sincerity. They were now at the head of Church Lane and she glanced up, then said quickly, 'Oh, I've just remembered: I promised to go into the village and buy some—er—onions for Elisabeth. Do go on—I'll catch you up.'

'Onions?' said Kathie in surprise, but Angela had hurried off. Kathie was about to continue on her way when she spotted what Angela had seen before her: Inspector Jameson standing by his motor-car, writing in his notebook. He saw her at the same time and stiffened.

'Hallo, Mrs. Montgomery,' he said formally as she approached, and then, since it would have looked odd not to mention it, went on, 'I'm glad they released you and Mr. Tipping so quickly. I hope you were well treated.'

'Yes, I was, thank you,' said Kathie. 'They were very kind in the circumstances.'

'I'm pleased to hear it,' he said.

'I suppose you are going back to London now,' she said.

'Yes. I only came down to write a report for Sergeant Primm, but I'm wanted back at Scotland Yard shortly,' he said.

They stood for a moment in awkward silence, then he smiled stiffly and turned to open the car door.

'I hope you don't think I blame you for what happened,' she said suddenly.

He turned back.

'How could you not blame me, when it was all my doing?' he said, and she saw pain in his eyes.

'Because you were doing your duty,' she said. 'The evidence pointed to Norman and me and so of course the police had to arrest us. It really wasn't very long, you know —not much more than a day and a half, all told. They let us go as soon as you found the real culprit.'

'I'm afraid that was all thanks to Angela Marchmont,' he said bitterly. 'I had nothing to do with it. I ran back to London with my tail between my legs when I ought to have stayed here and looked into the thing properly, for—for your sake, and for Mr. Tipping's. If I had, then I'm certain this could all have been avoided and you would never have been arrested in the first place. I don't think I shall ever forgive myself.'

'I'm sorry you feel like that,' she said, 'but really, there's nothing to forgive.' She moved a little closer, and he looked into her face and saw that she was smiling. 'Perhaps I ought to ask *you* to forgive *me*, since I seem to have made you feel so terribly bad about things.'

'You could never make me feel bad about anything,' he said quickly. He recollected himself and said, 'I had better go.'

'You seem rather anxious to get away from me,' said Kathie, 'and I don't quite understand it. Is it something I've done?'

'No, it's nothing you've done,' he said.

'I'm glad of that,' she said. 'You see, I rather thought you—liked me.'

'Of course I like you,' he said crossly. 'I fell hopelessly in love with you the moment I first laid eyes on you, and the thought of you belonging to someone else has been tearing me apart ever since.'

'Oh!' she said, in momentary surprise. 'Is *that* why you're going away?'

'Yes. Why did you think I was going?' he said.

'I don't know,' she said. 'I'm not used to this sort of thing, you see—falling in love, I mean. Of course, I loved Peter's father, but it was all such a long time ago, and I'm fairly sure it was all very simple then.'

'It's simple enough now,' he said. 'You're engaged to someone else—or as good as—and so I shall leave you to it and wish you all the best.'

'But I'm not,' she said. 'I'm not engaged. Norman has never asked me—and besides, how could I possibly marry him? I couldn't, not after what's happened.'

'But everyone knows he's innocent now,' said Jameson. 'There's nothing to stop you.'

'I wasn't talking about the murder,' said Kathie quietly.

They stared at one another for a moment, and a dim light of hope began to flicker in Jameson's breast.

'Are you really in love with me?' went on Kathie. 'I mean, *really* in love? You don't think it's a sort of temporary madness, or something like that?'

'Not as far as I'm aware,' he said. 'Do I seem mad to you?'

'No, but I've been wondering whether I am,' said Kathie. 'I was going along quite happily—or so I believed —but then *you* came, and something happened and I couldn't stop thinking about you, and then you nearly kissed me and I wished so terribly much that you had, and I thought that perhaps all the confusion over Tom's death had made me lose my head somehow. Don't you think it's the same with you?'

'Of course not,' he said. 'I'm a detective. I investigate this sort of thing every day. You don't think I fall in love with everyone I meet, do you? Why, if I did that, they'd have to lock me up.'

'I suppose they would,' she said. 'I hadn't thought of it like that. Then perhaps I'm not mad—perhaps it is real after all.'

'You don't mean to say you feel the same way?' he said.

'Why, I rather think I do,' she said. 'Isn't it absurd?'

She laughed with sudden delight, and he gazed at her, momentarily dumbfounded. He could not quite believe what he had heard. Without thinking he caught up her hand.

'Are you sure you're not going to marry Norman?' he managed at last.

'Quite sure,' she said firmly.

'Good,' he said before he could stop himself. 'Then you can marry me instead.'

She drew in her breath, and he was suddenly filled with self-doubt.

'I'm sorry,' he said. 'It's a ridiculous thing to ask. Why, you hardly know me.'

He made to let go of her hand but she would not let him. She was shaking her head.

'Yes, it *is* ridiculous,' she said. 'It's ridiculous that I should feel so happy after all that's occurred this week, but I do and I can't help it. I still can't explain what's happened to me, but I do know it's because of you and I don't want the feeling to stop. Please don't say we hardly know each other. It's only been a few days, but somehow I feel as though I've known you forever. I felt it as soon as we met, truly I did. Yes, of course I'll marry you.'

'Darling Kathie, are you sure? I realize I've rather sprung it on you.'

'Yes,' she said, half-laughing and half-crying. 'You have,

haven't you? It's completely absurd, and yet I've never been so sure of anything in my life.'

Then somehow she was in his arms and he was gazing into those bright blue eyes of hers, which bewitched him and invited him so irresistibly that he could not help kissing her, as he had so nearly done the other day. He apologized immediately—for after all, the whole thing *had* been rather sudden—and she said it was quite all right and he might do it again if he liked, so he did. A few minutes passed, then she said they were making rather an exhibition of themselves and perhaps they ought to stop. Besides, she was sure he wasn't supposed to do this sort of thing while on duty, and wasn't he meant to be getting back to London? At that he glanced at his watch and saw that he was late again, and so he let go of her reluctantly and opened the car door.

'You must go, or you'll get into trouble,' she said when he showed signs of hesitation. 'Please don't stay away too long, though, or I might start to think I dreamed all this.'

'I'll come back tomorrow, I promise,' he said. 'Nothing will keep me away, you'll see.'

'Yes, tomorrow,' she said. 'I can wait until then. After all, I've been waiting for you for years, so a few more hours won't make much difference, will it?'

'How odd,' said Jameson. 'I was just thinking exactly the same thing.'

They stared at each other in a moment of surprise and shared understanding, then she smiled.

'Go,' she said. 'I'll be waiting for you. Come to dinner tomorrow with me and Peter. As a matter of fact, it might be as well to get that out of the way as soon as possible—after all,' she went on practically, 'you might loathe my cooking and it's only fair to let you find it out well in advance so you can back out if you want to.'

He laughed.

'You could serve me a plate of cold ashes and I shouldn't back out,' he said.

'You oughtn't to say things like that,' she said mischievously. 'You're tempting me to do it, just to test you.'

A sudden concern struck him.

'How do you think Peter will take it?' he said. 'I should hate him to think I was intruding. It's not as though I can replace his father.'

'Peter hardly remembers his father,' she replied, 'and he's talked of nothing but you since you first came here, so I couldn't have forgotten you even if I'd wanted to. I don't think we need worry. You *will* come back tomorrow, though, won't you?' she went on, suddenly looking rather lost. 'This has all happened so suddenly that I'm not quite certain it's real.'

'I feel rather the same,' he admitted. 'I only wish I had a ring to give you, but I don't tend to carry one around on the off-chance that a beautiful woman with the bluest eyes I've ever seen will agree to marry me. But I must give you *something* to demonstrate my good faith, mustn't I?'

In the end all he could find with which to plight his troth was a gold propelling pencil that had been a present from an elderly aunt. She accepted it with an attempt at solemnity, but then at the look on his face she began to giggle and did not stop until he kissed her again. Then he got into the car and set off—very late now—with his head in a whirl, and it was presumably only by a miracle that he managed to get back to London without driving into a tree.

Chapter Twenty-Eight

'THERE YOU ARE,' said Elisabeth, as Kathie entered the drawing-room some time later. 'Wherever have you been?'

Kathie answered vaguely and sat down as though not quite certain of where she was.

'I was just saying to Humphrey that we ought to invite Norman to dinner one day,' went on Elisabeth. 'Just to show everyone our feelings on the subject of this unpleasant business, and make it quite clear that we have no intention of shunning him.'

'Oh,' said Kathie. 'I don't think that would be a good idea at all. You see, I'm getting married.'

The last words burst out of her as though she were unable to contain them any longer, and everyone looked up in surprise.

'That is excellent news,' said Humphrey in his usual pompous manner. 'I must congratulate you.'

'Well, thank goodness Norman has got to the point at last,' said Elisabeth. 'I was beginning to think he never would.'

'He didn't,' said Kathie. 'I'm not marrying him. I'm going to marry Inspector Jameson.'

'Oh, how simply splendid!' exclaimed Angela, clapping her hands together in delight.

'Inspector Jameson?' said Elisabeth in astonishment. 'Are you quite sure?'

'I think so,' said Kathie. 'He gave me a pencil.'

She began giggling, and Elisabeth glanced at Humphrey, who said:

'Perhaps you ought to go and lie down, Kathie. I'm afraid this whole business has affected you badly.'

'No, no it hasn't,' said Kathie. 'In fact, I don't think I've ever felt better in my life.' She saw the blank faces around her, and said, 'Perhaps it is rather sudden, and I don't think I've quite taken it in myself, but you *are* pleased for me, aren't you? You've wanted me to get married for such a long time, and now I am.'

'Yes, but—we thought—I don't—' said Elisabeth, then gave up, momentarily nonplussed.

Humphrey stood up with great dignity.

'Naturally, we want you to be happy, Kathie,' he said, 'but there are other considerations. This Jameson fellow—does he have any money? Can he support you and Peter?'

'I haven't the faintest idea,' said Kathie. 'And to be perfectly honest, I don't care.'

Humphrey drew himself up, and was about to hold forth when Angela decided to interject on Kathie's behalf.

'I know a little of his family,' she said, 'and I don't think you need worry on that score, Humphrey. As a matter of fact, you yourself may know his brother Henry.'

'The intelligence man?' said Humphrey. 'Oh, he's from *that* family, is he?' There was a moment of silence in which he mentally adjusted his ideas, then he went on, 'Well, then —ahem—I think that will be quite acceptable.'

'What will Peter say?' said Elisabeth. 'Do you think it's quite fair on him?'

'Peter is terribly excited,' said Kathie. 'Perhaps even more than I am. There's no need for you to worry about him.'

Since all the material points seemed to have been dealt with for the present, Humphrey and Elisabeth subsided into temporary silence. They were not the sort of people who liked surprises, and it would take some time for them to get used to this one, but it was plain to see that Kathie had quite made her mind up, and so they resolved to make no more objections—at least until they had heard what Inspector Jameson had to say for himself.

Mrs. Randall then surprised everyone by congratulating her younger daughter.

'I never liked that Tipping fellow,' she said. 'And if Angela says this Jameson is worth having, then we ought to believe her. Angela is a sport.'

Angela looked up in astonishment, and was almost certain she saw Mrs. Randall wink at her.

'She most certainly *is* a sport,' said Kathie. 'Did you get the onions, by the way, Angela?'

'Don't be silly,' said Angela, and they both laughed merrily.

'Onions? What on earth are you talking about?' said Elisabeth, but nobody replied.

Angela said, 'Kathie, I'm so tremendously pleased for you both that I'm afraid I shall have to kiss you.'

She jumped up and suited the action to the word, and then for good measure kissed Elisabeth, Mrs. Randall and even Humphrey, who looked taken aback. Then Peter turned up and had to be kissed too, much to his disgust, and then tea arrived and the rest of the time until dinner was taken up with talk.

As she looked at Kathie's beaming face, Angela smiled to herself. She was sincerely pleased for her and Inspector Jameson—they seemed eminently suited to each other and would no doubt settle down and be blissfully happy together—but she could not help sighing a little at the contrast between their future and her own. Her experience of marriage had not been a positive one, and perhaps it had spoiled her chances of happiness in love, for she seemed to make the most unsuitable choices in that regard. She could only assume that she was one of those women who were best off alone—and thank heaven at least that she was fortunate enough to have her own money and not to need a husband to support her. She looked wistfully down at her Venetian bracelet. It was an attractive but insubstantial thing—much like the man who had given it to her. She should wear it for a while and then put it away, perhaps to bring out and look at occasionally as a souvenir of a place to which she would never return. Angela sat for a moment in thought, and then shook herself. Today was a day for happiness and she would not become maudlin. She pushed the bracelet firmly up her sleeve and challenged Peter to a game of Snap.

On Tuesday Angela was to return to London, and so that morning she went down to breakfast promptly, determined to be punctual for at least *one* meal during her visit. When she went into the breakfast-parlour she found Humphrey sitting alone, reading his newspaper.

'Good morning, Angela,' he said. 'And so today you leave us to return to the busy whirl of London.'

'Yes,' said Angela. 'It's been very good of you both to put up with me for so long.'

'Not at all,' he said. 'I only hope you haven't found it too dull.'

'On the contrary, the whole visit has been very eventful,' said Angela.

'I suppose it has,' he said. 'Yes, the whole village will be talking about the murder for years to come, I don't doubt.' There was a pause, and then he coughed. 'Thank you,' he said.

'That's quite all right,' said Angela. 'I couldn't let Kathie be put in prison for something she didn't do.'

'I meant thank you for not crowing,' he said, looking slightly shamefaced, 'although you'd have been perfectly within your rights to do so. I understand that you were responsible for solving the whole thing.'

'Well—' began Angela, but he went on:

'I fear I may have been a little too concerned with appearances in the beginning, but I am very glad you forgot our differences and agreed to help.'

'You're more than welcome,' said Angela. 'I know you find my goings-on a little hard to swallow, but I hope you believe I don't do anything deliberately to offend.'

'No, no, I'm sure you don't,' he said.

'There's no denying we're very different people,' she continued, 'but after all, we are brother and sister, so perhaps we ought to make a little more effort to get on. Look, Kathie is going to be married soon, and I'm sure she'd hate to think of her wedding being spoiled by family rows.'

'Perhaps you are right,' he said. 'Very well, I shall do my best in future.'

'And so shall I,' said Angela.

The truce having been declared, they smiled at one another and Humphrey poured his sister some tea, and they took their breakfast together in a not unfriendly silence.

After lunch Angela was ready to leave, and was

standing in front of the house speaking to William as he loaded the luggage into the Bentley when she looked up and saw Kathie and Inspector Jameson approaching. She ran to greet them, and after shaking hands with Jameson and congratulating him, said mischievously:

'Are you off to beard the lion in his den?'

'Not at all,' said Kathie, as Jameson assumed an expression of mock alarm. 'We've just come to reassure Humphrey that Alec isn't planning to run off and that he was perfectly sober when he asked me to marry him.'

'I'm not certain I was,' said Jameson. 'As a matter of fact, I've felt slightly drunk ever since yesterday.'

Kathie laughed and scolded him, and Angela smiled at them both in their happiness.

'So you are going now, Angela,' said Kathie. 'You must come to the wedding, of course. You were responsible for it, after all.'

'Try and keep me away,' said Angela. 'I shall wear a new hat and pretend to cry.'

'I don't believe I've thanked you properly for your help with the Tipping case, Mrs. Marchmont,' said Inspector Jameson.

'Think nothing of it,' said Angela. 'And by the way, now that we're practically related I think it's about time we stopped all this Mrs. Marchmont nonsense. It's Angela, and I shall call you Alec.'

'Of course you're Angela,' said Jameson. 'I never think of you as anything else, really. The formality is just force of habit.'

'Splendid,' said Angela. 'Then that's settled.'

They all beamed at each other, and then Kathie and Jameson bade her farewell and went into the house. Angela returned to the Bentley, where Marthe and William were waiting to get in.

'Have we got everything?' said Angela. 'Well, then, I suppose we had better be off. I expect there will be a mountain of post to see to. I do hope I haven't missed anything exciting.'

'Isn't murder exciting enough?' said William.

'I suppose it is,' said Angela. 'But even murder seems rather a quiet affair down here in the country. Dear me!' she said, recollecting herself. 'And to think only a few days ago I denied being anything like those jaded society women. Why, I ought to be ashamed of myself.'

She was saved from too much self-recrimination by the arrival of Elisabeth, who had come to bid her goodbye.

'Thank you so much for coming, Angela,' she said. 'It has been a pleasure to have you.'

It appeared to be costing her some effort, but her manner was almost friendly.

'The pleasure was all mine,' said Angela graciously, trying not to think about the incident with the cocktails in the garden.

'I do hope you will come again soon,' said Elisabeth. 'As a matter of fact, I've been thinking—I don't believe your old room is quite the thing. Next time you shall have the blue room. It's much more comfortable and suitable for guests.'

'Oh,' said Angela, somewhat stumped for a reply. 'I shall look forward to it,' she said inadequately.

The two ladies smiled politely but warily at each other, much as the ambassadors of two warring nations might approach one another with a view to opening talks on a peace treaty. Then, to Angela's utter astonishment, Elisabeth stepped forward and kissed her stiffly on the cheek.

'Well, goodbye,' she said, and hurried off before Angela could respond.

Angela stood dumbfounded for a second, then turned

and prepared to get into the car. Just then, her attention was caught by William and Marthe, who were staring determinedly at the ground, and she glared at them.

'What are you laughing at?' she said. 'Come on, let's go.'

———

New Releases

If you'd like to receive news of further releases by Clara Benson, you can sign up to my mailing list here: clarabenson.com/newsletter.

Books by Clara Benson

THE ANGELA MARCHMONT MYSTERIES

THE FREDDY PILKINGTON-SOAMES ADVENTURES

SHORT STORIES

Angela's Christmas Adventure

The Man on the Train

A Question of Hats

COLLECTIONS

Angela Marchmont Mysteries Books 1-3

Angela Marchmont Mysteries Books 4-6

Freddy Pilkington-Soames Adventures Books 1-3

HISTORICAL FICTION

In Darkness, Look for Stars (published by Bookouture)

The Stolen Letter (published by Bookouture)

OTHER

The Lucases of Lucas Lodge

Printed in Great Britain
by Amazon

17374516R00144